A MACE BAUER MYSTERY

MAMA RIDES SHOTGUN

DEBORAH SHARP

THORNDIKE
C H I V E R S

This Large Print edition is published by Thorndike Press, Waterville, Maine, USA and by BBC Audiobooks Ltd, Bath, England.
Thorndike Press, a part of Gale, Cengage Learning.
The text of this Large Print edition is unabridged.
Other aspects of the book may vary from the original edition.
Set in 16 pt. Plantin.
Printed on permanent paper.

LIBRARY OF CONGRESS CATALOGING-IN-PUBLICATION DATA

Sharp, Deborah, 1954–
    Mama rides shotgun : a Mace Bauer mystery / by Deborah Sharp.
        p. cm. — (Thorndike Press large print mystery)
    ISBN-13: 978-1-4104-1944-6 (alk. paper)
    ISBN-10: 1-4104-1944-4 (alk. paper)
    1. Mothers and daughters—Fiction. 2. Florida—Fiction.
3. Large type books. I. Title.
    PS3619.H35645M367 2009b
    813'.6—dc22   2009025753

BRITISH LIBRARY CATALOGUING-IN-PUBLICATION DATA AVAILABLE

Published in 2009 in the U.S. by arrangement with Midnight Ink, Llewellyn Publications, Woodbury, MN 55125-2989 USA.
Published in 2010 in the U.K. by arrangement with Llewellyn Worldwide Ltd.

U.K. Hardcover: 978 1 408 45776 4 (Chivers Large Print)
U.K. Softcover: 978 1 408 45777 1 (Camden Large Print)

Printed in the United States of America
1 2 3 4 5 6 7 13 12 11 10 09

To my brother Kevin Sharp . . . gone too soon, just like Daddy. With strong hearts in heaven, I hope they're knocking those baseballs out of the park.

ONE

"Why don't you move over a little so that setting sun hits your hair, Mace? You look so pretty when it sparkles like that."

Mama grabbed my chin, cranking it in a westward direction like I was a baby doll with a pop-off head. I'd been savoring the moment, gazing upon a still pristine stretch of our once vast central Florida prairie.

"Quit," I snapped at her, jerking my chin away. Val, the horse I'd borrowed for the annual Florida Cracker Trail Ride, shifted beneath me and shook her own head. Equine empathy, maybe. Val must have had a mother who drove her crazy, too.

"Well, you don't need to get snippy." Mama edged her horse a little closer and whispered. "I was just trying to present you in your most flattering light, darlin'." She nodded significantly toward a weekend cowboy astride a big palomino, heading into the evening camp.

"Oh, for God's sake, Mama!" I whispered back. "Can't we spend any time at all together without you trying to find me a man?"

I glanced at the cowboy. He was bald, twenty years older than me, and about a hundred pounds overweight. The gelding he was riding was plenty big. Still, the horse looked relieved the ride was stopping for the day so he could get a break.

Turning Val away from the long line of riders, I trotted toward a remote corner of ranch land I'd already chosen for our campsite. Mama spurred her horse to catch up, her mouth hooked downward in a pout.

"I don't know why you've got us way out here in Siberia, Mace. There's not a soul nearby for me to talk to."

"I like the quiet, Mama. And you can socialize up a storm at dinner. Besides, I thought this trip was all about the two of us bonding."

With Mama's impending marriage just a few months away, it had been her idea to saddle up and hit the week-long camping and riding trip along the Cracker Trail. She drove me crazy about it until I finally caved in.

"We need us some bonding time, Mace," she'd said. "We're the last two single gals in the family." I think there was even a tear in her eye.

I got all nostalgic about Florida's early cattle-driving days, and how we'd traced the historic trail as a family when Daddy was alive. Insanely, I went along with Mama's plan. My sisters, Marty and Maddie, couldn't take a whole week off work. But they were going to drive the hour and a half from Himmarshee to the Atlantic coast. They'd meet us for the big parade in Fort Pierce, the end point for the hundred or so riders who make the cross-state trek.

If I made it that far without killing Mama, that is.

Combine her upcoming nuptials with the fact that my former flame moved back to Miami and out of my life, and Mama's matchmaking compulsion had hit overdrive. We were only on day two of the six-day ride, and already she'd eyed every male she'd seen as my possible mate: from the pimply clerk at the mega-store, who bagged up our trail provisions, to the ride's middle-aged cowboy poet, even after two of his girlfriends got into a scuffle near the stage last night. By this point, I was praying for an off-season hurricane that might force us to cancel the rest of the trip.

We'd just pulled up the horses to a tree

line that marked our evening camp, when I suddenly felt Val's muscular body tense beneath me. Her ears went up. A moment later, I heard the sound myself: Something was moving out there through the shadows of a dense oak hammock.

"Well, as I live and breathe." A deep, booming voice. "If it isn't the prettiest girl ever to grace the halls at Himmarshee High."

Mama's hand flew to her hair, and she batted her lashes becomingly. I didn't even bother to turn around. I'm not awful to look at: thirty-one; five-foot-ten; slender, well-muscled build. But Mama and I both know which one of us would be described as the prettiest girl ever at Himmarshee High. She'd been homecoming queen *and* head cheerleader. I'd received special permission to compete with the boys at bulldogging for the high school rodeo.

"Mace, honey, look who's here. You've met Lawton Bramble before, haven't you? Law and I were an item back in high school, a hundred years ago."

Given that the wedding in four months would be Mama's fifth, I was surprised she could still keep all her "items" straight. Then again, you don't forget a man like Lawton Bramble.

He sauntered out of the trees toward Mama and me. In expensive custom boots and worn Wrangler jeans, he was still gorgeous in his sixties; so tall he barely had to raise his head to look us in the eye on our horses.

"Whoo-eee! Aren't you something, Mace," Lawton said. "You turned out just as pretty as your mama."

I hoped I wasn't blushing. I didn't care much for the way Lawton treated his land, or for his politics or business practices. Gossip was he was cruel; but he was all charm today. Magnetism oozed off him like musk. And there was no ignoring the force of those blue eyes. No wonder everyone from the governor on down asked how high when Lawton said jump.

Mama patted the hand he'd placed on the horn of her saddle. "I've tried to tell Mace exactly the same thing about how pretty she is, Law. I mean, look at that hair: so thick and black. The girl at Hair Today, Dyed Tomorrow says Mace looks just like a silent movie queen. But she doesn't do a thing with what God gave her. She goes around looking like one of those critters she traps crawled up on her head and built itself a nest. Mace, honey, turn around so Law can see all those snarls in the back of your hair."

I shot Mama a murderous look.

"I'm not a heifer at auction!"

Lawton rocked back a little and hunched his shoulders up to his ears. He might be rich and powerful, but this discourse on my poor grooming was turning him into the Shrinking Man.

"Mama, as much as I'm enjoying your hair-care tips," I said, "I'm hungry. I want to get out of the saddle, get these horses taken care of, and get some grub."

Relief passed over Lawton's face. He took off his hat and brushed a hand through hair that was steel-gray, but still thick. "That's just what I came to tell y'all. I've got a cook site just over in that next clearing, and I'm making a batch of my famous Cow Hunter Chili. I'm gonna serve it at supper, so you better be hungry."

Mama's hand fluttered up to cup the side of her face. It was the left hand, the one with the enormous diamond engagement ring from Sal Provenza.

"Oh, Law, my constitution is much too delicate for that five-alarm recipe of yours."

Truth is, Mama has a stomach like an iron-sided battleship. I've seen her down jalapeños whole on Mexican Fiesta Night at her church.

"But if your handsome son is going to be

at supper," Mama continued, "we'd sure like to stop by and say hello."

I noticed the slightest pressure at Lawton's mouth. "Trey's here." He didn't elaborate.

"How is that darlin' boy?" Mama pressed ahead, her matchmaking obsession overriding her observational powers.

"Fine." The set of Lawton's mouth was grimmer than mine.

"You must be so proud of him. I heard he's stepping into the family cattle business," Mama plowed on, oblivious.

"Don't believe everything you hear, Rosalee."

Mama finally caught on to Lawton's cold tone of voice. Even in the dim light of the dying sun, I could see a muscle twitching in his clenched jaw. What had gone on between father and son?

"Oh . . . oh, my," Mama sputtered. "I certainly didn't mean . . ."

Lawton cut her off with a smile. "Don't worry your pretty head, Rosalee. It's just family stuff. You know how families are."

"Don't I ever," I said.

"Anyway, I've gotta get back to my chili and ratchet up the spices. We'll see y'all in a couple of hours, okay?"

As Lawton left, Mama swung out of her saddle. I did the same. We worked silently for some time, putting up a temporary paddock; trading the horses' bridles for halters, tethering them by lead ropes to the trailer. I'd just lifted off Val's blanket and saddle, when Mama could stand the silence no longer.

"What do you think that was all about, Mace?" She whispered, though Lawton was well out of hearing range. "He turned as cold as a mother-in-law's kiss, didn't he? All I did was ask about Trey."

Lawton Bramble III — Trey — had been three years ahead of me in high school. Quarterback on the football team, straight-A student, the air of privilege that comes from being the son of the richest cattleman in three counties. He was exactly the kind of boy Mama would have loved for me to date. And exactly the kind who wouldn't have given a second glance to a tomboy like me.

"Don't ask me, Mama," I shrugged, stowing Val's saddle in the trailer. Predictably, Mama had made no move to finish with her horse. I lifted off Brandy's saddle, too. "Just family I guess, like Lawton said."

Dusk was coming on fast now. Crickets sang. A barred owl called. The air was crisp and chilled. The ride is held every year in February, when it can get cold in the center of Florida. But it rarely freezes. And most riders would rather bundle up with a couple of extra layers than camp along the Cracker Trail in the summer, when it's so hot the hens are laying hard-boiled eggs.

By the time I watered and fed the horses, my own stomach was grumbling. I had to wait for Mama to decide what outfit to wear, then fix her hair and apply fresh makeup. Who brings mascara and blush-on to a trail ride? I glanced at my watch: More than two hours had passed since we spoke to Lawton. His chili would be spicy enough to peel paint by now.

Finally, we were ready to head over to the Bramble homestead. Several cattle-raising families along the trail generously opened their land each year to the trail riders. The cynic in me always figured that in Lawton's case, he did it mostly so he could show off.

We started through the hammock, dodging low branches above and clumps of palmetto at our feet. A full moon was just beginning to peek above the clouds on the horizon, adding its glow to the flashlight I carried to find our way. Something small and wild scurried through the dry brush and leaves.

I held back a thorny vine so Mama could pass under. We came out of the oaks and onto a treeless pasture. Light shone from a lantern and campfire in the distance. Just as we started toward it, a woman's scream stopped both of us short. With barely a glance at each other, we began running toward the sound.

"Oh, my God," the woman screamed again. "It's Lawton. He's dead."

Two

A young woman stood wringing her hands over Lawton Bramble's body. He was stretched out on the ground at his cook site, a dark stain spreading around him. Mama grabbed my arm. I drew her close, and we approached the scene together.

"I don't know what happened." Tears on the woman's face glistened in the firelight. She stared down at Lawton. "I came to check on him and his crazy chili. This is how I found him. I don't know what happened," she repeated, her voice getting smaller.

She was pulling so hard at the skin of her hands I thought she might strip it off. The eyes she aimed at Lawton were glassy.

"Mama, check to see if you can find a pulse." I spoke softly, already suspecting by the unnatural body position and the blood that Lawton was dead. "I'm going to tend to this one here. I think she might be going

17

into shock."

Mama stretched up to whisper in my ear before she hurried away. "Her name's Wynonna, Mace. She's Lawton's brand-new wife."

Guiding Wynonna to a low plank bench, I gently sat her down. I removed the fleece vest I wore over my turtleneck, and zipped it tightly around her. It barely fit across her bust.

"Now, put your head down on your knees." I spoke as distinctly and calmly as I could. "Take some slow, deep breaths. That's good. In. Out."

Basic first aid is a job requirement at Himmarshee Park, where I work. We've had some experience at the park with emergencies, medical and otherwise. Wynonna did just as I told her, which was an encouraging sign.

"In and out. You're doing fine." I rubbed her back, feeling her breathing start to slow.

I glanced toward Mama. Kneeling, her fingers resting lightly at the side of Lawton's throat, she looked at me and shook her head. No pulse.

She drew a compact from her jacket pocket and whipped it open. Mama couldn't possibly be checking her lipstick at a time like this. Could she? I was relieved when she held the glass of the mirror down low, close to Lawton's mouth.

After a moment, she raised the mirror and looked toward us again. She shook her head. No sign of breath.

Mama might be ditsy, but she's not squeamish about death. She grew up on a farm. She volunteers at the hospital. And, less than a year ago, she discovered the body of a murder victim in the trunk of her turquoise convertible.

Giving Lawton's cheek a gentle pat, Mama stood and started toward us. The sharp snap of her compact closing seemed to bring Wynonna back into the world. She lifted her face from her knees, two dark streaks of mascara marring her creamy skin.

"Our five-month anniversary is next Thursday." She sniffled. "Lawton was taking me to Paris. I guess I'll never get to see that Eiffel Tower now."

I immediately raised my eyebrows at Mama, now standing beside us at the bench. She leaned down to whisper, "Let it go, Mace. The woman's just had an awful shock. Folks can't be held accountable for what they say when a loved one dies so suddenly."

She laid a hand on Wynonna's hair, stroking blond highlights. "Honey, do you want us to take you over to the house? Can we call someone to be with you?"

Wynonna jumped off the wooden bench, her eyes focused now. "Oh, my Lord! What am I going to tell Trey? And Lawton's daughter, Belle? They've been after him something fierce to listen to his doctors about his cholesterol."

"So, you think he had a heart attack," I said.

"His last report from Dr. Perloff was real bad." Her green eyes widened in alarm. "Why? Don't you think that's what it was?"

All three of us looked across the campfire at Lawton's body. A horse whinnied in the distance, answered by a second horse's whicker.

"Well, there is the blood," I finally said, hesitant to bring up something so gruesome to so recent a widow. At least I didn't add how many people feared or hated Lawton Bramble, and might want to see him dead.

"What blood?" Confusion played across Wynonna's pretty features.

"Uhm, Mace, honey?" Grabbing at my arm, Mama tugged me off the bench toward the body.

"Quit, Mama," I said, trying to shake her off.

She didn't say anything, just kept dragging me closer. Finally, she stopped next to him, out of Wynonna's hearing. "Take a deep breath, honey."

I did as I was told. And as I breathed, the aroma of spicy Cow Hunter Chili filled my nose.

"Oh," I said, embarrassed.

The pot of chili Lawton had been tending must have toppled when he collapsed. Examining the scene more closely now, I saw a scattering of beans and ground beef mixed into the dark stain on the sandy ground. He wore a white chef's apron over his jeans and Western-style shirt. Bright red letters on the apron proclaimed, *It Ain't Hot Enuf Yet!* An oversized soup mug, decorated with a tongue in flames, sat sideways on the ground a few feet from his body. It still had about a fourth of a cup of Lawton's chili inside.

Neither of us noticed that Wynonna had crept up behind us. Then we heard her gasp.

"That big ol' mug is his special tasting cup," she said, tears choking her voice. "Nobody ever touches that chili cup but Lawton."

Sobbing, Wynonna collapsed onto Mama. In high-heeled boots, she towered nearly a foot over Mama's four-foot-eleven-inch frame. When Mama staggered under the onslaught, I stepped in to provide some ballast.

"We should get a doctor, or at least an ambulance, out here to do what's right for Lawton," Mama said, craning her neck around Wynonna's generous bustline to find me. "Mace, honey, why don't you call somebody on your cell-o-phone?"

"My *cell* phone is in the saddlebag, Mama."

"There's . . . no . . . reception . . ." Wynonna said between sobs. "We'll have to walk up to the house . . . to . . . place a . . . to place a . . . call."

She seemed to be making an effort to control herself. She stepped away from us and gave her tight blouse a tug to rearrange it at the waist. She ran her hands through her hair, lifting and patting it back into place. Mama offered her a handkerchief from the pocket of her own powder-blue jeans. Taking the lacy blue hanky, Wynonna dabbed daintily at her nose.

"I think I'm ready to go up to the house," she said, squaring her shoulders. "I'd just like to pick up that chili cup and take it with me. I want something to remember him by."

Something about the way Wynonna had gotten a hold of herself so quickly rubbed me the wrong way. It seemed brave, yes. But brave like she was playing the role of a distraught but determined widow in a movie. Then again, everybody grieves in different ways. Who am I to say what's normal and not?

The three of us walked back to Lawton's body. Now that the initial shock had passed, I immediately noticed that the air was thick with the smell of tomatoes, spiced beef, and beans. Wynonna gave us a shaky smile.

"With Lawton, it was always Cow Hunter Chili this, and Cow Hunter Chili that. 'Cow hunters' is what they called the old-time Florida cowboys, you know?"

I nodded.

"He sure loved making that chili, Lawton did."

Mama cleared her throat. "Do you want to say your goodbyes, honey? Mace and I will stand right here with you 'til you're done."

Wynonna's tears glistened again in the light of the fire. She closed her eyes and started murmuring something that sounded like a prayer. Mama put an arm around her waist. I stood awkwardly on Wynonna's other side, hands dangling from my wrists. As she went on, I lowered my eyes out of respect.

Gazing down, I noticed something silvery

23

shimmering near Lawton's right leg. Probably a tasting spoon or a cooking utensil of some sort, I thought. But it looked too bulky for that. I took a couple of steps closer. Wynonna stopped praying.

I squinted in the flashlight beam. The object was nearly hidden under Lawton's thick leg, but the shape was unmistakable. It was a gun.

THREE

Bending at the waist, I took a better look. Lawton wore an old-fashioned holster, a nod to the turn-of-the-century Florida frontier men who once rode the Cracker Trail. I got on my knees, lowered my head, and peered as close as I could at his right thigh. The gun was a Colt .44, lifted free of the holster.

Now, why would Lawton have had to pull that six-shooter if all he was doing when he died was making chili?

"Mace, honey? What's going on? What're you doin' crawling around down there on the ground?"

"That's a good question." Wynonna echoed Mama, her voice as cool as the darkening night. "What is it you find so interesting about my husband's body?"

I stood and brushed dirt and bits of dead grass from the knees of my jeans. "I'm sorry, Wynonna. I didn't mean any disrespect."

She narrowed her eyes at me.

"Fact is, I don't think it's a good idea for us to touch anything else. Or, for you to cart off that chili-tasting mug of Lawton's." I worked at keeping my voice neutral. Respectful. "I think we ought to leave everything here, just as we found it."

Nary a tear shone in Wynonna's eyes now. "So that's what you think, is it? And why is that?"

"Because I don't think your husband died of natural causes."

Mama took a sharp breath. "Mace, mind your manners! Wynonna's already told us her husband wasn't a well man. She's struggling with an awful loss. The last thing she needs is you playing detective. It's just plain cruel."

"Sorry," I said, lifting my eyes to Lawton's widow. "I just think we should get the authorities out here to determine exactly what happened."

"I'm going to apologize for my daughter." Mama's tone was confiding. "Mace is used to being in charge — at least she is when her big sister Maddie's not around. Maddie bosses everyone she sees, but she doesn't mean any harm by it." Mama put her hands on her hips, settling in for a gal-to-gal chat. "Truth is, we had us a bit of trouble last

26

summer after I found that poor dead man in the trunk of my convertible. It's made Mace awful suspicious about anything that could, possibly, in any way, no matter how remote . . . be murder."

Wynonna was listening to Mama, but she hadn't taken her eyes off me.

"What makes you think Lawton was muh . ." she swallowed like the word was stuck in her throat, then tried again. "What makes you think Lawton's death wasn't a heart attack?"

I pointed out the Colt on the ground under Lawton.

"Is that all?" She shook her head, her frosted blonde bangs falling prettily into her eyes. "Lawton was probably out here practicing his quick draw. I used to come in on him all the time, showboating in front of the mirror. He thought he was something out of an old Clint Eastwood movie with all those big ol' guns of his. 'Make my day,' he'd say into the mirror, his eyes all squinty like a gunslinger. When I'd catch him, and bust out laughing, he'd get so embarrassed. Y'all should see him do it. It's real funny."

The half-smile died on Wynonna's lips as she caught herself using the present tense. A tear coursed down her cheek. Mama reached over and rubbed her shoulder.

"I really loved him, you know?" Her voice was soft, pleading with us to believe her. "I'm well aware of what people think about me. I'm sure y'all think it, too."

"Oh, honey. Nobody thinks anything bad about you."

I thought Mama was laying it on a bit thick, but Wynonna looked at her hopefully.

"That's nice of you to say. But yes. Yes, they do. They think I'm a gold digger."

Mama opened her mouth to protest. Wynonna waved a hand to ward off whatever lie Mama was about to tell.

"No, it's all right. I'm used to it. People have always thought the worst of me, ever since I was a girl in North Carolina. I've never really understood why; but I think it's the reason I've grown such a hard shell. I could say it until I'm blue in the face, but people will just not believe how much I loved Lawton. He was the first man who ever 'got' me. Soul to soul. And not just because I'm nice to look at, either. I think he would have proposed even if I was big and fat and plain as a fence post."

I doubted that, but I held my tongue.

"Truth is, I would have married Lawton Bramble if he didn't have a pot to piss in. My own mother married for money. She always said it was the hardest work she ever

28

did. We kids grew up with anything we wanted, but not a bit of love in the house. My father was rich, but he could be a cold son of a bitch."

Not unlike Lawton himself, I thought.

"My mother died alone and unhappy," she said. "People blamed it on the stress of having been married to my dad. I'd be the last woman in the world to set my sights on a man just because he had money."

Wynonna stared into the dying cook fire, a far-away look in her eyes. I wondered if she was thinking about her present heartache, or about that loveless childhood home?

We sure didn't have much money after Daddy died. And, more often than not, Mama's antics drove my two sisters and me to distraction. But love was one thing all of us always had enough of. I suddenly felt sorry for Wynonna.

We were silent for a few moments, even Mama. An owl flew by, so low I felt a whoosh of wind as it passed. Frogs formed a chorus from the alligator grass in a creek on the Bramble land. Finally, Wynonna cleared her throat.

"Well, I guess we should head over to the house; get somebody to come on out here, like Mace said." She ran a graceful hand through her hair. "I want everything to be on the up and up. I know people will imagine the worst about me. I'm not going to give them any cause to talk."

She looked at Lawton's tasting mug. "I'll leave his chili cup just where it is, too. At least 'til we get everything straightened out."

"Don't worry, Wynonna. You'll carry Lawton right here." Mama put her palm to her own chest, patting at her heart. "That's the way it is when someone you love dies."

Wynonna nodded, brushing at the fresh tears that spilled onto her cheeks.

I reached for her arm to steer her away. "C'mon. Let's get you home," I said.

I was surprised when she grabbed at my outstretched hand and hung on.

"Thanks, Mace. I mean it. I'm sorry I blew up at you before. I know you only have Lawton's best interests at heart."

"Well, honey, of course we do," Mama butted in. "Lawton's a very dear old friend."

I prayed Mama wouldn't get into just how dear their friendship had been. I sent her a warning look. Wynonna didn't seem to notice.

"Will y'all stay with me when I break the news to Lawton's kids?" she asked. "I don't want to do that alone."

"Whatever you need, honey. We'll be right

beside you." Mama patted Wynonna's free hand.

With her other hand, Wynonna clutched at me like a drowning woman. She held on so tight, my fingers were going white.

We picked our way through oak trees and scrub between Lawton's outdoor fire pit and the Bramble home. Wild hogs had torn through, digging up roots in the dirt. The ground was rough and uneven. We all cast our eyes downward, so as not to stumble in the dim light.

"Watch out, Mama. There's a big rotten log just ahead."

Wynonna, at least thirty years younger than Mama and twice as strong, dropped my hand. She stepped behind me, nearly lifting Mama off her feet to help her over the log.

We started out again, single file, as the path narrowed through the hammock's thick trees. Just then, a faint noise floated toward us on the night air. Low, droning, it was unlike the evening song of any bird I'd ever heard. I strained to catch it more clearly. Animal? Human? I couldn't be sure. I turned and motioned for Mama and Wynonna to hold up.

"Hear that?" I whispered.

Mama cocked her head to listen. "Whistle

While You Work," she finally said. "Sorriest rendition I've ever heard."

She was right. The melody was there, but just barely. What should have been a happy, peppy tune sounded more like a dirge. Combine the thought of Lawton's body growing cold in the clearing with that odd, cheerless song, and it was enough to raise a prickle along the back of my neck.

For a moment, the whistle seemed familiar. And then, suddenly, a sound exploded in the woods just ahead. I stopped pondering the unhappy tune. I stopped thinking about anything at all. Something crashed through the brush. It was big. It was loud. And it was coming straight for us.

FOUR

"Dammit!"

A heavy-set man muttered curses as he hopped on one foot. He flailed at a vine encircling his ankle. He beat at a low-growing sabal palm that threatened to knock an already battered straw hat off his head.

"I hate the woods!" He swore again under his breath.

He seemed unaware of our presence, probably because of the racket he was raising in the brush. Either that, or Dr. Frank Abel had lost what was left of his hearing at the same time he'd gained about three pant sizes around the waist. He was already old, and on the heavy side, when I last saw him, some ten years before. Doc Abel treated a wrist I'd sprained when a horse threw me in a riding accident a couple of hours north of Himmarshee, near Holopaw, Florida. I'd have guessed he would have retired by now.

Wynonna rushed toward him, surprisingly nimble for a woman in high-heel boots in thick undergrowth. "I'm so glad you're here, Doc. Something awful has happened." Reaching him, she offered an arm for him to hang onto. "Lawton's had a heart attack. He's at his cook site."

"Oh God, no! I need to see to him, Wynonna. Help me out of this mess." He struggled some more as Wynonna leaned to untangle him from the grip of the vines.

"He's dead, Doc. I told them how you and his other doctors tried to make him control his cholesterol. Now, Lawton's beyond your help," she said.

Doc Abel's hand went to his own chest. Given his advanced age and the purple tint to his face, I hoped we weren't going to have another casualty along the Cracker Trail.

"Are you sure he's dead?" he asked. "I need to make sure." Finally extricating himself from the clutch of the woods, Doc Abel was all business now.

I glanced at Wynonna. Her face was pale and drawn. The evening's events were finally sinking in. She reached for my hand again.

"Mama, why don't you take Doc over to see Lawton?"

As she looked at Doc, I could almost see the gears spinning. Mama was actually

34

weighing him as a match for me. But whether it was our age difference of at least forty-five years, or the fact that Lawton was lying in the woods unprotected from who-knows-what animal, she thought better of her timing.

"I'll do it, Mace. But you know you're better with details and I'm better with people. I should be with Wynonna once she gets to the house."

I shot Mama a look. Her eyes followed mine down to the vise grip Lawton's widow had on my hand. For some reason, Wynonna had attached herself, even though I'm not generally the comforting type.

"Make sure you tell Doc *everything* we talked about," I said.

Mama nodded. "Everything," she repeated.

"The rest of the riders will be gathering for dinner soon," I said. "We need to let Lawton's kin know what happened before word starts to spread."

After they left, Wynonna and I waited a few moments to make sure they found their way. The sound of the physician stomping through the woods had just begun to fade, when we heard a loud snap of brush.

"Watch that log, Doc!" Mama yelled from the distance.

I pictured him toppling over, pulling down an acre of skunk vine. "I guess the doctor doesn't do nature," I said.

"Oh, my Lord, no." Dropping my hand, Wynonna stepped in front to lead the way. "That man's idea of physical activity is strolling the buffet line at the Kountry Kitchen. He's never met a smothered pork chop or a chicken-fried steak he doesn't like."

She pulled back a branch from a hickory sapling so I could pass.

"Sounds like the old saying: Do as I say, not as I do. Did Doc Abel really think Lawton would listen to him about diet and exercise, considering Doc's own bad habits?" I asked.

"Oh, he wasn't really Lawton's main doctor anymore. Lawton started seeing a fancy cardiologist a few years back. Doc's been slipping a bit, but he still gives out flu shots and the occasional prescription. He and Lawton go way back, and Lawton's loyal. Doc took care of him ever since he was a little boy, you know?"

I shook my head, and felt the web of a banana spider clinging to my eyelashes.

"Yep, Lawton and his folks were among Doc's first patients when he was just starting out. And he kept going to him until he was a grown man, with grown kids of his own." Wynonna looked over her shoulder in the direction we'd come. I wondered if she was thinking about how Doc Abel might be examining her husband's body right now.

To distract her, I told Wynonna how Doc had iced and wrapped my wrist a decade before. As I spoke, I had a flash of him leaning over me in his exam room, reading glasses slid low on his nose. He asked me where it hurt, then gently lifted my hand this way and that. And as he did, I now remembered, he whistled that same tuneless song we'd heard in the woods tonight. That's why his awful version of "Whistle While You Work" had sounded familiar.

Wynonna led the way up three cypress wood steps to the Bramble ranch house. A wide porch encircled the house. A line of wooden rocking chairs sat under outdoor ceiling fans. Two big front windows were open, bringing in cool air to a structure that sat in the center of flat pastureland. Since the last hurricane, only two oak trees remained for shade. For most of the year, the house baked under a scorching sun, making it intolerable without air-conditioning.

But this was February. The crisp weather was welcome. In Florida, steam baths aren't a luxury to indulge at a spa. They're a hardship to endure every time we walk out the front door from June straight through to October.

Wynonna's hand was on the doorknob when we heard shouting from inside.

"And I told you I wouldn't sch-tand for it," a man yelled, his voice slurred. He waited, apparently listening, though we heard no one else speak. "Goddammit, I said no. Ab-showlutely not!"

Something hit the wall on the other side of the door, and then clattered to the floor. Unsteady footsteps lurched inside. A few seconds later came a heavy thump, followed by the sound of shattering glass.

"Ouc-sh! That hurt!" The same man yelled.

Wynonna's hand froze on the knob. "I don't want to deal with this," she whispered.

I cocked an eyebrow.

"It's Lawton's son, Trey. I wasn't looking forward to breaking the news under the best circumstances. And now this. He's drunk."

We both looked at the door. She straightened, seeming to gather her strength as she had at the cook site.

"Now or never." She breathed deeply. I patted awkwardly at her shoulder, trying to do as I'd seen Mama do.

She opened the door. I followed her in, stepping carefully around the cell phone that lay in pieces near the door jamb.

Trey sat cross-legged on the floor of a large living room, next to an overturned lamp. There was a rip in the wagon-wheel shaped shade. Light bulb shards were scattered across the legs of his jeans. His head hung in his hands. Scratches crisscrossed his muscled forearms, exposed by the rolled up sleeves of a Western-cut shirt.

"Trey?" Wynonna's voice was soft, tentative.

He looked up, lifting blood-shot eyes. A nasty gash left a reddish-brown streak across one cheek. His shirt, minus its top three buttons, gaped open to show a broad chest. Trey looked like he'd been on the losing side of a bar brawl.

His eyes were the same startling shade of blue as his father's. I remembered how they'd sparkled with fun and mischief when we were in high school. I'd never seen the cruelty in Trey's eyes that I saw the moment he focused on Wynonna.

"Well, if it ish-n't the wicked stepmother," he slurred. "Come to shake her moneymaker and bust my balls."

The haughty expression from the cook site returned to Wynonna's face. She looked at

Trey like he was something she'd dragged in from the paddock on the bottom of her pointy-toed boot. When she spoke, her voice was as chilly as the air rustling the curtains at the window.

"You're pathetic, Trey."

I suspected the only thing keeping Wynonna from spitting on the floor as she said his name were company manners and a pricey-looking bearskin rug.

"Why don't you stay right there on the floor, lowdown as you belong, while I make us some coffee? I'm afraid I've got some bad news for you, stepson."

"Don't tell me, Wynonna. Let me guess-sh. You've finally managed to figure out a way to get all my Daddy's money."

FIVE

"So then Lawton told me I'd been the prettiest girl ever at Himmarshee High. I believe that's the last thing I heard the poor man say."

As Mama's voice floated from the front porch through the open window, I quickly looked at Trey. Not even a twitch. He'd moved from the floor to a couch, where he was sitting straight up, sound asleep. Or passed out, one.

I wasn't at all surprised that Mama would choose to remember a compliment to her as Lawton Bramble's final words on this earth.

"The man always did have charm, may he rest in peace," she was saying to Doc Abel, as the door opened.

I put a finger to my lips and glared at her, pointing at Trey. Mama clapped a hand over her mouth, at least having the good grace to look embarrassed. Hurrying over, she perched like a small bird on the fat arm of the leather chair where I sat.

"Sorry, Mace," she whispered in my ear. "My stars! That poor boy looks like something the dog's dragged out from under the porch. He doesn't know about his daddy yet?"

"No thanks to you," I whispered back.

Across the big room, Trey's legs were stretched out to a low coffee table. His head slumped forward onto his chest.

"He's been drinking," I said. "I'm not even sure he noticed I was here. Wynonna's gone to make some coffee. No sign of Belle."

Barely glancing at Trey, Doc plodded toward us. "That boy's gonna have to straighten up now," he said in a purposely loud voice. "It's time for Mr. Lawton Bramble III to put aside all his foolishness and become a man."

That seemed harsh, considering Trey wasn't even aware yet he'd lost his father. Then again, I didn't know the family dynamics as well as Doc Abel did. I'd never met Trey's sister. She was younger, and I'd heard she studied art and languages at boarding schools in Europe.

"I'm gonna head out to my car and get my medical bag," he said, speaking more softly now. "I want to be ready in case I need to administer anything to the family members tonight."

"Hang on a sec, Doc. I'll step out with you," I said.

The night was dark enough now to see stars scattered across the sky. Orange blossoms from surrounding groves scented the air. Sounds from the Cracker Trail riders carried from the campsite, a quarter-mile or so away. Someone strummed a guitar, the melody faint. Someone else showed off with a cow whip, loud as a gunshot.

"Listen to that whip crack," Doc Abel said. "That's why they called the old-time Florida cow hunters 'Crackers.' "

I walked with him across a rutted dirt driveway to his ancient station wagon. Doc Abel had to be the only person in three counties with a Saab. It's mainly trucks and SUVs in this part of Florida, where cows still outnumber people and all the wild land has yet to be paved. I drive a beat-up Jeep. Mama has a 1967 Bonneville convertible. Her car's turquoise, which is about as exotic as it gets in our little hometown of Himmarshee. We're in the middle of the state: three-and-a-half hours north of Miami's sin and sunshine, south enough of Orlando to stay out of Mickey Mouse's big shadow.

Doc opened his car door and leaned into the back seat.

"Mama showed you the body, right? What'd you think?" I asked him. "Was it a heart attack?"

"That seems fairly certain, given Lawton's poor health." He straightened, holding his black bag.

"But he should still be checked out, right?"

"I checked him out," Doc said, "and the cause of death is clear. Everything I saw is consistent with cardiac arrest."

When I didn't say anything, Doc added, "That means a heart attack."

"I know," I said. "That's how my daddy died."

Doc closed the backseat door and leaned against it. "I'm sorry. How old were you when you lost him?"

"Ten. Maddie was almost fourteen. Marty was just eight."

"That's tough for girls, growing up without a father."

"Well, we had a few stepfathers along the way."

"It's not the same, though, is it?"

I shook my head. As I did, I caught a glimpse of something circular and ceramic on the front passenger seat of Doc's Saab. He saw me staring at it through the window.

"Your mother told me about the trouble

y'all had last summer, and about how you want to make sure there's nothing suspicious about Lawton's death. She said you were worried someone might mess with that tasting mug. So I brought it with me, for safekeeping."

I started to protest. He held up a hand.

"I'll hang onto the cup and the crusty stuff inside until the cause of death is absolutely certain. But I can tell you right now, with nearly sixty years of medical experience, the man died of a heart attack. It happens."

He shrugged, like Lawton's death was of minor consequence.

I know it happens, I felt like saying. I just got through telling you it happened to my own daddy. I was having trouble getting a read on Doc Abel. One moment, he seemed kindly; the next, almost mean.

Before I had the chance to figure out what I thought about him, Wynonna called out from the porch. "Doc?" Her voice trembled. "You better come on in here."

We hurried inside to find Mama gently shaking Trey by the shoulders. He was now stretched out on the couch.

"We tried to get him up and get some coffee into him so we could tell him what happened," Wynonna said.

"He's not responding," Mama added,

shaking hard enough now to loosen Trey's fillings.

Squeezing past Mama, Doc slowly lowered his bulk beside the couch. The floor seemed to shudder when his knees made contact with the bearskin rug. His fingers moved expertly to the pulse point at Trey's wrist. He leaned toward his mouth and sniffed.

"Stinkin' drunk, is all he is. Like usual." Wrinkling his nose, Doc dropped Trey's wrist like it was something nasty. "Other than a liver well on its way to being pickled, the boy's fine."

After the laborious process of rising from the rug, Doc collapsed into a heavy, cowhide-upholstered chair. As I listened to his ragged breathing, my eyes returned to Trey. Drool dribbled from his open mouth. His head lolled to one side. A brewery's worth of beer-stench escaped from his pores.

An image formed in my mind of a very different Trey. We were in high school. He'd just led the Himmarshee Brahmans to a state football championship. He strutted the halls with a perky blonde cheerleader on each arm — a king in a cowboy hat.

What in the world had happened to Trey Bramble?

Outside, a dog began to bark. A moment

later we heard clunks and squeaks as a vehicle jounced over the unpaved drive.

"That'll be Belle, Lawton's daughter." Wynonna was pulling at the skin on her hands again. "I called her earlier, and caught her on her cell. She was already on her way here for dinner. I didn't want to tell her about Lawton on the phone, you know?" She looked first at me, then at Mama, for reassurance.

"You did the right thing, honey." Mama covered Wynonna's nervous hands with her own. "That's not the kind of news anybody should get while they're driving."

The engine quit. A car door slammed. Keys jangled. Doc Abel huffed to his feet, holding his black bag ready. We all watched, waiting, as the front door opened.

"What's everybody looking at?"

The young woman who stepped into the room had coppery red hair, falling in wild curls past her shoulders. Her eyes were light green, the color of cypress needles in spring. The gaze she turned on us was curious, intelligent.

"Well?" she said.

Finally, Wynonna spoke. "Belle, why don't you sit down? Doc Abel has something he needs to tell you."

The news about her father's death left Belle's body rigid, her face pale. She gripped the arms of a cane-back chair like she was afraid it was going to fly away on her. The veins atop her hands bulged out, blue-grey against fair, sun-freckled skin.

"I want to go to Daddy's cook site right now," she said.

"Honey, I don't think you should . . ."

"Right now." Belle interrupted Mama. Her lower lip quivered, but her eyes were dry.

"All right, then. This is Rosalee, Belle." Doc nodded toward Mama. "She and I will take you over to see your father." He glanced at Wynonna. "Are you up to making the call to the funeral home?"

Pressing her lips together, Wynonna nodded.

"I wrote the number for you on the pad in the kitchen, by the phone," Doc said.

After Doc left with Mama and Belle, the big living room was quiet, except for Trey's snores. Wynonna's voice was a low murmur from the kitchen. Here, it was just me and Trey, sleeping off his drunk. I hated to admit it, but he was still a handsome guy —

even with a line of drool on his chin. Was it a bar fight, or something else, that had left him scratched and bruised? Where were the buttons off his shirt, which hung open to reveal his smooth chest?

I sat and studied Trey, like he was an animal in the wild. On the side, I make a little extra money trapping nuisance critters for newcomers. These are people who move to Himmarshee imagining they'll love the country, until the country comes to call. And then they're desperate to evict it, from the attic or the swimming pool or whatever part of their home the country has crashed.

My business depends on understanding animals well enough to predict their behavior. I like to do the same with the human animal, but that's usually a lot more complicated.

I understood how Trey grew up: Money. Privilege. God-given talent. But I couldn't have predicted this behavior: Drunk. Passed out. Failing to achieve his potential. He seemed wounded. I always stop to help injured animals. I just hoped Trey wouldn't bite.

"Mace?" Wynonna's voice snapped me out of my reverie. She handed me a cup of coffee, and put one for herself on an end table mounted on a wagon wheel. "Thanks for

49

sticking around."

"Don't mention it," I said. "Listen, would you mind if I used your phone? I'll keep it short. I just want to let my sisters know Mama and I are okay, in case they hear something happened on the Cracker Trail."

Waving me toward the kitchen, she sank into a chair next to the couch. Wynonna looked like she could use that cup of coffee.

Fortunately, I reached Maddie's answering machine. No half-hour back-and-forth about how if Mama and I were more careful, we wouldn't be in the position of finding another dead body, and by the way, we should watch out for snakes if we're foolhardy enough to sleep out in the wilderness in a tent. At the sound of the beep, I simply said:

"Maddie, it's Mace. It looks like Lawton Bramble had a fatal heart attack just as the Cracker Trail riders were arriving on his land. Wanted to let you know Mama and I are fine. I'm not sure if the rest of the ride is off or on, but I'll be in touch. Be sure and tell Marty everything's okay. We haven't seen a single snake."

That last part was a lie. But I didn't want to worry our little sister, Marty.

I used the toilet and washed up, using a bathroom off the kitchen. By the time I was done, my coffee had gone cold on the counter. I nuked it in the microwave, looking for the sugar bowl while I waited. I added two teaspoons to my cup, and then rooted around in the 'fridge for some half-and-half. All I saw was skim milk. I'd sooner drink it black than ruin good coffee with that thin gruel.

Carrying my cup, I tiptoed back into the living room. If Wynonna had managed to catch some sleep, I didn't want to disturb her. She leaned forward off the chair, angled toward Trey. Her long hair had fallen like a cloak over her face. I couldn't tell if she was awake or sleeping.

As I got closer, I saw one of Wynonna's arms stretched out toward the couch, resting on Trey's chest. She'd slipped her hand beneath his ripped-open shirt. Her big diamond ring glinted as she moved her hand back and forth, back and forth, massaging the bare chest of her dead husband's son.

SIX

"Leave that dog be, Mace. We've got to get over to the camp."

A Florida cur, a cow-working dog, lay with his head on his paws on the hard-pine porch of an outbuilding on the Bramble property. He watched with sad eyes as we walked past.

"I think he was Lawton's dog, Mama." I bent to check the name on his collar. *Tuck.* "Look how lost he looks."

I'd slipped out of the Brambles' living room without letting on what I'd seen between Wynonna and Trey. I certainly wasn't ready to spill the beans to Mama. I didn't want speculation about the young widow and her stepson spreading all over middle Florida until I had it clearer in my mind what was going on.

Mama and I met as she was coming back from Lawton's cook site. Doc Abel was still there, with the body. He and Lawton's daughter, Belle, were waiting for the van from the funeral home.

I kneeled on the pine board and stroked the dog's head. "Hey, Tuck, old boy. How you doin'?"

A snort came from Mama's direction. "Maybe Carlos Martinez wouldn't have moved back to Miamuh," she said, using the old Florida pronunciation, "if you'd of paid as much attention to him as you're paying to that hound."

Not this again.

"I told you, Mama, Carlos had a lot of history to reconcile with in Miami. The timing wasn't right. We both knew it."

I scratched behind Tuck's right ear. He rolled to his back so I could rub his belly.

"All I'm saying is Carlos is a good man. I know I wouldn't have been so quick to let him get away." Mama smoothed at her hair.

"I know all about it, Mama. If you were just twenty-five years younger, you'd be wearing his engagement ring by now."

One of her convenient memory lapses had allowed Mama to forget that Detective Carlos Martinez had nearly sent her to the slammer the previous summer for murder. Back then, he'd have been more likely to slip a pair of handcuffs around her wrists than an engagement ring around her finger.

The dog got up and shook itself as we

continued across Bramble property. He followed us, tags jangling on his collar. Mama turned sideways and waved a hand in Tuck's direction. "Go on, shoo!" she yelled. "Git, you rascal."

He stopped, cocking his head at me.

"Quit it, Mama!" I said. "Can't you see the poor thing is lonely?" I slapped my thigh and whistled. "C'mon, Tuck. You can come with us." The dog loped to my side.

Mama rolled her eyes. "Just one ounce, Mace. If you'd use just an ounce of your power to attract animals on men, you'd be married by now. You're a smart girl, honey. But when it comes to men, you ain't got the brains God gave a possum."

"Who says I want to be married?" I snapped at her. "You've marched down the aisle enough for the both of us. Enough for half the female population in Himmarshee, in fact."

She ignored me, leveling a firm look at Tuck. "That flea-bitten animal is not sleeping in the tent with us."

"You'll be glad to have him if it gets as cold tonight as it's supposed to get."

"Some women might prefer a man to a dog for warmth, Mace." She arched her perfectly plucked eyebrows. "Think about it, honey."

The parched Bermuda grass and sharp stobs sticking up from the pasture crackled under our boots. The light of the moon edged white clouds with silver, brightening the sky above us.

"Speaking of men, Mace, you might be curled up alone with Lawton's cur in the tent tonight. I called Sally from the ranch house earlier. He's driving over to meet us on the ride."

"Sally" is Mama's irritating nickname for her fiancé, Salvatore Provenza — would-be husband No. 5. Somehow, I couldn't picture the ex–New Yorker with the mysterious past as Cracker Trail material.

"What in the world is a guy from the Bronx going to do on a trail ride where everyone else is on horseback?"

"Don't ask me, Mace. He got a burr under his saddle about me being out here in the woods when I told him about Lawton. Why does everyone think I'm gonna get into trouble every time someone I know turns up dead?"

Yeah, imagine that, I thought.

"Anyhoo, Sally says he wants to come up here and poke around. He says he'll keep a low profile."

I pictured Sal: three-hundred-some pounds; a taste for pastel-colored golfing duds; and a Bronx honk that could stop the D train at Yankee Stadium. Amid a group of slow-talking, jeans-wearing, native Florida crackers, Big Sal screamed "high-profile."

"I'm not sure that's a good idea, Mama."

"I couldn't persuade him otherwise, Mace. After all, the man is crazy about me." She fluffed her platinum-hued hairdo. Amazingly, it hadn't lost much height at all after a full day's ride. "He wants to be here to protect me if problems arise."

Big Sal may have been terrific in his mystery profession up north in New York. But down south, he was out of his element. Suppose someone had killed Lawton? If Sal pushed too hard, too fast, there was no telling what might happen. Desperate people do desperate things.

Mama stopped in the pasture. "Which way, Mace?"

We'd come to a fork along the unpaved road that wound through the Bramble property. To the right, I could hear the distant sound of traffic on State Road 64. The shell-and-sand surface was also more compressed in that direction, indicating heavier travel.

"Let's go left," I said. "That'll probably take us to the back pasture, where the camp is set up."

As we set out, Mama picked up where she left off. "Personally, Mace, I think it's a waste of time for Sally to come all the way up here. Doc Abel was Lawton's doctor forever, and he seems certain his heart killed him."

The image of Wynonna rubbing Trey's chest on the living room couch popped into my mind. I was just about to open my mouth to tell Mama what I'd seen when the loud crack of a cow whip snapped the sense back into my head. An aspiring cow hunter was brushing up on technique. We'd almost arrived at the camp where the rest of the riders had gathered.

"We'd better get it straight what we're gonna say about Lawton, Mama." I unwound the chain that secured the gate between the Bramble homestead and the outlying pastures. A hand-lettered sign hung from the barbed wire fence:

Cracker Trail Campers:
Please close gate behind you. Cattle will scatter.

As Mama and I stepped through, Tuck whined and looked back in the direction of the ranch house.

"C'mon, boy. It's okay," I said.

He sat down in the sandy road and hung his head.

"All right, then. We'll see you later."

I gave him a parting pat, and then swung the gate shut, wrapping the chain around twice.

"Poor thing," Mama said. "He's waiting for Lawton."

Before long, we'd found our way to the center of camp. Wood smoke rose from a big fire. The smell of steaks sizzling wafted from the cook wagon. A Toby Keith CD blasted from the speakers inside somebody's RV.

"Daddy would roll over in his grave if he saw the fancy rigs people bring on the Cracker Trail these days." I gazed around at gleaming trucks and matching horse trailers, luxury RVs and campers.

"Nonsense, Mace. Your daddy went with the times. You can put all the disapproval you want into your voice. But that doesn't change the fact that there's nothing noble about sleeping on the cold, hard ground inside a tent that stinks of mildew." Mama pouted. "And I still don't see why we couldn't rent us a nice little pop-up camper to bring."

"Because the original Florida cow hunters didn't have campers, Mama. Or heated horse trailers. Or recreational vehicles. The ride is supposed to honor our Florida pioneer history. It ought to be authentic."

"Yeah? Well, I notice you don't mind doing your business in the portable potties the Cracker Trail Association hauls along."

A low chuckle sounded behind us, coming from the food trailer.

"Your Mama's got you there, darlin'."

We turned to see a strapping older man with a full head of wiry grey hair. Stacks of paper plates and napkins in plastic bags nearly hid his face. Mama's hand flew to smooth her 'do. She tried to get a glance at her reflection in the generator used to power the electric lights around the chuck wagon.

"The first Florida Crackers didn't have disposable utensils, neither. Nor wet coconut cake nor cold banana pudding for dessert," the man said. "But that hasn't stopped anyone with a sweet tooth from trying to weasel seconds out of my servers."

"Why, I don't believe we've had the pleasure," Mama said, eyelashes fluttering in time to her words. "I'm Rosalee Deveraux, and this is my middle daughter, Mace."

He shifted the paper goods away to reveal his face. Strong cheekbones. A cheerful smile, which stopped just short of his dark eyes. "Hell, Rosalee, I'd never forget you!

I'm Johnny Adams. Remember, I moved away to Sebring during high school?"

Mama's flirtatiousness disappeared, replaced by a mournful tone. "Oh, Johnny! I'm afraid I have some awful news about Lawton Bramble. I know y'all were as close as brothers once."

A hard look flitted across his face. "That was a long time ago, Rosalee."

"I'm sorry to have to tell you this, standing right here by the food trailer." Mama glanced around, like there might be a better spot for breaking bad news. Then she blurted out, "Lawton's gone, Johnny. He had a heart attack and died."

She reached out a comforting hand, but Johnny didn't seem to need it. When Mama revealed that Lawton was dead, the hard look never left his face.

SEVEN

The big campfire roared, sending sparks into the night. Johnny Adams stared at the white-hot logs as they collapsed in the flames. His face was unreadable. Mama said he'd been as close as a brother once to Lawton. What memories was he calling up out of that fire?

"All right, then. We need to tell the trail boss," Johnny finally said. "He'll bring everybody together, and we'll make the announcement about Lawton just before dinner."

"I'll go and tell him," Mama said. "Jack will probably have some questions about how it happened and all."

I pictured Jack Hollister, our trail boss, trying to get a straight story from Mama. She might get distracted onto a tangent about Wynonna's high-heeled boots, and forget to mention that Lawton was dead.

"I'll come with you," I said to Mama.

"Well, I for one am shocked that Lawton and that new wife aren't nowhere to be seen. You'd think they'd have been out here to greet us by now."

The whisper in the dinner chow line came from a middle-aged cowgirl whose bottom was too broad for her jeans.

"Oh, I'm sure he would have been here, strutting, if not for that young wife," sniffed her companion, a woman in a Western-style blouse and tight permanent curls. "She's probably convinced him to take her out for caviar in Palm Beach instead of coming out to stand around here, serving Cow Hunter Chili to a bunch of ol' Crackers."

I was about to set the gossipy pair of them straight, but Mama put her finger to her lips and shook her head. "Wait for the trail boss," she said into my ear. "He'll tell everybody at once."

A few minutes later, Jack Hollister was about to do just that. With his compact, well-muscled build and sun-beaten face, Jack's age could have been anywhere from forty to fifty. But I guessed closer to forty, based on his physical ease climbing onto an up-ended length of log. He didn't seem as comfortable when it came to actually speaking.

He cleared his throat a couple of times, and then spoke too softly. "Can I get everybody's attention?"

People shifted and jostled, wanting to see what Jack had to say, but not wanting to lose their place in the supper line. Some of those in position near the front muttered as other riders crowded in around them.

Suddenly, someone gave a loud, long whistle. The shrill sound silenced the crowd. Jack removed his stained cowboy hat.

"I don't know how else to say this but to get right to it. Lawton Bramble died this afternoon. Looks like a heart attack. All of us are already here, a hundred or more. So, we're gonna go ahead and camp tonight on his land, just as we planned. Then, we'll ride out in the morning, so we can make our next scheduled stop."

The only sound now was the hum of the generators that powered the cook trailer. I looked over at the big-bottomed woman and her friend. Both of them looked ashamed of themselves, which served them right.

"Lawton was a good friend to the Florida Cracker Trail," Jack continued. "He'll be missed. Now, I'm sure the Bramble family would appreciate your prayers. Let's all bow our heads for a few moments, why don't we?"

As Jack lowered his head, a ripple of prayer rose over the line. I said my own brief piece, asking for safe passage to heaven for Lawton. I looked up and saw that many others were still praying, Mama included. She always did have more than me to say to the Lord.

I used the time to scan the crowd. The fifty-something cowgirls were whispering to one another. The trail boss snuck a quick look at his watch. And Johnny Adams knuckled away a single tear that rolled down his cheek.

Later, as Mama and I were sitting in our camp chairs with chicken-fried steaks on plastic plates, I asked her about Johnny and Lawton.

"Oh, my stars, Mace. Those boys were tighter than ticks on a skinny dog when all of us were young. Lawton's daddy used to have a rodeo arena on the ranch they had in Himmarshee back then. When those two would saddle up for team roping, nobody else could touch their times. The steers never had a chance when it came to getting past Lawton and Johnny. It was like the two of them thought with a single mind."

I speared a cheesy potato before it slid

from my plate. "What happened?"

"Mostly, it was over a woman — like so many men's battles. And then, later, there was some business falling-out, too. Johnny got the short end of the stick, of course, like most people did with Lawton. But the love triangle was the real issue. Lawton swept in and stole the girl that Johnny was engaged to marry. And then Lawton married her himself. Poor Johnny never did find another, and he never did get over it."

"Surely this wasn't Wynonna?"

"My goodness, no." Mama cut her steak into bite-size pieces. "Wynonna hadn't even got her first Barbie doll lunchbox for kindergarten when all this happened. It was Trey's mama. Lawton's first wife." She chewed her meat thoughtfully. "Barbara was her name, if I recall. I sort of lost track of the Bramble family, once they moved their cattle operation to the north of Himmarshee. But from what I heard, the marriage never was a happy one. Rumor was that Lawton had a roving eye. Poor Barb took to drinking hard, so as not to notice it."

I thought of Trey, and how I'd watched in awe with all the other peasants as he reigned over the hallways of Himmarshee High. With all the Bramble money and power, I'd always assumed he had the perfect life.

Guess it wasn't so perfect after all.

Mama sipped at her lemonade, then patted her mouth with her napkin. She looked around to see if anyone was listening. Then she lowered her voice to a whisper.

"That wasn't the worst of it, though. The poor woman ended up dying in some kind of accident at home, when Trey and Belle were still little. Everyone said she was drunk as could be. She probably never even knew the fall she took would turn out to be fatal."

Suspicion made the hairs on my arms stand up straight. "Where was Barbara's not-so-loving husband when she tripped and fell, Mama?"

"Lawton? He was up at the Capitol in Tallahassee, talking to the state legislature about agricultural exemptions for pasture land. It was an accident, pure and simple, Mace. She stumbled down some steps, is what I think I heard." She clucked her tongue. "That's not to say Lawton waited all that long before replacing the first Mrs. Bramble with the second."

I pushed the rest of my steak around on the plate. Suddenly, I didn't feel very hungry.

"Did you and Daddy go to the funeral?"

"We did. It was way over in Polk County. Those poor children looked like they didn't know what hit them. Lawton held onto them, one for each hand, as they lowered Barbara's casket into the ground. The flowers were awful pretty, though, I have to say that. Lots of white roses and baby's breath."

A rush of sympathy for Trey and Belle washed over me.

"How'd Lawton seem?" I asked.

"Guilty-looking, if you want the truth. He knew what kind of husband he'd been. But his eyes stayed dry the whole way through. I can't say the same for Johnny."

My eyes automatically shifted to where the cook stood, too far away to overhear us.

"Why not?" I asked.

"Johnny sobbed like a baby, poor thing. When he walked up to pay his respects, he collapsed onto one knee and pounded his fist on Barbara's casket. I think he might have thrown himself in there if some of Lawton's ranch hands hadn't pulled him away."

We both glanced over at Johnny, who seemed to be on automatic pilot as he passed out the last pieces of strawberry pie. The granite was back in his jaw.

I wondered if that tear I'd spotted earlier on his cheek had been shed for his old friend Lawton, or for Barbara, his one true love?

EIGHT

A funeral home van inched toward the gate that led from the Bramble ranch to State Road 64. Cracker Trail campers lined both sides of the narrow, crushed-shell road. Mama and I stood with the others, our flashlights and lanterns marking the route of Lawton's last ride.

The van stopped at the gate, its headlights shining into a vast blackness beyond the highway. The engine idled, a low rumble. Moths flitted in and out of the beams from our lights. One of Lawton's ranch hands ran to unlock the gate. The rest of us stood silently, waiting.

Doc Abel climbed from the passenger side of the van. Then he leaned in to talk to the driver, one arm resting on the open window. Finally, he straightened and gave a little pat to the side of the vehicle. The driver pulled on through the gate. We watched until his taillights on the highway turned to tiny red dots.

"It's a shame. He wasn't that old of a man," someone said.

"Sixty-three or four, I heard," someone else answered.

As the crowd began to break up, Doc Abel walked with heavy steps toward Mama and me.

"That part of the job never gets any easier." He sounded older and more tired than he had just a few hours before. "There's nothing like saying goodbye to a friend to make you realize your own mortality."

Mama aimed her flashlight into the sky. "Are you a religious man, Doc? Because you know, the Bible promises us a reunion in heaven with those we've cared for here on earth."

Doc was silent for a moment.

"I'm a man of medicine, Rosalee. A man of science. That's not the best foundation for a strong religious faith. I believe we should make the most of the time we're given. After that, there's no guarantee."

Mama swung her light into Doc's face. "Are you telling me you don't believe in life everlasting?"

He waited a beat, squinting into the light.

"I believe in life, Rosalee. Let's just leave it at that."

Her eyes searched his face for evidence he might need converting. From past experience, I knew she usually found such evidence, whether it existed or not. I cut her off at the pulpit.

"Doc probably has business to get to, don't you, Doc?" I looked at him meaningfully. "I'm sure he doesn't have time for a theological discussion."

"It's not theology, Mace." Mama shook her head. "It's salvation, pure and simple."

"Mama," I warned. "Now's not the time."

"There's always time for the Lord. He always makes time for us. *If you confess with your mouth that Jesus is Lord and believe in your heart that God raised him from the dead, you will be saved.* That's not just me; that's the Bible talking. Romans 10:9."

Mama's light was still trained on Doc. He was squirming like a shoplifter in the store security office.

"Mama, haven't you ever heard the saying 'To each his own'? Doc has every right to his own views on religion, or anything else."

"Even if his views mean he'll burn in eternal hellfire?"

Sweat was beginning to bead on Doc's upper lip, though the night was cool. Maybe he was starting to sizzle in anticipation.

"Mama, if Doc wants spiritual guidance, I'm sure he'll turn to you." When purple pigs fly, I thought. "Now, that's enough!"

Pressing her lips together, she lowered the light. The inquisition appeared to be over, leastwise for now. Doc gave me a grateful look.

"I should be getting back to the ranch house." He pulled an oversized handkerchief from his pocket and dabbed at his upper lip. "I need to check on Wynonna and the rest of the family. I'm worried about Belle. She's fragile. Lawton dying might be enough to break her."

I could see twin desires warring on Mama's face: redeeming a non-believer versus discovering a juicy tidbit about a Bramble family member.

"Is Belle crazy, Doc?" she blurted out.

"You know I can't discuss a patient, Rosalee. On the other hand, it is common knowledge Belle's had some problems growing up."

"Well, we don't hear much common knowledge from up here way down in Himmarshee," Mama said.

"That's right," I added. "We're too busy gossiping about our own to worry about gossiping about folks who live a few counties north."

Mama pulled herself to her full height. She still didn't reach my chin. "I am *not* a gossip, Mace. I'm merely concerned about Belle. Maybe I could do something to help her — right, Doc?"

Only if the poor girl needs a ride all the way 'round the crazy bend, I thought.

"I'd say just be as kind to Belle as you can," Doc said. "Now, I hate to change the subject, but do you suppose there's any food left from dinner? I missed it altogether."

By the looks of him, missing a meal was a rare event. Nonetheless, his mention of food sent Mama into Southern hostess mode.

"You're hungry?" She put a hand on his arm. "Well, why didn't you say something? That's awful! We'll get Johnny to scare you up a plate. He served chicken-fried steak and strawberry pie tonight. It'd be a shame to miss it. Mace and I will take you over and keep you company while you eat."

That meant Mama would angle for a little something for us, too, since it's rude to just sit there and watch someone else eat. I was tired. And I still had to check on our loaner horses. But I am my mama's daughter, sweet tooth and all. We turned our flashlights toward our cow-pasture-turned-campground and the promise of seconds on strawberry pie.

After a few false starts — "I'm positive it's a right at the sabal palm, Mace. Not the pine tree!" — we arrived back at the cook trailer.

Some of the other riders sat in small groups around the campfire. The mood was quiet, subdued. Someone picked a guitar. A few people sipped from coffee cups or beer cans. Johnny, the cook, wasn't around. But Mama persuaded one of his servers to fix a dinner plate for Doc. She also scored three pieces of pie. The girl left off the whipped cream on top, but Mama decided not to push her luck.

We'd just settled into the camp chairs we left earlier by the fire, when I thought I heard the unmistakable singing voice of Frank Sinatra. A moment later, Mama heard it, too, judging by the smile that spread across her face.

An awful, nasal voice arose, chiming in with the recording for Frank's big finish: *"Bam-ba-da-dum, Bump-bump-ba-da-dum . . ."*

"Sally!" Mama's smile broadened and her hand flew to her hair. "How's my lipstick, honey?" She bared her teeth at me in the firelight.

"Eaten off with your first piece of strawberry pie."

She fumbled through the pockets of her jeans, pulling out a tube of her favorite shade, Apricot Ice. "Hold still a sec, Mace. I can almost make out my reflection, shining in your eyes." She stuck her nose a few inches from mine and formed an O with her mouth.

"Who's Sally?" Doc Abel asked, before tucking into a tower of au gratin potatoes. Seeing his old friend off to the great unknown hadn't seemed to diminish his appetite.

Mama finished circling her lips. I dabbed with my napkin where she'd smeared Apricot Ice under her nose.

"Sally's my fiancé," she said, waving the rock on her left hand in Doc's direction. "Sal Provenza. He's from New York City."

No kidding, I thought. Sal's as New York as the subway, and just about as subtle.

The last strains of Sinatra wound down. Then, a heavy car door slammed. The smell of dollar store cologne drifted toward us in the night.

"Rosalee, honey? You dere?"

I'd know that Bronx accent anywhere.

When Sal shouldered his way into the dinner camp, I couldn't believe my eyes. He had on a ten-gallon hat and cowboy boots.

Both in white. His neon-blue jacket sported decorative lapels. On the left, a mounted cowboy tossed a lariat. On the right, the rope ensnared a white-piping calf. And were those rhinestones along the outside seams of Sal's pants, winking in the firelight?

Mama's boyfriend looked like John Wayne up and married Elton John.

She shouted, "We're over here, Sally."

"He can always use the glare off that suit to find his way," I cracked.

"Hush!" Mama whispered, and she pinched me. Hard.

NINE

Mama spooned the last bite of her strawberry pie into Sal's mouth. As nauseating as the display was, I knew it was a sign of true love. She's serious about sweets, never sharing lightly.

I'd given Sal my camp chair and taken a seat on the ground. I shifted, trying to avoid a sharp stob sticking up from the pasture. It was about to draw blood on my butt cheek, right through my jeans. After Sal finished chewing, he leaned back contentedly in my chair. I watched as the supposedly indestructible fabric strained at the seams. I'd bet Mama's fiancé exceeded the chair's load capacity, even before he Hoovered that strawberry pie.

"So, you say this Lawton guy keeled over while he was making chili?" Sal pulled a toothpick from behind his ear and stuck it in his mouth, staring all the while at Doc Abel.

"It was his heart. And it wasn't unexpected." Doc sat rigid in his chair, meeting Sal's stare head on.

"Sally's not suggesting anything to the contrary." Mama placed her hand on Doc's arm. Her immaculate manicure was a marvel, considering we were camping in the woods. "He's from the Bronx in New York, so his questions don't always come out sounding right."

Ring, ring, I thought. That's the kettle, calling the pot black.

"Rosie's right about that. I'm just a big bull in the teacup shop half the time." Sal clapped Doc's shoulder, causing him to wince. "Do you like cigars, Doc? I gotta couple of Cubans I've been saving. A buddy brought 'em for me through Mexico. We can have a smoke, so long as you don't squeal to nobody about where they came from."

Doc looked torn. "Smoking isn't good for your health. On the other hand, I haven't had a proper cigar in years. What the heck?" He shrugged. "Life's short, as Lawton's unfortunate death demonstrated today."

Sal reached into the neon blue expanse of his jacket and pulled out a leather cigar case, an engagement present from Mama. He handed a cigar to Doc, who sniffed as if it were a fine wine. Putting it between his lips, Doc puffed as Sal torched the tip with a cigar lighter. Once it was glowing, Doc leaned back, exhaling with a happy sigh. He looked like he'd died and gone to that heaven that he didn't believe in.

When Sal lit up, a cigar-scented cloud swirled around us, warring with the wood smoke from the campfire. Sitting across the way, the big-bottomed cowgirl sniffed, then made a big show of waving her hand in front of her face.

The smell of cigars has never bothered me. They remind me of Mama's Husband No. 3, who I liked. He was a nice man, just a bad match for Mama. Number 3 taught me to drive in an orange grove he managed west of Fort Pierce. I can still remember the smell in his pickup truck: cigar overlaid with orange blossoms.

"You're doing just fine, Mace," he'd say, as we bounced along the rows between trees. "Go ahead and give her some gas."

I'd floor it, and he'd smile around the cigar he planted between his lips.

Staring into the fire, I flashed back to being fifteen. I'd felt like the queen of the world high up in the cab of that old truck. Watching the flames, I drifted off, almost rolling again with the truck over the rough ground in that long-ago grove. I suddenly snapped back to the present when I heard Sal mention my name.

"What'd I miss?"

He flicked an ash. His cigar was about two-thirds gone. They must have been talking around me for a while. Had I dozed off?

"I was just telling Doc you're suspicious after that murder you and your mother got mixed up in last summer." *Mudder,* he pronounced it. "You're inclined to see foul play around every corner, even where there ain't none. It's only natural, Mace."

Mama scrubbed with Sal's hanky at a glob of pie he'd dropped on his gaudy Western wear.

"When you open the trunk of your convertible, like I did, and find a dead man stuffed inside like he was a Samsonite suitcase, foul play seems obvious," Mama said. "But, Mace, this looks completely different than my murder victim. It's clear that Lawton spent his time on earth, died of natural causes, and went on to meet his maker." Here Mama paused to look at Doc. "That's what Doc says, all except the part about Lawton going to heaven, of course."

Oh, Lord. Not the afterlife again.

"Y'all aren't looking at the whole picture, Mama. Don't forget Lawton had pulled his gun. And something about that scene just

79

didn't set right with me."

"You've seen a lot of crime scenes, huh, Mace?" Sal held out his cigar and gazed at it, confident he'd made his point.

I had no comeback. I twisted my body around in an effort to find a comfortable spot — and make Sal feel guilty about taking my chair. As I did, I noticed two teen-aged riders nearby, straining forward in their seats to hear what we'd say next. When the closest one saw me looking, she ducked her head and started fiddling with a big silver buckle on her belt.

"Little pitchers . . ." I whispered, nodding in the girls' direction.

". . . have big ears," Mama completed the old saying.

I shut up and went back to watching the fire. I was too tired to argue anyway. But I still had my doubts — about the natural causes, and also about heaven. Not that I didn't believe. I just wondered if Lawton would be asked to make a U-turn at the Pearly Gates. He'd womanized. He was estranged from his only son. And he'd done a friend wrong in love and business. And those were just the sins we knew about.

If there were things in Lawton Bramble's life bad enough to keep him out of heaven, wouldn't they be bad enough to get him murdered?

I was pondering that when an excited murmur began to ripple through the campfire crowd. The trail boss was leading Wynonna to the big oak log he'd already used to address the Cracker Trail gathering. People parted, like Wynonna was Princess Di brought back from the dead.

At the log, Jack offered Wynonna his arm. She steadied herself, climbing up in her high-heeled boots. I couldn't help but notice she'd had time to trade in the black pair she'd worn earlier for a fancier set. These were light blue suede, with a swirl of turquoise snaking up the sides.

Jack coughed a couple of times. But he didn't need to get anyone's attention. The dinner camp was as silent as a church, every eye riveted on Wynonna. The broad-beamed cowgirl and her curly-headed pal studied the Widow Bramble like they were in charge of phoning in a report to *People* magazine.

"I've just come to say a few words to welcome you to the Bramble ranch," Wynonna said, tears threatening to spill from her green eyes. "Lawton would have wanted that. He'd have wanted y'all to feel at home here, on family land. I'm sure everyone has heard by now that my husband suffered a fatal heart attack this afternoon."

The crowd murmured in affirmation.

"The trail boss passed along prayers and condolences from many of you. I want you to know the family — Trey and Belle and I — appreciate it."

I glanced around, and noticed the rest of Lawton's family hadn't come over with their young stepmother. Had they asked Wynonna to speak, or had she taken on the role on her own?

Brushing her frosted bangs from her forehead, she scanned the large crowd. "I just want y'all to know you're welcome here, despite Lawton's death. He really looked forward to being your host. He was all set to catch somebody's tongue a'fire with that Cow Hunter Chili." Her smile wavered. She touched a wadded up tissue gently to each eye. "I'm sorry," she said.

The crowd murmured its sympathy.

Jack reached for her arm to guide her down from the log. But Wynonna lingered, hanging tight to his hand.

"Just one more thing."

The crowd murmured a question.

"Y'all may hear all kinds of things about Lawton in the coming days. Some true. Most not. I just want you to know that, on balance, my husband was a good man. I loved him, faults and all, just the way he loved me. And although our marriage wasn't a long one, it was solid." Her shoulders began to shake. "I'm going to miss him something awful," she choked out.

Stepping down, Wynonna was sobbing. Jack put an arm around her, adding an awkward pat. First one rider, and then another, and then another stepped forward from the crowd. Hands reached out to comfort her.

"You poor thing," the big cowgirl said, as she stood in line to stroke Wynonna's arm.

"So brave!" The cowgirl's curly-haired friend dabbed her own teary eyes, and then peeled off a fresh tissue from her pack to hand to the new widow.

"Poor broad." Sal said, and then peered at Mama in the firelight. "I thought for sure you'd have the wadderworks turned on by now." He ran a finger down Mama's cheek, which was just as dry as mine. "What's wrong, Rosie? I've seen you get teary-eyed over a TV commercial."

Mama's lips were pressed together; her arms folded tight across her chest. She watched through narrowed eyes as a human surge of sympathy engulfed Wynonna.

"Mace?" Sal turned to me. "What's up with your mudder?

Mama shook her head at me, a barely

perceptible "no." She wouldn't speak ill of so recent a widow. But I knew she was thinking the same thing as I was. Wynonna's public grief smacked of performance. And the two of us had witnessed her dress rehearsal, standing beside her husband's body just a few hours before.

Ten

"Bravo! Bravo!"

The mocking shout came from the edge of the crowd. In the hushed silence that followed, Trey stood all alone, clapping. He must have slipped in while all eyes were on his stepmother.

"And the Oscar goes to Wynonna Bramble," Trey continued, "as the grieving widow." He swayed a bit, but his voice carried like a TV preacher's. "Oh my Lord, what will poor, young Wynonna do now? What *will* she do, without her beloved husband? Not to worry, folks. That pile of money she'll inherit will make it a whole lot easier for our heroine to answer that question."

Gasps rippled through the crowd. Heads swiveled to Trey and back to Wynonna. It was so quiet you could hear the wood sap popping in the campfire.

"Hello, Trey." Wynonna's eyes were bone-dry now. "I see you've been drinking. Again."

"And I see you've been play-acting about how much you loved my daddy. Again. You may have these fine people fooled, Wynonna. But I'm not nearly drunk enough to buy it. It's just a matter of time before you're found out. And I plan to be there when it happens, holding the rope for your pretty neck."

Wynonna's hands clenched at her sides. She took a couple of steadying breaths. When her voice came out, it was as unforgiving as a slab of ice.

"It's too bad you didn't take such an interest in your daddy before he died, Trey. He cried many a tear over you. Your drinking. Your business failures. Your refusal to grow up. I think it was all the stress you gave Lawton that finally broke his weak heart."

Trey's eyes were slits as he took a step toward Wynonna, a rattlesnake ready to strike. She backed up against the trail boss, who looked like he'd rather be off roping a calf somewhere. Moving fast for such a big man, Sal inserted himself between the widow and her stepson. With a hand like a bear paw, he grabbed Trey's arm.

"C'mon, pal. Let's you and me take a wawk," Sal said. "We'll have us a little tawk."

In tone, in size, in demeanor — Sal oozed menace. He had at least five inches and a hundred pounds on the younger man. And Trey wasn't that drunk that he'd argue with someone who looked and acted like a New York gangster. Sal had found it served his purpose to let people assume whatever they would about his colorful past, before retirement in Florida.

I grabbed a lantern and caught up with the two of them in time to overhear Trey ask, "Are you taking me to the woodshed?"

"Too late for that, pal. Your fadder should have done that a long time ago."

At the mention of Lawton, Trey's shoulders slumped. The tough-guy cast to his face crumbled. "Wynonna's a bitch, and she never loved my daddy. But she's right about one thing. I'm probably the reason his heart quit. I never gave that man a day of peace."

I took hold of Trey's other arm. "That's not true, and you know it," I said. "I remember Lawton sitting in the stands at Himmarshee High when you played football. He was so proud of you. He always wore that No. 1 Fan hat with the Brahma horns. He'd scream his head off with every touchdown pass you threw."

A half-smile appeared, making Trey's face handsome again. "Yeah, I remember that, too." The smile faded, faster than it came. "But high school was a long time ago. I'm talking about the mess I've made of my life since then."

I couldn't argue with him there. I'd already seen evidence of hard drinking. And I'd witnessed something fishy going on between Trey and his father's wife, although I still wasn't sure what.

"My screw-ups killed my daddy," Trey said, "as sure as if I took a gun and shot him."

Sal stopped short, which meant we did, too, since he was the engine pulling all of us away from the dinner camp. Like a kid's game of whip, we jerked around, too, from the brute force of Sal's action.

"You listen to me, son." Sal brought his big head close to Trey's. "I've seen a lot of people over the years do a lot of bad things. Stabbings and beatings. Fatal shootings, where one person aims a weapon to take another's life. That's murder. You being a bad son, maybe even a disappointing son? It doesn't come close to that level of evil."

Sal paused, letting his words sink in. Finally, he moved his huge hand from Trey's arm to his shoulder. He gave it a fatherly squeeze.

"It's not too late, you know. You can step

up and be a man. It's what your dad would have wanted. Maybe, somehow, he'll know you've straightened up and done right."

Trey dropped his head to his chest, and brushed quickly at his eyes. He coughed. When he raised his face, my heart ached at the grief I saw written there. I had the strangest urge to wrap my arms around him and comfort him with a kiss.

Trey stared at me with his daddy's blue eyes, and I wondered if he could read my thoughts. It surprised me to realize I wouldn't mind if he did.

Our eyes locked. A flash of desire arced between us. It must have spilled out into the cool air, because Sal dropped his hand from Trey's shoulder and took a step back. His gaze shifted, first to Trey and then to me.

"Guess I'll get back to the fire," he mumbled as he backed away from us. "See if Rosie needs anything."

I lifted my hand in a wave, not wanting to pull my eyes from Trey's. "Bye, Sal," I said.

"Bye," Trey echoed, never breaking my gaze. "And, Sal? Thanks."

The light in our clearing dimmed as Sal walked away, carrying the lantern I'd brought. Trey pulled a small flashlight from his pocket; flicked it on and off so I could see he had it. Neither of us said a word. Cattle lowed in a distant pasture. Crickets chirped. Clouds floated across a dinner plate moon.

"Do you . . ."

"Would you . . ."

Both of us spoke at the same time.

"You first," I said.

"I was just going to ask if you wanted to sit over there on that log for a while. I could really use a friend."

I wasn't about to say I wanted to be more than that. I wasn't even sure myself where that spark of desire for him had come from. Maybe it was a combination: My memories of him as Himmarshee High's golden boy. The sorrow I felt that he'd lost his daddy. The mess I'd made of my short-lived affair with Carlos Martinez.

I let Trey Bramble lead me to that fallen log.

Once we were settled side-by-side, our thighs almost touching, he offered a cigarette from his pack. I shook my head no.

"I'm down to a half-pack a day," he said, careful to blow the smoke away from me. "I've been trying to quit. But this sure isn't the time."

He wet his fingers to extinguish the match, then tucked it into the top pocket of his shirt. I liked that he was mindful about the threat of wildfires during Florida's winter dry season.

"I haven't had the chance to tell you, Trey. I'm sure sorry about your loss. My own daddy died when my sisters and I were little. It's an awful thing to bear."

"I still can't believe he's gone, Mace. Daddy was bigger than life."

He took two last drags, stubbing out the cigarette under his boot. As with the match, he put the crushed butt into his pocket.

"I just wish things had been right between us," Trey continued. "I'll never forgive myself for being such a bastard. I was a major disappointment."

My mind flashed back to the tight, angry set to Lawton's mouth when he'd talked about his son to Mama and me. I didn't know enough about their relationship to reassure Trey that his father had loved him. But I did know what I'd seen at the ranch house. I took the plunge.

"Was the trouble between you and Lawton over Wynonna?"

A look of pure surprise flitted across his face. "Wynonna? Hell, no. Things had gone sour between Daddy and me way before she came on the scene. But it didn't help I despised her. He wanted me and Belle to like her. But neither of us trusted her as far as we could toss her."

I watched a tiger beetle crawl over the rough bark of our downed tree. Finally, I said what I had to say.

"That's not how it looked to me tonight at the ranch house."

Trey raised his eyebrows. "How what looked?"

"You and Wynonna. I came in from making a phone call in the kitchen, and she was massaging your chest, real sexy-like. She didn't look like somebody you despised."

He touched the front of his shirt, as if feeling for evidence of Wynonna's caress. "I don't have any idea what you're talking about, Mace. I was pretty drunk tonight. Passed out. I don't even remember seeing Wynonna until out there at the campfire, after my sister Belle woke me up and broke the news about Daddy."

I stared into his eyes. "So, there's nothing between you two?"

"Good God, no. Well, nothing but a lot of hard feelings. I wouldn't put it past Wynonna, though, to set her sights on me now that Daddy's gone. That way she might guarantee there'd be no fight over his money. The woman is a conniver, plain and simple."

I looked down at the beetle again. It had stopped at my right leg to confront what must look like a mountain range of denim. I gently brushed the bug to the ground.

"You believe me, don't you?" Trey took my chin in his hand and lifted my face to his. His blue eyes were pleading. "Mace?"

I leaned forward, just a couple of inches. But it was enough. Trey met me more than halfway. I felt the rough edge of his beard against my face. He must have showered, because he smelled like soap. But he hadn't taken the time to shave. His lips brushed mine, softly at first and then more insistently. His hand moved to cup the back of my head. He entwined his fingers into my hair. He'd just pulled us even closer, when a woman's angry voice broke the spell.

"Well, that's a fine how-do-you-do. I drive all the way here to comfort you about your daddy, and you've already found some trashy little tramp to take my place."

I pushed away like Trey was radioactive. But the trashy tramp part of me wished we'd kissed a little longer before I did.

"Who's she?" The other woman shouted, as she stormed toward where we sat on the log. "I can tell you right now, whoever she is, you and her both are gonna be sorry, Trey."

She thrust a lantern into my face. I about tumbled backwards off the log, until Trey caught me.

"This is Mace Bauer," he said, seeming not the least bit embarrassed. "She's a good friend of mine from high school."

She lifted the light in her hand up and down, getting a good look at me. Her other hand was fastened at her tiny waist, just above the swell of her hip. Her jeans were painted on. Sun-tanned cleavage spilled from her tight, checkered Western blouse.

I wasn't sure of the greeting etiquette after someone has called you a tramp. A handshake? A head nod? I settled on saying, "Hey."

"Charmed, I'm sure." She tossed her perfect auburn curls in my direction. "And I'm Austin Close. Trey's fiancée."

ELEVEN

"She was Trey's fiancée, Val. Can you imagine?"

Val seemed less interested in my plight than in the pad of hay I was dividing to drop on the ground.

"You should have seen it, girl. It was pure humiliation." I leaned my face against her muscular neck and whispered into her mane. "Oh, Trey tried to explain. Not that there could be any explanation. 'Save it for somebody who gives a shit,' I told him. And, no, I'm not real proud that I cussed a man who just lost his daddy."

Val nudged my hip with the top of her head. It might have been sympathy; then again, she might just have ear mites.

My sister Maddie says it's weird that I talk to animals. I don't agree. It's not like I think they're going to talk back.

Brandy, Mama's loaner horse for the trail ride, ambled over to get her share of the late-night snack. I tossed half the hay to her and half to Val, the quarter horse I'd borrowed to ride.

Nothing like food to create a captive audience.

"So," I continued, edging closer to Val, "I just grabbed the flashlight Trey left on the log and hightailed it out of there. Of course, I lost a little steam when I ran into a clump of palmetto so thick I had to turn around and stalk right back past to find a way out."

Brandy munched away. Val shook her head.

"We'll get the vet to take a look at those ears, girl." I ran a hand over Val's back and across her broad chest. She was the perfect horse for working cattle: strong, quick, and agile. My family quit keeping stock after Daddy lost our ranch. But we still had plenty of friends in the cattle business. I'd had no trouble scaring up two horses and a trailer when Mama announced we were making the ride.

"Okay, then." I gave Val a last pat on her rump. "Time for me to turn in and dream about what an idiot I am."

I heard the *whirr* of a power window sliding down. Sinatra crooned softly in the near-distance.

"Mace!" Mama's whisper came from the

front seat of Sal's enormous Cadillac. He'd parked on one side of our makeshift horse paddock; my tent was on the other. "Quit talking to the horses and get some sleep. Are you sure you don't want to join us, honey? The temperature's supposed to really drop, and this sure beats the heck out of the ground. I can bunk in the back seat with Sal, and you'll have the front all to yourself."

I couldn't think of anyplace I'd rather *not* be.

"No, thanks. Mama," I whispered back. "The tent will do just fine."

The ground under my sleeping bag felt like a slab of concrete that someone had left overnight in the freezer. In addition to my thermal long johns, I had a long-sleeved T-shirt tied around my head and the turtleneck of my sweater pulled up over my mouth. I'd slipped a dirty pair of socks over my hands. My nose was the only body part I hadn't covered, and I could no longer feel it on the front of my face. My version of cold-weather wear was no match for the temperature plunge. It had to be in the thirties, which feels sub-zero to a native Floridian like me. I envied the horses the thicker coats they grow each winter.

Holding my breath against the onslaught of cold, I climbed out of my sleeping bag, pulled on boots and a parka, and fled my tent for Sal's car.

"Let me in. I changed my mind," I hissed, rapping on the passenger-side window. "I need to get warm."

Mama pushed open the car door and scooted over on the wide leather seat. Her hair looked like a platinum-colored soufflé, except collapsed to one side. "C'mon in, honey. We'll turn the heater on for a little bit." She cranked the car engine and put a hand to my face. "My stars, Mace! Your cheek is like ice. And are those socks clean?"

Sal grumbled something, stirring in the back seat like a poked bear in hibernation.

"I left my gloves in the horse trailer." I held up my hands. "This is what I could find."

"Sally, honey, toss Mace that extra blanket from the floor back there."

An unintelligible mumble sounded from behind us. A few seconds later, a wool blanket sailed over the seat.

"Who'd have thought I'd need an Arctic-rated sleeping bag in the Sunshine State?"

"I've got some hot chocolate in my thermos. Want a cup?" Mama asked.

I nodded from beneath the blanket, willing the car's heater to hurry up and blow warm.

Before long, I was sipping chocolate and feeling almost toasty. The gauges and dials on the dashboard glowed, burnishing the golden interior of Sal's car. I felt as snug as a honeybee inside its hive.

"Feeling better, darlin'?"

"Mmm-hmm." I savored the hot chocolate. "Thanks, Mama."

"Then maybe you'd like to tell me," she leaned back and crossed her arms over her chest. "What in the world is going on between you and Trey Bramble?"

I groaned.

"Sally told me he left the two of you alone in the woods."

"There's nothing going on, Mama. We talked, that's all."

"Sally said it looked like talking was the last thing on your minds."

"Mama, I'm tired. Can we dissect my dating life tomorrow?" Or never, I thought.

"So, you're dating now? I'm not sure that's a good idea, Mace. The man is obviously a drinker." Mama should know. We both remembered Husband No. 2.

"We're not dating. It's just an expression. Besides, Trey is engaged."

"Engaged?" Mama screeched. "Honey, if

99

he's engaged and coming on to you, then he's not worth a milk bucket under a bull."

Sal sat up in the backseat. I swear I felt the big car sway.

"The way that guy looked at you?" His voice was thick from sleep. "Fuh-geddaboutit. That's not the way a guy getting married should be looking at another girl."

"Could we change the subject, please? How 'bout this weather change?" I said. "Brrr! Did you know it was supposed to get this cold?"

"All I know is when you gotta girl you really love, you're not looking for something on the side." Sal rested his crossed arms, like hairy hams, over the back of the seat and gazed at Mama.

I motioned to her to fluff the smashed side of her hair. But she didn't see me, since she was busy returning cow eyes at Sal.

"I thought Mace might find that kind of relationship with Carlos Martinez, but that love affair didn't take either," Mama said to Sal, her tone confiding.

"Hello? I'm right here. Stop talking about me like I'm not."

"Yeah, what happened between the two of youse, Mace? Martinez is a good man."

"How about some Sinatra?" I said.

"Wouldn't a little music sound good right now?"

"I'll tell you what happened, Sally," Mama said, as if I hadn't spoken. "Carlos wanted to coddle her, and Mace felt smothered. You can't blame the man for trying to keep her safe, not after what happened to his poor wife. But Mace likes to be the one who takes care of people. And she takes pride in being independent and strong. Well, except for cold weather." She patted my cheek. "You're a bit of a baby when the temperature drops below fifty, honey."

"Listen, Dr. Phil, as much as I want to stick around for the psychotherapy, I'm going back to my tent. Thanks for the chocolate and the extra blanket." I slid toward the car door.

"Hang on there, Mace. I gotta reason for asking about Martinez," Sal said. "He's coming back to Himmarshee."

My heart felt like it wanted to sprout wings and fly out of my mouth. I swallowed, but it seemed to have lodged in my throat. I guess I wasn't over Carlos after all.

"Is that so?" I finally said, forcing my voice to be steady. "Good for him. I guess that means he dealt with the stuff he had to deal with down in Miami."

"Guess so," Sal said. "And you won't

believe this: he's signed up to join the Cracker Trail for a couple of days. Says it's the perfect way to ease back into the pace up here before he starts work again."

Mama said, "Now, I like Carlos a lot — especially after he stopped trying to send me to the Big House. But the man doesn't seem like he'd know a fetlock from a forelock. I cannot picture him on a horse."

Sal shrugged. "He says he knows how to ride. I offered to tell him where to buy some Western-style clothes. But he said he was all set."

A smart decision for Carlos, I thought, fighting off an image of the two Urban Cowboys in matching electric blue.

"Okay, then. G'night, now," I said, slipping out the door before they could grill me further — or see how my hands were shaking from the news about Carlos.

As I walked back to the tent, my mind was spinning so fast I barely noticed the cold. I took a few deep breaths, trying to imagine how I'd react the first time I saw him. Sal hadn't said when Carlos planned on coming. Did I have time to prepare myself? I couldn't believe it. Cold as it was, my palms were damp with nervous sweat underneath those stupid socks.

I glanced at the horses, secure in their

enclosure. Then I stared into the sky, searching for answers in the spray of stars that glittered there. Something small rustled through the drought-dry grass of the pasture. I could smell hay and spilled feed through the open slats of our horse trailer.

The sound of whistling drifted toward me on the night air. *Whistle While You Work.* I had to smile, thinking that poor Doc Abel really could use a course on melody. Before, his tuneless whistle had seemed creepy; now it was somehow comforting. It meant someone else was up. I wasn't the only one unable to get to sleep. Or, maybe Doc was just taking a potty break.

Dodging horse and cow patties on the ground, I hummed along. As I drew nearer to the tent, I was almost enjoying my part in our Disney-movie duet. And then, just a few yards from the tent, my song went silent. I stopped in my tracks, staring straight ahead in the moonlight. I could just make out my sleeping bag, sticking halfway out on the ground through the tent's open entry flap. I distinctly remembered closing it, since working a zipper in hand socks was a challenge.

I fumbled for Trey's flashlight, still in my coat pocket. It flickered, then lit to show the shredded sides of the tent, gaping open like wounds. Down filling spilled onto the ground from deep gashes in the sleeping bag. Feathers clung to a wet, sticky-looking substance. It turned the pale orange of the bag into something dark; something frightening.

Under the dimming beam of the flashlight, the stain on my bag looked an awful lot like blood.

TWELVE

Snores rumbled from inside Sal's Cadillac. How in the world could he sleep with Mama rattling the windows like that? I tapped at the glass by her head.

"Wake up," I whispered. "It's me again."

I'd left my campsite without touching anything, backing away from my shredded tent the way I'd come. I didn't want to trample any evidence that might be collected. Not that my case would be a high priority for the crime lab at the Florida Department of Law Enforcement. On further inspection, the dark stain on my sleeping bag turned out to be red wine. Merlot, probably. When I got close enough to sniff, my campsite smelled like Happy Hour at a yuppie bar.

I rapped harder on the car window.

"Mama, open up. It's colder out here than a freezer full of sheared sheep."

The front-seat car door swung open.

Mama had shifted in her sleep, and now the other side of her bouffant 'do drooped, too. At least she was symmetrical.

"What in the blue blazes is wrong with you, Mace?" She rubbed her eyes. "We shouldn't all have to suffer just 'cause you're too stubborn to admit you can't take the cold."

"Scoot over, Mama." I slid in. The seat was blessedly warm where she'd slept. "This isn't about the temperature. My tent's not an option. Somebody took a hunting knife or a kitchen cleaver to it. My sleeping bag, too. They're both ripped to ribbons."

Mama gasped. Sal stirred in the back seat.

"Are you okay?" She put a hand on my cheek, making sure I was whole.

"I'm fine. Just pissed off. I wasn't there when it happened. But I think I might know who did it." I pulled a corner of Mama's down comforter over my lap.

"Did what?" Sal grumbled.

"Somebody stabbed Mace's tent, Sally." She turned to me. "Who was it, honey?"

I told her about Trey's girlfriend, how she'd walked in on us in the woods and called me a tramp.

"She's pretty, so she's used to getting what she wants. And she acted like a girl who doesn't like to be crossed. I wouldn't put vandalism past her at all."

Sal's big head popped up from the back seat. His hair looked better than Mama's. Maybe she should try his styling mousse.

"Mace has a point about vandalism, Rosie." He rested those ham-like arms on the seat back and leaned in close. "Men move right to physical violence; women often target property. It's a known fact."

Mama took some breath spray from her purse and handed it to Sal.

"Don't you remember that cheerleader at Himmarshee High, Mama?" I asked. "The one who was so jealous of Marty? When her ex asked Marty to the prom, the cheerleader threw acid on Marty's Ford Escort. Marty had to drive it until she could scrape together the insurance deductible. Her poor car looked like a speckled Dalmatian."

Sal squirted, and passed the breath spray back to Mama. She handed it to me.

"I haven't even been to sleep yet, Mama." Offended, I tossed it back to her.

"Couldn't hurt, darlin'." She put it in my lap. "And I do remember that cheerleader. I remember your sister couldn't do anything about it because we couldn't prove the girl did it. The Himmarshee Police didn't take Marty very seriously."

"Sounds about right." Sal's freshened

breath hit us in the front seat like a cinnamon tsunami. "Unless there's a threat of violence, or the damaged goods are supervaluable, vandalism's the bottom of the totem pole for most cops. Maybe you should talk to Martinez about it when he gets here, Mace."

The idea of talking to Carlos about anything made the two pieces of pie I'd eaten earlier somersault over each other. I swallowed my emotions, along with a tiny, strawberry-flavored burp.

"He's seventy-some miles out of his jurisdiction up here." My voice was so measured, I might have been discussing interest rates, not the man I once thought I loved. "Besides, I'm going to handle it myself."

"I don't like the way that sounds, Mace." Mama shook her finger at me.

"Me neither," Sal said. "You're not gonna whack her, are ya?"

My mouth opened wide in a laugh, and I realized Mama had been right about that breath spray. I aimed a blast at my tongue. "Nobody's whacking anybody. I'm just saying I intend to prove Austin's the one who ripped up my stuff, then drenched it with wine."

Mama and Sal were silent. Tired, probably. I know I was. As I wondered where I'd bunk for the rest of the ride, I glanced at Sal's watch, sitting on the dashboard. Saucer-sized, encrusted with diamonds, the face read two-thirty-five a.m. I had to be up in less than four hours to groom, saddle, and water the horses. I expected Mama to help, manicure or not.

But I wasn't going to tell her that now. Now, I needed to be sweet since I had nowhere else to lay my head.

"Listen, if you meant it before, Mama, I'll take you up on your offer to sleep here."

"Say no more, darlin'." She vaulted over the seat with entirely too much familiarity for a woman about to celebrate her sixty-third birthday on the Fourth of July. "Sal and I will be snug as two bugs back here."

I heard the rustle of clothes and blankets. Sal grunted. Mama *oofed,* as the two of them shifted this way and that, getting comfortable. Soon, she was snoring again. Taking as brief a glance as I could into the back, I was surprised to find they fit, given Sal's size. My fingers covered my eyes like a kid at a scary movie, trying not to see too much.

The last thing I remember before sleep was me pretending I wasn't sharing a Caddy in a cow pasture with my mama and her beau — spooned together on the back seat like two teenagers.

Mama sauntered to breakfast like a celebrity, bestowing pats and kisses in her wake. Sal trailed behind, her beefy bodyguard. Meal service was late getting started. I'd been holding Mama's place in line for fifteen minutes, while she re-poufed her hair and fixed her makeup. I don't know how she did it. We were going on our third day without a shower. I'd already scared myself earlier, when I saw my matted locks and dirty face reflected in the horses' watering trough. Yet Mama managed to look like she'd just finished a beauty treatment at Hair Today, Dyed Tomorrow. And all with a few baby wipes, a teasing comb, and a tube of Apricot Ice. Her jeans matched her Western-style shirt, both in honeydew-green. They were spotless, too, since she'd managed to convince me she needed to find a good spot to call my sisters while I did all the work of getting the horses ready. Now, she moved as gracefully as if she were two-stepping across a dance floor. That was another thing that irritated me: Mama's tiny enough to fit almost anywhere and get a comfortable night's sleep. I'm five-ten. Sal's car was roomy, but I'd still managed to wedge my head between the end of the seat and the armrest. My back ached and my neck had a crick. Had somebody hung me on a hook and used me as a punching bag when I wasn't looking?

My mood brightened a bit when I saw that Sal was also moving stiffly. Even so, I still had to rotate my entire body, just so I could watch anything else but Mama gliding around all chipper and ache free.

Early-morning fog settled in the holes and gullies of the pasture. Horses pawed at the ground and snorted, their warm breath making puffs of steam in the cold air. The trail outriders were already saddled up, ready to supervise and set the day's pace. Their orange reflective vests seemed out-of-place over cowboy garb. But much of the Cracker Trail snakes along the two-lane highways that cross the state's mid-section. The vests increase our visibility, reducing the chance of a rider getting clipped by one of Florida's famously bad drivers.

I was thinking of the seventeen-some miles we'd have to cover to make our next camp, near Zolfo Springs, when suddenly I felt the pressure of a hand on the small of my back.

"Who's there?" I asked, because it hurt too much to turn my head to look.

"It's me. Trey." His whisper was warm on my sore neck. "You didn't give me a chance to explain last night."

"And I don't intend to." I knocked his hand off my back and took a step forward. Lawton's dog, Tuck, was with Trey. He plopped himself in front of me, wagging his tail.

"Please, Mace." Trey drew closer, trapped as I was by the dog. "I didn't know what to do when Austin showed up," he murmured, mouth against my ear. "She's a loose cannon. We've been split for over two months, but she can't get it through her head that we're through."

"She was wearing an engagement ring," I pointed out.

He paused for a moment.

"I let her keep it," Trey said. "God only knows how she'd react if I tried to get it back. Breaking my engagement to that psycho is the only smart thing I've done in recent memory."

Trey stood so close his body heat warmed me. I could feel the hard muscles in his chest and shoulder. I imagined backing up just a step. I imagined how his arms would rise up, enfolding me in his warmth and soap-clean smell.

"Trey, I . . ."

And those two words were all I managed to utter before Mama's excited shriek rang out across the breakfast crowd.

"Well, I declare," she shouted. "Sally, dar-lin', lookit who's here!"

I whipped my head around, regretting it immediately, to see whose arrival had Mama so worked up.

Carlos Martinez stood glaring across the now-cold campfire. It looked like all the sparks from last night had somehow found their way to his black eyes. And now that burning hot gaze was searing two holes, right through Trey and me.

THIRTEEN

I barely had time to wonder why a man who'd "moved on" to Miami was glowering at me and my would-be new suitor, before Mama squealed again.

"My stars and garters!" Her pitch was so high, Tuck shook his head and whined. "Now all three of my darlin' girls are here!"

Maddie and Marty peered through the fog, trying to place Mama's location. I stepped around Tuck and hurried to greet my sisters, leaving Trey standing in Carlos Martinez's line of ire. The dog followed after me, chain collar jangling.

"Mace! C'mere where I can get a good look at you." Maddie's voice cut through the fog like the crack of a cow whip. "Mama said some slasher ripped your campsite to shreds. It's a miracle you survived."

I had a moment's satisfaction as a worried look crossed Carlos' face. Until I realized Maddie was broadcasting my business to a hundred-plus hungry riders.

"Hush, Maddie. Mama's exaggerating again. It was minor vandalism — probably just a prank. And I wasn't even in my tent when it happened."

Carlos's scowl returned. By the time I rotated my body back to look at Trey, he'd moved on. His face was mournful as he accepted condolences from folks in the breakfast line. I couldn't be sure Trey had even heard my big sister. He'd be the only one in the camp who hadn't.

Maddie lowered her voice, but added her disapproving principal tone. "You mean Marty and I took off work and broke the speed limit all the way up here and you're not even hurt?"

Marty punched her arm. "That's not nice, Maddie!"

"Ouch!" Maddie jerked back in surprise. "You know that's not how I meant it. Of course I'm glad Mace is safe. But we could have saved an hour's-plus drive and the money for gas if Mama got her story straight in the first place."

Mama, joining us just then, looked wounded. "It wasn't my fault, Maddie. It was Sally's cell-o-phone. It must have been a bad reception."

I doubted that. Mama may not have

mastered cell phone lingo, but she'd been getting her stories screwed up since long before they were invented.

Rubbing her arm, Maddie grumbled at Marty, "I liked you better when you were afraid of your own shadow."

Our little sister is still scared of a lot of things: snakes, the dark, closed-in places, and people who scream at each other in rage. But, last year, she got a big promotion at the library. Then, Sal shared a secret with her, showing her extraordinary respect. Ever since, she's just as sweet as ever, but she doesn't let Maddie push her around like before. It annoys the hell out of my big sister, which tickles me to pieces.

I looked at the two of them, a cowgirl version of Mutt and Jeff. Big-boned Maddie, in a string tie and ankle-length denim culottes, towered over Marty. Like Mama, Marty's tiny, except for a thick head of blond hair, which she'd swept up neatly this morning under a black hat. The cute jeans and silver-buckled belt she wore came from the little girls' department at Home on the Range Feed Supply and Clothing Emporium.

I fit somewhere between my two sisters: Not as pretty as Marty, but only half as mean as Maddie.

"All right, you two." I played peacemaker. "Y'all are here now. You can stay for breakfast, and we'll find a couple of horses you can borrow."

By this time, my sisters had spotted Carlos, watching us from the edge of the campfire. Of course, they knew all about our breakup. Mama's never met a morsel of gossip she can't chew. Maddie stared at him, and then raised her eyebrows at me. Marty looked confused and upset on my behalf. Mama, who'd left Sal holding her place in line, wriggled her fingers at my ex.

"So nice to see you, darlin'," she trilled. "You haven't come to arrest me again, I hope."

What might have been a smile made a brief appearance on his lips.

"What's he doing here, Mace?" Maddie hissed under her breath. "Hasn't he done enough?"

I crouched down to pet Tuck, so Carlos wouldn't see me talking about him. Welcome to high school.

"Maddie, I told you, it was mutual when we parted ways," I whispered.

"Humph!" She crossed her arms over her chest and glared at him. "He could have tried a little harder. You're not *that* hard to love."

"Thanks, I guess," I said.

Marty stooped down, patting my shoulder. "You're impossible *not* to love, Mace. And, don't look now, but he's coming this way."

I wondered whether Tuck would respond to a *Sic 'em* command? If so, I wasn't sure if I wanted the dog to go after Carlos, or just tear through my jugular and kill me on the spot.

"*Buenos días,* ladies." He smirked, giving us an overly courtly bow. "The four of you are looking lovely this morning."

Oh, please. I almost preferred the surly cop from last summer, the one who'd wanted to toss Mama in the slammer.

"Detective," Maddie said, arms still folded.

Marty nodded hello, smiling shyly before lowering her eyes.

Mama stood on tiptoes to kiss him on the cheek.

Then everybody looked at me, waiting to see what I'd do.

Luckily, I didn't have to do anything. At just that moment, a long, loud whistle shut off all the conversation in the cook site. Tuck barked. Marty put her hands over her ears. I hunched up my shoulders, feeling a fresh stab of pain to my sore neck.

"Listen up, everybody," Jack Hollister

118

shouted, as he clambered onto the oak log again.

This was probably more talking than the trail boss had done in the full month before Lawton died. But he seemed to be growing more at ease in front of the crowd.

"This fog is gonna put us behind schedule. But we'll ride out as soon as it lifts, and we'll make up the time this afternoon." He cleared his throat. "And, uhm, Lawton's daughter, Belle, is here, standing right over there with her big brother, Trey. She's got something she'd like to say to y'all."

Jack looked down, smiling encouragingly. My gaze followed his until I found Belle, leaning on Trey for support. He had a firm arm around her shoulders. She cocked her head, resting it on her brother's broad chest. As fragile-seeming as a baby sparrow, Belle had obviously been crying. Her pretty green eyes were swollen, and rimmed with red.

Trey squeezed her shoulders, and then nudged her to climb the log.

"Hey, everybody." Belle's voice was low, barely a whisper. People strained to listen. Some even abandoned spots in the breakfast line to crowd in. I lost sight of Carlos in the shuffle.

Tucking a wild curl behind her ear, Belle tried again, louder this time.

"I'm so glad everybody's here. Daddy would have been happy to know the ride wasn't cancelled on his account. He loved Florida history, and especially the Cracker Trail. I can remember him telling us stories about the old-timey cowmen, hunting up half-wild cattle right here in this brush." She waved her arm to the distance, taking in palmetto scrub and stands of sabal palms shrouded in fog. "Growing up, we always had a dog named after the cattle catchdogs Patrick Smith wrote about in *A Land Remembered*. It was always a Nip or a Tuck."

Lawton's dog, hearing his name, gave a little yip.

"Remember Daddy reading to us from that book?" She looked into the crowd, her eyes meeting Trey's.

"I do," he said, his voice thick.

"Trey and I have decided we'd like to ride along with y'all for a couple of days, if you'll have us."

"Of course we will," someone yelled. "Glad to," shouted someone else.

"Daddy left a capable ranch foreman in charge and detailed instructions about what to do in the event that he ever . . ." Belle paused, swallowing hard. "In the event he passed away."

Trey stepped closer to the log, reaching

up to hold his sister's hand.

"Anyway, there's not a whole lot for the two of us to do until the funeral," she said. "We'd like to honor him by riding along, honor how much he cherished our Florida land."

Maddie leaned over to whisper in my ear, " 'Cherish' might be too strong a word. I heard Lawton planned to carve up most of his land to sell as ten-acre ranchettes."

"No!" I whispered back.

"Hand to God," Maddie said, relishing telling me news I hadn't known.

"Shhh!" Marty shushed us.

Lawton's daughter opened her mouth to speak again, just as a murmur spread through the crowd. People began to push and move this way and that. Someone in the rear shouted, "Let her through!"

Belle put a hand to her forehead and peered toward the back of the clearing, trying to see what the interruption was. Heads turned. The crowd parted. Everyone stared at Wynonna, making her way to the front. She moved in fits and starts, stopping every few feet as people reached out with shoulder pats and comforting hugs.

"As I was saying . . ." Belle tried unsuccessfully to regain the crowd's attention. Most eyes were on Wynonna now, who was dressed in widow's black from silver-banded hat to ostrich-skin boots. She even clutched a black neckerchief, which she lifted every moment or two to dab at her eyes. Finally, at the front, she stepped past Trey. Stopping at the foot of the log, she looked up to Belle's perch.

"Go ahead, sweetie," she said, waving the black neck scarf up at Belle. "I didn't mean to cause a fuss."

Sure, I thought. And Eve never meant to tempt Adam with that apple, either.

"Did you have something you wanted to say, Wynonna?" Belle's voice was as cold as the ground under my tent last night.

"Well, I don't want to interrupt." Wynonna was already climbing onto the log before her last word was out. Belle stepped down, yielding the spotlight to her father's young wife.

"Thanks, sweetie." Wynonna smiled at Belle, who stared at the ground. "I know my stepdaughter told y'all that she and Trey plan to tag along on the ride. I wasn't sure if she mentioned I'd like to come, too."

Belle's head jerked up. Trey's mouth hung open.

"Lawton's business manager will follow his instructions in the next day or so. We won't be missed. And I think doing what

Lawton would have loved to do is the best way for us to remember him. As a family."

"Belle and Trey look like they'd rather be mothered by a rabid she-wolf," Maddie said in my ear.

Trey's mouth was closed now, his face a furious red. Belle didn't seem as fragile as before. Her back was plank straight. Her tiny hands were clenched into fists. And the eyes she turned on Wynonna were furious, and filled with pure hate.

FOURTEEN

The breakfast line inched forward like pickups in the parking lot after a Monster Truck rally. The smell of bacon and fresh coffee was painfully mouthwatering. I reached around my sisters, trying to grab a plate and plastic utensils so I'd be ready when I finally did get to the front. Maddie slapped my hand.

"I don't believe it's your turn yet, is it Mace?"

"Maddie, I left middle school twenty years ago. Stop principaling me."

"Well, Lord knows somebody's got to watch your manners. You spend too much time out in the woods with the animals. You're starting to act like one."

Marty picked up a plastic serving set, making a show of handing it around Maddie to me.

"Stop fussing, you two. We're all hungry. And nobody's an animal. Now, Mace, tell

124

us what's going on with Carlos. Is it true he plans to ride?"

The speeches from Belle and Wynonna interrupted us earlier. Afterward, Carlos left the cook site to ready his horse without so much as a goodbye.

"I haven't actually talked to the man, Marty. But that's what he told Sal. Carlos came up this morning with that group from Homestead. Somebody down there loaned him a horse. Though it's hard for me to believe he knows much about trail riding. I'll bet the closest he's ever come is cruising asphalt in a squad car on Tamiami Trail."

We finally loaded up our plates — eggs and bacon with a side of biscuits and sausage gravy for Maddie and me; the same minus the meat for Marty. Mama waved us over to where she sat with Sal.

As we passed by the riders still standing in the chow line, I overheard a snatch of conversation that almost made me drop the breakfast I'd waited so long to get.

". . . and this gal doesn't think Lawton had a heart attack. My daughter Amber told me she and Lauren heard all of them discussing it last night at the campfire."

I slowed down to listen in on two women in their thirties, standing with their backs to me. "Do you know her?" one asked the other.

"Never met her."

"Well, I heard she cracked a murder case last summer down in Himmarshee, so she must know something."

"Really? I heard it was her mama who actually caught the murderer."

I nearly poked my head in to say they had it all wrong about what happened last summer. Mama didn't catch a murderer. She was accused of *being* the murderer.

"Hurry up, Mace," Maddie called over her shoulder, her face scrunched in annoyance. "My breakfast is getting cold."

The two teen-aged eavesdroppers from the campfire sat right next to Mama and Sal. The girls stared as my sisters and I walked up. They were probably trying to gauge if I was packing a pistol in my jeans.

"Y'know," I announced in a loud voice to our little group, "it's not nice to spread gossip about people you don't even know."

"I was not gossiping, Mace!"

"I'm not talking about you, Mama." I nodded pointedly at the two girls, who blushed and looked at the ground.

"Well, I *never* gossip," Maddie said with a huff.

"Not talking about you either, Maddie.

Though I'd never say never."

I continued to stare at the girls, who seemed fascinated by the scraps of biscuits and rinds of cantaloupe left on their plates.

Sitting down, I put a hand on the arm of the closest teen. "I didn't catch your names last night, girls. I'm Mace Bauer, by the way."

"Lauren," the closest one mumbled. "She's Amber."

"Well, it's very nice to meet you," I said.

"We'vegottago." Amber's words tumbled out as she tugged at Lauren's sleeve.

"Okay, y'all be good, hear?" I said, as they stumbled over one another running away from me.

As the girls left, Mama shoveled a final forkful of sausage patty into Sal's mouth. Marty said, "What was that all about, Mace?"

I lowered my voice. "I overheard the mama of one of those girls saying I suspect Lawton didn't die of a heart attack. I don't want that bit of gossip getting out of hand."

"Looks like the cat's already out of the bag," Maddie said, spooning up some biscuit and gravy.

"Mama told us about your suspicions, Mace. You might have tried just asking those two kids not to talk about it, instead of scaring them with those mean looks," Marty said.

"Mace thinks she can intimidate people into doing what she wants, girls. It's because she's so tall," Mama said, patting her napkin to a smear of grease on Sal's jacket.

"Who's tall?"

I turned toward the voice behind me, and immediately clapped a hand on my stiff neck.

"Mornin', Trey," Mama said. "Why don't you join us?"

I resisted the urge to stab her in the hand with my plastic fork.

"We're all so sorry about your daddy, hon," Mama said.

Now I felt guilty for being mean to a man who was in mourning.

"Please, Trey. Sit down," I said. "Did you ever meet my sisters? Maddie was a class ahead of you at Himmarshee High; Marty was a couple of years behind me."

Trey took one of the chairs the teens had forgotten when they fled. He removed his cowboy hat, put it on his lap, and shook both my sisters' hands.

"I just came by to apologize for the way I acted last night."

Ohmigod! He wouldn't do this in front of everybody, would he?

"Sal, I sure do appreciate you hauling me away to cool off before I got really nasty to Wynonna."

I breathed a sigh of relief.

"Fuhgeddaboutit." Sal waved his tooth-pick at Trey, a forgiving gesture. "You're under a lot of stress."

"That doesn't excuse it. Even before I found out Daddy died, I was already plastered last night. I wasn't even able to take care of my little sister, Belle, when she needed me most."

He looked down at his hat, working the brim with his fingers. None of us spoke.

"I've been a mess these last few years, but I'm ready to change. They always say admitting you have a problem is the first step, right?" He raised his head, looking hopefully at me.

"Admitting it and doing something about it are two different things." Maddie's tone revealed that she disapproved of drinking, like she did so many other things. "My advice is to go home right now and pour out every drop. Just take and pour the bottles down the drain."

"Maddie, as much as Trey surely appreciates the counsel of someone who's never had a drink, he doesn't have time to go home right now," I said. "We're riding out when the fog lifts."

"Sorry to say, there's nuthin' left at home to pour out anyway," Trey said. "I pretty much drank it all up."

He ducked his head. The shame on his face about broke my heart.

"What do you think made you start drinking so heavy, Trey?" Mama placed a hand on his arm. "I don't remember your daddy being bad to drink."

"No, ma'am. My daddy was a lot of things that I'm not."

We all stared at our boots. I couldn't help but notice Maddie's feet looked like bulldozers, while Marty's looked as dainty as a baby doll's in the same style lace-up.

"Fadders and sons can be complicated," Sal finally said, pointing the toothpick at Trey. "My dad was a decorated war hero. That's a tough act to follow. I never felt I measured up. My own boy went in the opposite direction. He didn't even try to walk in his old man's footsteps. He dances for the New York City Ballet."

Sal looked around as if daring one of us to comment.

"He's damn good, too." He jammed the toothpick back in his mouth, clamping his lips around it.

"I just never knew if people liked me for

myself, or because I was Lawton Bramble III." Trey swung in his chair to face me, blue eyes beaming with sincerity. "Even with Austin, it was that way, Mace."

Uh-oh. Here it comes.

"Who's Austin?" Marty asked.

"That's the gal who called Mace a tramp last night when Mace and Trey were making out in the woods. Mace thinks Austin took a knife and shredded her tent and sleeping bag for revenge," Mama said.

Earth, please swallow me now, I prayed.

"What?!!" came a chorus from Marty, Maddie, and Trey.

Mama took her Apricot Ice from her pocket and circled her lips. She folded her napkin in half and closed her mouth over it to blot.

"What?" she asked innocently. "I figured we were all being honest. Go ahead and tell them, Mace."

I mumbled out an explanation about Austin, not even sure of what I said.

Trey looked thoughtful. "I swear to God, I wouldn't put it past her. The girl's not the sharpest tool in the box, and she's got a hell of a temper. Austin could start a fight in an empty house. Did she threaten you, Mace?"

"Not in words, no."

"Well, I'm going to find out what's what,"

he said. "If it was Austin, she'll pay for your tent and bag and whatever else she ruined."

"I can take care of myself." I heard the huffiness in my own voice.

Marty took pity on me and changed the subject.

"Trey, you were saying you're never sure if people like you for yourself," her voice was soft, caring. "That must be really hard."

"I wouldn't think it's so hard," Maddie said. "You've just got to make sure you give people something to like."

"Maddie knows all about that subject, Trey," I said.

Before my big sister and I could really begin to bicker, one of the trail outriders loped up to the breakfast crowd. She pulled up on her horse's reins, leaned back in the saddle, and whistled for everyone's attention.

"Twenty minutes, everybody," she yelled. "It's clear enough to go, so we leave in twenty. Remember to stay behind the mule wagons."

She turned and sped off to spread the news to the rest of the camp. We all stood and started packing up our breakfast trash.

"I'll take that," Trey said, piling plates and napkins into his arms. "And, yes, Marty. It is hard. Folks have always looked at my family's land and money, and thought I was lucky. They thought it was a breeze being Lawton Bramble III. But my daddy wore some pretty big boots. And no matter how hard I tried, I never seemed able to fill them."

As Trey carried our trash off toward the garbage cans, Marty *tsked*. "That is *so* sad."

"That's one way of looking at it." Maddie folded her arms as she watched him disappear. "Another is that Trey doesn't have to worry so much now about those big ol' boots of Lawton's."

FIFTEEN

The outriders patrolled the mounted and waiting crowd, their eyes never still. They looked for any problem that had the potential to become a crisis. Here, a weekend cowboy needed a red ribbon tied to his horse's tail, a sign to steer clear because the horse kicked. There, another horse spooked at the sharp snap of a cow whip. Embarrassed but unhurt, the rider landed hard on the sandy ground.

Little got by the outriders.

"Listen up," the one closest to us shouted. "We can't say it enough about them cow whips. This is called the Cracker Trail Ride. It honors the Florida pioneers. They used to call 'em Crackers for those loud-assed whips they used." He looked down the line of riders, not focusing on any one person. Still, all of us knew what was coming next. "Now, if your horse don't like the sound of a cow whip, that's your problem. Not the

Cracker Trail's. You need to get 'em used to that sound, 'cause you're gonna be hearing it a lot." He shifted a wad of tobacco under his lip. "And if they can't get used to it, you and your horse are gonna have to find another trail to ride." The outrider gazed down the line again, lingering for a moment on the woman whose horse dumped her off. She got busy fiddling with a leather strap on her saddle.

"We just can't take the chance of a horse bolting out into the road or knocking somebody off whenever they hear a whip crack." He spat a stream of tobacco juice onto the pasture. It hit a soda apple, poisonous to cattle. I wondered whether tobacco worked as a weed control.

"We'll be off in a few minutes," the outrider said. "Let's have us a good ride."

He gave a quick smile, but the serious look stayed in his eyes. Keeping track of more than a hundred riders of various ages and abilities is hard work and heavy responsibility. It's definitely more challenging than working cattle. More like herding cats.

Mama took the opportunity of our delay to catch up on her socializing. The last I'd seen her, she was jabbering away, somewhere near the back of the crowd.

Sal enlisted another non-rider to help him

move my Jeep and the horse trailer, as well as his own car, to our next camp. The organizers provide buses to ferry riders at each day's lunch break. While the horses rest, the riders travel back to the morning camp, collect their rigs, and then drive everything ahead and park it at the night camp. Then it's back on the buses to the lunch spot, meet up with the rest of the ride, and continue all afternoon on horseback to the new camp.

Everybody hates all that back-and-forth and gobbling lunch, so I was grateful to Sal for letting me bypass the bus rides and leapfrogging. He said he was comfortable doing the driving, and if God had intended for him to learn to ride, he'd have put a herd of horses in the Bronx.

With the fog nearly cleared, the sun was starting to heat up the day. A yellow sulphur butterfly floated past. A scrub jay called from the low branch of a pine. I lifted my face to the warmth. As I was praying the temperature wouldn't plunge again overnight, I felt Marty nudge my left leg with her stirrup.

"There's Carlos," she whispered out of the side of her mouth. "On your right. About four o'clock."

Oh, crap. My poor neck.

Once I got my head turned, I couldn't believe my eyes. Carlos had traded in his driving-up-from-Miami clothes — a navy blue crewneck sweater and tennis shoes — for riding gear. And, unlike Sal with his gaudy glitter, Carlos had got it exactly right. His brown boots were appropriately scuffed. He'd angled his straw cowboy hat — a Resistol — just so. He wore a long-sleeved denim shirt, faded and soft. And his jeans were by Wrangler — the brand favored at rodeos from Florida to Washington State.

"The man looks gorgeous, Mace. I'll give him that. That white hat with his dark eyes and skin? Umm-umm," Maddie leaned in close from my right side so I could hear her lips smack.

Begrudgingly, I agreed that he looked hotter than a stolen pistol.

"But let's see if he knows the north end of that horse from the south," I said. "That's a thoroughbred he's riding, and he looks like a handful."

Carlos eased his horse to the front of the line, where the mule- and horse-drawn wagons were gathered. Even the most placid of horses will sometimes get spooky around pulled wagons. The look of them and the sounds they make can take some getting used to. And a thoroughbred, with its high spirits and often nervous temperament, is far from placid. I watched to see how Carlos would handle the horse.

One of the wagons had been having a problem with a brake that rubbed. As the driver circled the pasture to test his repair, Carlos urged his bay-colored horse toward the mule-drawn contraption. The thoroughbred's ears went back. He rolled his big eyes until the whites showed, looking at the wagon as if to say "What in the hell is that, and how's it going to hurt me?"

The wagon clattered by, squeaking and rattling. The horse went into a fast sidestep, trying to flee. Carlos turned the reins, shifted in the saddle, and used the pressure of his legs on the horse's belly to force him straight back to what he feared. Tossing his head, the horse turned round and round in a tight circle. Carlos repeated the same actions again, firm but not cruel. By the time he'd done it a third and fourth time, the horse walked along behind the wagon, as docile as the family dog.

"Looks like he has a little more experience than riding a police car through Miami's concrete jungle," Marty said.

"Hmmm." I left it at that, not caring to add that the man whose skills I'd mocked could handle a horse just as well as I could.

At just that moment, he glanced my way. If my neck had been in better shape, I would have snapped my head around before he caught me looking. But it wasn't, so he did. I could hardly ignore him now. Especially since he was heading my way.

"Hey," I said as he rode up.

"Mace." He stopped, and touched the brim of his hat. No smile. "Where's your cowboy friend from earlier this morning? You looked like such good buddies, I thought maybe you two would be riding double on the same horse."

Maddie snorted. Marty giggled. I ignored his comment.

"Speaking of riding," I said, "how come you never told me you were so at home on a horse?"

"What, and spoil your notion that you were Ms. Rodeo Rider and I was just a city boy who wouldn't know a saddle from a squad car?"

I think I might have blushed. That sounded just like the way I'd have put it.

"Where'd you learn to ride?" Maddie asked.

"My grandfather had cattle in Cuba. After Castro took over, my family didn't own the ranch anymore." His eyes got a pained, far-away look. "My dad still worked there, though. And he taught me everything he knew about horses."

"Well, he must have taught you well," Marty said. 'You ride like a dream."

"*Gracias,*" he said, giving Marty a grin that showed off his white teeth.

When he turned back to me, the smile was gone. "You know, *niña,* you don't have the market cornered on cowboys. We had them in Cuba, too. We called them *guajiros.*"

With that, he tipped his hat and galloped away.

"It's a good sign he's angry about seeing you with Trey," Marty said. "It means he still cares."

"Or, it means he doesn't like her well enough to even try to be nice," Maddie said.

I didn't reply to the theories of either of my sisters. I just sat there, thinking of the sight of his strong thighs in the saddle, and of the thrill I'd felt the first time he called me *niña.* Then, his voice had been low and sexy. The Spanish word for girl had sounded like a caress. Now, it sounded like a slap.

"Headin' out!" came the call, repeated by riders up and down the length of the pasture. "Headin' oooooouuuuuttt!"

County sheriff's deputies had pulled their squad cars onto State Road 64, lights flashing, near the entrance to Bramble land. They blocked traffic so the long line of riders could cross the highway and proceed onto a grassy, roadside swale that makes up much of the Cracker Trail. Today's highways follow the old paths made by the state's cattle-raising pioneers. In the old days, cowmen moved their herds from east to west, where they'd load the cattle onto ships on Florida's Gulf Coast, bound for markets in Cuba. Our ride reverses the direction, signifying their return trip — minus their cattle, and, hopefully, with some money in their pockets.

Once we'd crossed the road and got on our way, the ride began to settle into a pattern. Horses and riders found their strides. Maddie and Marty had been able to rustle up two horses from a group that brings abused and abandoned animals on the ride — partly as rehabilitation, partly in an effort to find homes for the horses. Maddie's mount walked faster than mine; Marty's a bit slower. So, it wasn't long before I was on my own in the line. I enjoyed the passing scenery: an orange grove to the right; a fenced horse pasture to the left. Whinnying loudly, an Appaloosa mare cantered along on her side of the fence, looking like she wanted to break out and join the herd of

Cracker Trail horses passing by.

I knew from the last couple of days that Mama's horse and mine kept a similar pace. Just as I began to wonder where she'd gotten to, I heard her voice behind me.

"Oh, yes, my daughter Mace and I were right there when Wynonna found poor Lawton. She was so distraught. But, of course, I did what I could to make her feel better. I don't know what it is, but people just naturally turn to me in times of trouble."

I heard whoever Mama was bragging to murmur politely, not that she needed any encouragement to continue.

"Now, my daughter Mace, on the other hand, she doesn't have a natural gift with people. She's better with animals, quite frankly."

"Aw, the poor thing! She's a loner, then. No boyfriend?"

I recognized that other voice. I pulled up on the reins to slow Val.

"Well, speak of the devil! That's Mace riding, right up there. The gal with the snarly hair and big shoulders. Howdy, darlin'," Mama called to the back of my head. "I've just been talking to the sweetest, prettiest girl."

Pretty, yes. Sweet? Not even close.

"Hello again, Austin," I said as the two of them came abreast.

Sixteen

Austin tossed her hair, picked up her pace, and pulled ahead of us without a word.

The look on Mama's face almost made it worth it, getting my tent ripped to shreds. Her head swiveled back and forth, forth and back like a one-eyed man at a strip club. Finally, her gaze lit on me.

"Well, I never! You could have told me what the girl looked like, Mace," she whispered. Then, raising her voice to Austin's retreating back, she yelled out, "And she ain't all *that* pretty, either!"

"How much did you tell her about me, Mama?"

Mama's guilty look hinted she'd had a lot to say to Austin in the hour-and-half we'd been on the trail.

"Did you brag about my college grades?"

A nod and a proud smile.

"Did you complain that I never do anything with my hair or fix my face with makeup?"

A nod, no smile.

"Did you tell her you've just about given up hope I'll ever get married?"

Mama pursed her lips.

"That's what I thought." I turned Val's reins toward an open spot ahead and pushed my heels to her sides.

"Where you going, Mace?" Mama called after me.

"I'm going to show that even if I am too smart for my own good, plain, and pityingly single, I won't be pushed around."

Within moments, I'd caught up with Austin. Like Mama, she had on a full face. Rosy lips. Mascara-ed eyes. Blush expertly blended on perfect cheekbones. I hoped the sun would get really hot, so I could watch all that makeup melt.

I pulled up Val beside her.

"I want to talk to you, Austin."

I used the work tone I reserve for visitors to Himmarshee Park who steal rare plants or taunt Ollie, our alligator.

"Well, I don't want to talk to you."

She swung her face away from me. I wondered how she made her curls bounce like that. Hair rollers? An electric curling iron? If so, where would she plug it in on the trail? Did they make them with little chargers you could use with your car's cigarette lighter, like they do for cell phones?

I edged Val closer to Austin's little horse. It was a flashy Arabian mare, the equine world's equivalent of a beauty queen. How appropriate.

"You're going to listen to me, whether you like it or not." Seeing a couple of other riders turn their heads, I lowered my voice to a hiss. "Number one. I didn't know Trey was involved with you. Which he says he isn't anymore, by the way."

"That's just temporary." She waved her hand like I was a pesky horsefly, engagement ring glinting in the sun. "We've broken up and gotten back a dozen times. He'll come around. *If* a certain tramp I could name would just leave him alone."

That started my blood to simmer.

"Number two, I'd appreciate it if you'd stop calling me a tramp. You don't even know me."

Austin arched her plucked eyebrows. "I know *plenty.*"

Thanks, Mama, I thought.

"And number three, have you got a knife hidden somewhere in those tight jeans? Did you have anything to do with my tent getting ruined last night?"

Confusion played across her face. It

looked genuine. I imagined it was the same look Austin's high school math teacher had seen a hundred times.

"What are you talking about?" she snapped. "Why would I care about your stupid tent?"

I stared, trying to gauge if she was lying.

"What kind of wine do you drink, Austin?"

A blank look. "Your mama was right, Mace. You have zero people skills. First you accuse me of whatever with a tent. Now, you want to buy me a gift to make up for trying to steal my fiancé. If you're serious, I prefer white wine."

"Don't hold your breath," I said, as I turned Val away.

Trey had already said that Austin was none too bright. I graduated cum laude from the University of Central Florida. So, how come I was the one who felt stupid?

Maddie and I held the reins of all four horses as Marty and Mama went off to scout the snack line. We'd pulled in at a wide spot along the trail to give horses and riders a midmorning break. I stretched and did knee bends. Maddie did a one-hand massage of her lower back. Funny, I didn't remember as many pains and aches the last time we rode.

Riders lined up at a flatbed truck hauling the water and lemonade supply. The queue was even longer for the portable potties, trailered from stop to stop like a smelly caboose. You could tell at a glance which occupied john had a broken lock. A cowboy hat propped at the door served as a Do Not Enter sign.

Soon, Mama and Marty returned with lemonades all around, as well as peanut butter crackers and four apples. The horses, of course, got the apples.

"Do you want my crackers, Mace?" Mama sweetly offered her package. "I'll give you half my lemonade, too."

She was trying to make up for spilling my secrets to Austin. I didn't feel like being nice yet.

"No, that's all right." I sighed. "I don't really feel much like eating."

That was a lie. It'd take much more than a shredded tent and a tiff with Austin to put me off my feed.

"I'll take your crackers, Mama," Maddie said.

"I wasn't offering them to you, Maddie. Who knows how many calories are in these things!"

I thought that was mean, since Mama

knows Maddie is sensitive about her size. I always tell her if she really wants to lose some weight, she should spend more time walking the track at Himmarshee High and less time at the Pork Pit restaurant.

Marty handed Maddie two crackers from her pack.

"What's gotten into you and Mama, Mace?" Marty asked. "Y'all are acting crazier than sprayed roaches."

Mama glanced at me. I got busy trying to get a tangle out of Val's mane.

"Well?" Marty asked again.

Never one to embrace a silence, Mama blurted, "I accidentally became friends with Trey's ex this morning."

I glared at her. "Austin pumped Mama for all kinds of information. Which we all know is easy to do, since that particular well never goes dry."

"Are you saying I talk too much, Mace?"

"Mama, if talk was money, you'd be a millionaire."

Smiling in anticipation, Maddie draped an arm across her horse's saddle. She leaned on the animal to get comfortable, in case Mama and I really got to arguing.

Marty, on the other hand, looked like she wanted to flee.

"Now, let's not fight," she fretted. "We're

here to enjoy ourselves. Remember the last time we all rode the Cracker Trail together? It was the year before Daddy died. Mace, you and I were too little to ride the whole way, so we sat in a mule wagon on two bales of hay. Remember?"

Of course I did. And I could tell my sisters and Mama were thinking back, too, from the far-away expressions in their eyes.

"Okay," I finally said. "Marty's right. Let's call a truce. We're here to have fun, aren't we?"

I didn't know that fun would soon be in short supply.

An hour out from our lunch stop, the sun beat on our backs. The horses kicked up dust. Many of the riders, including me, looked like train robbers with our neckerchiefs up over our faces. We didn't plan to loot the Cattle Rustler drive-thru on SR 64, though. The bandanas were to keep dirt and stirred-up pollen from trampled plants and grasses out of our mouths and noses.

I was by myself again on the trail. Maddie was in front; Marty somewhere behind. Mama was off in the middle, probably revealing dark family secrets to a stranger. Between the hot sun, Val's rolling walk, and the rhythmic sound of a hundred horses' hooves, I was about to doze off.

At least I was until I spotted Carlos riding in front of me. I'd know him anywhere, with that broad back and the cowlick that curled on his neck, just below his hat. I remembered tracing that circle of hair one night as I cuddled behind him in his bed.

Better not to think about that now.

I closed a bit of distance between us, moving to where I could watch Carlos, but he wouldn't see me. He leaned in his saddle to the right, his head cocked toward the rider by his side. She was small, thin-shouldered, and delicate. She reached a hand up to adjust her cowboy hat, and a copper-colored tendril of hair fell down her back.

Belle Bramble. How perfect: Carlos has a need to take care of somebody. Doc Abel said Belle is fragile, and needs taking care of. I backed off, and let them move well ahead of me. But just seeing them was enough to send my imagination into overdrive. I pictured her crying into his chest; her tiny body trembling in his strong arms. I imagined him stroking that fiery-colored hair. I played out their wedding day in my head, complete with a black tux and boutonniere for him, and her in a diamond-encrusted, size two gown. Just as I was picturing the two of them shopping together

151

for baby clothes, I heard a whip crack. It seemed awfully close.

Val stayed steady. But the loud retort snapped me out of my jealous daydream. I noticed that we'd drifted too close to the adjacent highway while I wasn't paying attention. A stream of traffic flowed by. Logging trucks moved cypress. Locals drove pickups. Lost tourists in rental cars tried to find Disney World.

I started to ease Val back onto the grassy swale, but another horse moved up beside us, blocking our way. Just as I turned my stiff neck to see who rode so near, the whip cracked again. I felt a rush of air behind me as the leather tip connected with Val's sensitive flank.

And then everything happened really fast.

Val lurched beneath me and skittered to the side, metal shoes scraping asphalt. I leaned over, searching for the reins I'd dropped when the whip hit. My fingertips clutched them, then missed, then grabbed the reins again. As I raised my head, I realized we were in trouble.

Val galloped down the middle of the highway. From the oncoming lane, a semi-truck hauling oranges bore down on us, headlights flashing a frantic rhythm.

SEVENTEEN

Brrraapp! brraapp! brraapp!

The horn on the orange truck blasted. Air brakes hissed. Riders screamed, "Watch out! Watch out!"

You know how they say your whole life flashes in front of your eyes in the final seconds before you die? Well, mine didn't. I saw the glint of the sun on the truck's chrome trim. I smelled the oranges in the back. And then I got a quick mental picture of what a mess it would be if the driver hit us, jackknifed his rig, and spilled 45,000 pounds of citrus across State Road 64.

I didn't want to be roadkill in a sea of orange juice. My instincts kicked in. I knew exactly what to do.

I crouched low over Val's neck, keeping my hand in contact with the sensitive spot just where her mane ends. "Whoa, girl." My voice was low, and as calm as I could make it. "Easy, Val."

With a tight rein, I threw my whole upper body into turning her to the left. Well-trained and responsive, she wanted to go where the reins and the weight of my body were telling her to. But her shoes were slick against the pavement. Her left front leg slid out. She stumbled. I prayed. She recovered; and we cut to the left in the nick of time. The orange hauler veered right, passing so close that I could see the terror in his eyes and read his name embroidered in dark thread on his light blue work shirt. *Juan.*

Now, Val and I were safely on the grass swale, across the highway from the rest of the ride. Val slowed, first to a trot, and then to a walk. My heart pounded. My lungs felt like they couldn't get enough air. Looking at the reins looped around my fingers, I saw my hands were shaking. My legs in the stirrups felt like boiled spaghetti.

Before I could dismount to check on Val's condition, a clatter of hooves came across the road. The outrider who'd given us the lecture about cow whips moved toward me, his face dark with fear and fury. Mama and Marty rode on either side of him. Maddie wasn't with them. It had all happened so quickly, she must have been too far up the line to even realize I was in danger. Carlos wasn't there, either. Had he been so taken with Belle that he didn't even register the drama unfolding behind him?

And, speaking of drama, the fourth rider hurrying across the highway was Austin. Except for two cherry-colored splotches of blush-on, her face was ghostly white. Her lower lip quivered. A cow whip dangled from her right hand.

Mama was the first to reach me. She was out of her saddle and by my side in a flash.

"Darlin', are you hurt?" She reached up to squeeze my knee. "I thought you and that horse were done for."

"I'm fine, Mama. Just shaken up."

Marty shuddered. "I've never been so scared in my life, Mace."

Tell me about it, I thought.

"I am so, so sorry." Tears spilled from Austin's eyes. "I was just fooling around, learning how to snap the whip. I never thought I'd get it to work."

"Looked like it worked just fine," I said. "You hit my horse. Were you trying for her, or for me?"

"Ohmigod, Mace!" The hand with the whip flew to her mouth. The tears really started flowing now. "I never, never, meant to hit you." She stared, her wide eyes lingering on each of us. "Y'all have got to believe me!"

The outrider was silent, working the tobacco in his jaw. Mama glared at Austin, her hands on her hips. Marty looked like she was about to cry, too.

"Right now, I'm worried about Val," I said. "I just want to make sure she's okay."

I climbed down. Mama flung both arms around my waist. She hung on as I stepped to Val's side and ran a hand over her coat. I gently touched her right flank.

"It's starting to welt, but the skin's not broken," I said. "So that's good."

I leaned down, checking the horse's legs and feet. Mama, still hanging on, leaned with me.

"Mama, let go." I unwound her fingers from my waist. "I'm fine." I kissed her on the forehead. "I promise."

The outrider had been watching all of this — tears, kissing, emotion — with a pained look. He spit a stream of tobacco juice, raising a tiny puff of dust where it hit the ground.

"This is what we're gonna do," he finally said. "I was thinking about banning you from the ride, Miss." He pointed at Austin, who lowered her eyes to the ground. Her shoulders shook with sobs.

"I'm not gonna do that. But I am gonna take away that cow whip of yours. You'll get it back when you show me you can behave. Now, I don't know what's between the two of you gals, and I don't want to know." He looked at me. "You say one thing; she says another. I don't have the time to try to straighten it out." He glanced at his watch. "We should be making our lunch stop about now with the rest of the ride. All of this has put us behind."

"Sorry if my almost getting squashed by a semi-truck screwed up your schedule."

"Hush, Mace!" Mama said. "Nobody likes a smart aleck."

He held out his hand to Austin. "Give it over."

She coiled the whip and laid it into his open palm, tears still streaming down her cheeks.

"I am so sorry. I never, ever meant to do her or that horse any harm."

"So you've said." He spit again and narrowed his eyes. "I'm watching you, Miss. Another careless stunt like that and you're off of this ride for good."

The outrider started back across the road, and Mama and I followed him. We were almost to the other side before I noticed that Marty and Austin weren't with us. I shifted sideways so I wouldn't have to turn my head to see what was holding them up.

Marty had moved her borrowed horse to block Austin's path. She leaned out from her saddle, her little face just inches from Austin's. As Marty's lips moved, Austin's eyes got wide again. Her face went pale. Then, she spun her little Arabian and high-tailed it away from my little sister.

Marty trotted across the road. Her usual sweet smile had returned.

"What in the world did you just say?" I asked, watching Austin's horse kicking up dust as they raced away. "She looks like she's not gonna stop 'til she gets to the ocean inlet at Fort Pierce."

Marty's gaze followed the fleeing Austin. Under the brim of her hat, my little sister's eyes were colder than I'd ever seen them.

"I just told her we're watching, too. I said if she harms you in any way, she won't have to worry about getting banned from the Cracker Trail. I told her that before that happened, Maddie and I'd break both her legs so bad she'd never ride a horse again."

And with that, Marty tucked some stray hair under her hat and turned her horse to the trail.

EIGHTEEN

The scent of pulled pork rose into the air as we turned off the trail and into a sprawling pasture set up for lunch. I pointed to a line of trees in the distance. It'd be a good place to tie up the horses out of the sun. Due to the delay of me almost getting killed, most of the other riders had already taken care of their horses. We had the water troughs nearly to ourselves. Val had just lowered her muzzle into the tub to drink when Maddie and Sal ran up.

"Where in the blazes have you three been?" Maddie asked.

"We wuz starting to get worried." Sal's furrowed brow revealed he was well past "starting" to worry.

"We had a little accident, but everybody's fine," I said.

"An accident?" Maddie's voice caught in her throat.

"Rosie, get down off that animal so I can

see for myself you're okay."

Sal stood about ten feet from Mama's horse, his hands clasped behind his back. His anxious gaze moved from her face to the horse's hindquarters. He'd take a step forward, and then step right back again like someone had drawn a line he couldn't cross in the grass.

I couldn't believe it! Big Sal was afraid of horses. Mama was riding a tiny Paso Fino, hardly bigger than a pony. If her horse and Sal were in a tug-of-war, I'd put my money on Sal. Yet, he was eyeing the horse like it was as big as a Clydesdale but crazy, ready to turn and trample him at any moment.

"I'm fine, Sally," Mama said, waving her ring hand at him. "It was Mace. She nearly got hit by a tractor-trailer hauling grape-fruit."

"Oranges, Mama," I said.

We filled them in on Austin's whip-cracking "practice" and my close call.

"The only good thing about the whole incident was Marty," I said. "You should have seen her, Maddie. She'd have made you proud. She got right up in Austin's face and gave her what-for."

Marty blushed. "And I'm feeling really guilty about that. I was so angry and scared, I threatened that girl. You know, Buddhism teaches us to never harm a living thing."

One of Marty's college boyfriends had been a Buddhist. The boy was long gone, but the religion stuck — a perfect match for our normally gentle sister.

"Don't worry about it, honey. I'm sure you can get at least one of your gods to forgive you."

Mama had mostly come to accept Marty's beliefs, but she'd still get in a dig where she could over no meat and multiple gods.

I was about to stick up for Marty and freedom of religion, but a scene unfolding under the canopy of trees captured my attention. Belle Bramble sat on a log, her horse tied to an oak branch. She was crying. Carlos was crouched in front of her. I watched as he took the bandana from his neck. Holding her chin in one hand, he dabbed ever so gently at her wet face. When she gave him a brave smile, I felt the sting of unshed tears behind my own eyes.

"Mace! Mama's on about false gods again. Marty could use your help here. What is so darned interesting in the woods?" Maddie's gaze followed mine. "Well, crap," she said. "Looks like Carlos has found him someone who doesn't mind being taken care of."

I blinked hard.

Mama said, "If he's so fired up about saving somebody, where was he when Mace was about to get squashed like a gopher turtle on the highway?"

Good question. Looks like I'd missed my moment. Not that the damsel in distress role suits me. I'd have to leave that — and Carlos, too, from the looks of it — to poor, fragile Belle.

After I stalked off alone, I found a spot in the back of the pasture to pick at my sandwich and work on my sulk. A cattle egret hunted bugs in the tall grass by some ancient cow pens. A meadow lark warbled nearby. The cloudless sky was swimming-pool blue. Sitting in the sun with my back against the worn wood of a pen, I nursed my hurt feelings — along with the last of my lemonade. I kept replaying Mama's litany, about how I'd probably end up all by myself.

It's not like I didn't have my choice of men: There was the alcoholic with the psycho girlfriend, who may or may not be his ex. And, oh yeah, he might also be diddling his daddy's recent widow. And then there was the other one — who I had to admit I still wanted, even though he clearly didn't want me.

Just as I was imagining a solitary life with

a houseful of cats, I heard throat-clearing beside me.

"Mace, can we talk to you?"

Deep voice; the slightest Spanish accent. Carlos. I turned my shoulders. My stiff neck followed reluctantly.

"Sure," I said, careful to keep my voice even.

I tried not to stare at the hands that he and Belle had linked together. But since they were standing and I was sitting, they were right there at my eye level. A camera hung from her neck.

"Why don't y'all have a seat?"

That was even worse. He actually brushed a spot for her to sit on the ground. She lowered herself gracefully, like a flower folding up for the night. As soon as he sat, she reached for his hand again. His was strong, the color of buttered caramel; hers was small, as delicate-looking as a child's. I forced myself to raise my eyes to Belle's.

"I didn't get the chance at the ranch house to tell you how sorry I am," I said. "We saw your daddy not too long before he died. He looked happy, like he was having the time of his life. I hope there's some comfort in that."

I didn't mention Lawton's less-than-happy reaction when Mama asked him about Trey.

"Thank you, Mace," she said in a whispery voice. "It does mean something to hear you say that."

She was clasping Carlos' hand so hard, the freckles were nearly jumping off her skin.

He said, "Belle and I have been talking this morning about her father's death. There are some things that don't seem to add up."

No kidding, I thought. That's what I've been trying to tell everybody.

She said, "Daddy was a wealthy, powerful man. He had enemies. What if someone killed him, maybe with poison? If you look around, you'll see people with motives, starting with his own wife."

Belle's intelligent eyes searched mine. I figured now was a good time to bring up some of those motives. I told them about seeing Wynonna rubbing Trey's chest.

"Is there something between her and your brother, Belle?"

"No way." She shook her head firmly. "I don't know what her game was, but he was passed out drunk. Besides, Trey can't stand Wynonna. Both of us knew she married Daddy for his money. Now it looks like she'll get what she wanted."

I told them about Johnny Adams, and the

trouble he'd had with Lawton, both business and personal.

"So Johnny was in love with my mother?"

"That's what Mama told me," I said.

Carlos rolled his eyes.

"I saw that," I said. "Anyway, there was Johnny's odd reaction, too. He acted so strange when Mama and I told him about your daddy dying."

Another eye roll from Carlos.

"If you don't stop doing that," I told him, "you'll give yourself a headache."

He sighed. "You're talking about feelings and observations, Mace, not evidence."

"Well, I know it's not *evidence*, Carlos. I'm just telling you and Belle what I've seen. How come cops can have hunches and real people can't?"

"So now I'm not a real person?"

I ignored that. I was on a roll.

"Not to mention, I seem to remember a certain detective's hunch last summer that turned out dead wrong. My mama went to jail because of it. I'm being extra careful to notice *everything* this time around."

"*Coño,* Mace." There was that Cuban cuss word I'd come to know. "How many times do I have to say I'm sorry?"

As I was trying to think of a snappy comeback, I glanced at Belle. She was tak-

165

ing everything in. I imagined not much got by those green eyes of hers, or her camera, either.

"Whatever," I finally said, not at all snappily.

I swigged from my lemonade cup. It was mostly ice, but I crunched away, as if the cubes weren't freezing my molars into glaciers. Carlos glared at me. I glared back. Belle unclasped her fingers from his and folded her hands in her lap. Then she lifted her camera and took a picture of the egret perched on a fence post. The stony silence stretched out between Carlos and me.

Just then, I heard a muffled cough from around the side of the pen. The grass rustled as someone hurried away. By the time I got up to look through the weathered slats, there was no one to see. Whoever had been there had slipped into the woods and vanished. Was it someone listening in, or just a passerby?

"What?" Carlos asked me.

"I heard something."

"I didn't," Belle said.

"Mace works in a nature park and traps animals as a sideline. She's got hearing like a bat," Carlos said.

"What's that supposed to mean? That I'm as crazy as a bat, like the old saying?"

"Give it a break, would you?" He got up and brushed off his Wranglers. "It was a compliment, Mace, not that you ever knew how to take one. All I meant was you have highly developed tracking skills and senses in the wild."

Belle got up, too, interrupting us before we could start another round.

"Mace, I know you had some questions about Daddy's death, too. Your mama told me all about it when she took me to see his bod . . . bahd . . . uhm, to see him."

Of course she did.

"She said you were concerned about what might have been in that chili cup."

I nodded, waiting for Belle to go on.

"Carlos told me this morning he was a police detective, and that he'd also lost someone close to him." She glanced at him. He smiled his encouragement. I felt something twist in my gut. "We talked on the trail about how you feel powerless when someone you love dies. I just want to make sure I've done everything I can for Daddy. If someone killed him, we need to find out who it was."

She looked at Carlos. He grabbed her hand and squeezed. I felt like throwing up.

"Even though I'm out of my jurisdiction, and technically between jobs, I can call in a favor," he said. "The least we can do is get some tests run on the chili left in that cup."

"That's what I've been saying," I said.

"Well, where is it then?" he asked.

"The cup?"

"No, Mace. The Empire State Building." The scowl again. "Isn't the cup what we've been talking about?"

I wondered how soon he'd start taking that surly, Miami tone with Belle. Probably never. Something about me seemed to bring out the worst in Carlos. I bit back a smart-tass remark on account of Belle being in mourning.

"The *cup*," I said, drawing out the word, "was in Doc Abel's front seat the last time I saw it. He seems sure a heart attack killed Lawton; but he said he'd hang onto the cup on the off chance he's wrong."

A funny look flitted across Belle's face. "Hmm," she said.

"What?" I asked her.

"Well, it's just that I saw Doc, riding in one of the wagons this morning. I asked him about Daddy's chili cup. He said Wynonna took it."

NINETEEN

Carlos and I went looking for Doc, and found Johnny Adams, breaking down the last of lunch. He carried two big stainless steel serving pans, one stacked sideways on top of the other. The cole slaw was all but gone; a bit of potato salad was left. I looked around for plastic bowls or a stray fork, but most everything had been put away. Too bad, too. In my jealous funk, I'd imagined I was too upset to eat more than half my sandwich. Now, I could have eaten two, along with something on the side. I was starving.

Belle left to help Trey move their big RV and horse trailer to the evening's campsite. Carlos and I stopped arguing long enough to agree we should find Doc to ask him what happened to Lawton's cup. We'd left our horses in Maddie's care. Mama and Marty were pitching in with Sal, helping leapfrog our vehicles and equipment ahead to tonight's camp.

"Hey, Johnny," I called. "We're looking for Doc. You seen him around?"

He shook his head as he kept walking. "Not since breakfast, but I've been busy."

"I don't suppose you've got a bag of chips or an extra sandwich hanging around in the trailer, do you?" I asked.

"Nope, sorry." He didn't break stride, merely shifted the pans so he could watch the ground for holes or horse paddies. "Lunch ended more than a half-hour ago."

To be honest, he didn't sound all that sorry. I wondered if Mama still had that pack of crackers she offered me on the trail?

"No problem," I said. "Last night, Mama got somebody to rustle up a late dinner plate for Doc. But I know y'all are rushed after lunch, trying to finish up and move everything ahead for tonight."

He stopped and looked around the tins at me. "You're Rosalee's girl, aren't you?"

I nodded.

"Well, why didn't you say so? I'll get you a couple of pork sandwiches out of the stash I hid for myself." He rubbed the swell of his stomach above his belt. "I sure don't need 'em. I'm getting as fat as a fixed dog."

"I couldn't take your food," I said, knowing I'd do just that if he offered again.

"I insist."

Thank God!

"Audrey!" He put the tins on a folding table and yelled toward the trailer. "Bring a couple of those leftover sandwiches out here, would you?"

He raised his eyebrows at Carlos. "Can I get you anything?"

"No, Mace is the one with the hollow leg. She's always hungry." He leaned past me and offered his hand to Johnny, introducing himself.

As the two men shook, I said, "I'm sorry, hunger must have fogged up the manners part of my brain. Carlos, this is Johnny Adams. He knew Mama and Lawton Bramble way back when. He and Lawton were very old friends."

Johnny's jaw went tight at the mention of Lawton's name, but he covered it with a joke.

"Hell, Mace, I ain't *that* old."

"Carlos is a police detective," I said, watching Johnny to see how he'd react.

To my surprise, his smile broadened, though it still didn't light those almost black eyes.

"A detective, huh? I got a nephew on the job up in Pensacola. I sure admire what y'all do. But it can be dangerous, can't it? I think

I'll stick to the barbecue business. So far as I know, a pork rib never learned to aim a gun."

He glanced toward the trailer again.

"Audrey! Where the hell are them sandwiches? We don't have all day."

"Hold your horses, you old grouch." A pretty woman in her forties with short hair and lively eyes hurried down the steps of the trailer, two foil-wrapped sandwiches in her hand. She smiled at me. "You must have something on Johnny for him to dip into his own stash."

"Go on now, woman!" He took the sandwiches and waved her away. Audrey didn't budge. "She thinks she can talk to me thataway because she's worked for me forever. But if she makes me mad enough, I just might fire her." His voice was gruff, but his mouth curved with the hint of a smile. It was the first one I'd seen to reach his eyes.

Audrey cupped her hand to her mouth, secret-style. "He wouldn't survive two days without me," she said in a stage whisper.

"That's what you think, you uppity woman. You can be replaced. Just keep testing me," he grumbled as he gathered up the serving trays and stalked off. "Enjoy the sandwiches."

I turned to offer my sympathies to Audrey

for having such a crabby boss, when the joke I was about to crack died in my mouth. She was looking after Johnny with yearning all over her face. He might be oblivious, but any woman could tell in an instant; Audrey was in love.

I filed away the observation. Audrey might have an interesting viewpoint to share on how Johnny hadn't been able to get over his tragic first love.

"There's Doc, up ahead in that mule wagon. Passenger side."

I nodded toward a bright green wagon in front of us. An American flag waved from one rear corner; Florida's red-on-white colors flew from the other. The wagon, about fifty yards ahead of Carlos and me, was listing to the right. The driver was a skinny old guy in suspenders and a beat-up Florida Cracker hat. Doc outweighed him by at least a hundred pounds. I'd find a tactful way later to let the driver know to add a couple of bales of hay to the left if Doc intended to go the distance.

"C'mon, let's catch up," I said, lifting Val's reins as I clucked my tongue.

Carlos' thoroughbred didn't need much encouragement. The big bay was off, like the racehorse he must have been. I admired the view from the rear. The man's butt barely left the saddle; he moved like he was melded onto the horse. Marty was right. Carlos rode like a dream. I dug in my heels and brought Val alongside.

"Hey, cowpoke, wait up. Sorry, I guess that should be 'guabero.' "

He winced.

"Pronunciation's that bad, huh?"

"*Guajiro.* Gwa-yee-row," he sounded it out for me.

I had a flash of the two of us in his kitchen one morning, fooling around as he made me breakfast. Picking up common items, he'd drilled me in Spanish: *café,* he said, holding up a vacuum-packed bag of strong Cuban coffee. *Cuchara,* he said, handing me a spoon. *Beso,* he whispered, as he leaned down and gave me a kiss.

Oh, crap. Why had I screwed things up?

"Listen, let me do the talking with Doc," I said, more sharply than I intended.

"Whatever you say, Mace. You're the boss."

"No offense," I semi-apologized.

"None taken," he said with his irritating smirk.

I eased Val closer to the wagon. "Afternoon, Doc," I said. "Enjoying the ride?"

The Oak Ridge Boys' gospel classic, "I'm

in Love With Jesus," blasted from a CD player in the front of the wagon. The driver sang along. His volume was in inverse proportion to his talent. I had a moment's sympathy for the non-believing Doc.

"Hello, Mace." Doc raised his voice, hunching up his shoulders to protect his ears. "Where's your mother?"

"She and my sisters are riding along somewhere, yakking it up." After three days of Mama all to myself, I was more than happy to let Marty and Maddie enjoy her company for a while.

I performed quick introductions. Doc's brow wrinkled when I mentioned Carlos was a police detective.

"I hope you're not still on that kick about Lawton's cause of death, Mace."

I was trying to think of what to say about my "kick" when Carlos butted in.

"Mace told me Lawton was using a cup just before he died. I agree with her it should be tested, if only to allay any doubts that anyone, including his family, might have."

Leave it to him to come right to the point. And, so much for letting me do the talking.

"I have no doubt what killed him. But I'm not averse to testing the cup, either." Doc narrowed his eyes at me. "As I've already told Mace."

I narrowed my eyes right back. "Then why'd you give the cup to Wynonna?"

He shook his head. "I didn't. It's still sitting in my car, as far as I know."

"Lawton's daughter Belle said you did," I said.

"Well, she's wrong. Belle is a high-strung girl. She doesn't always think clearly. She has problems keeping things straight, among other difficulties. I may have said Wynonna wanted the cup. I didn't say I handed it over."

The Oak Ridge Boys launched into "Closer to Thee." The mule-driver cranked the volume of his sing-along even higher. Doc put a discreet finger into the ear closest to the CD player.

"So you wouldn't mind giving the cup to me for analysis?" Carlos asked.

"Not at all, officer." Doc turned his palms up in a friendly gesture, but his voice had an edge. "I've worked with enough policemen over the years to know you're a suspicious breed."

"Actually, it's *Detective,* not officer," Carlos said. "And having suspicions comes with the territory."

"Hmm, yes. I would imagine it does," Doc said. "I'll make sure you get that cup, once we reach camp."

"Mace, you need to pull that corner tighter," Maddie instructed. "The tent looks all lopsided on this side."

Despite the morning's delay, we made camp near Zolfo Springs by late afternoon. Maddie's four-man monstrosity belonged at the Smithsonian as an example of early man's recreational practices. Canvas, it weighed about two hundred pounds, reeked of mildew, and was missing a quarter of its stakes. I was doing the best I could under the circumstances.

"Maddie, instead of standing there criticizing, why don't you go see if you can find a dead sabal frond? I can break it into long stakes for this sandy ground."

"You want me to go into the woods?" she looked like I'd asked her to cross a scorching desert on her hands and knees.

"Yes. The woods, Maddie. I know you and Kenny's idea of camping is when the Cracker Barrel restaurant's more than a block from your hotel, but you've got to help out." I raised my head from untangling one of the ropes for the antique tent. "Look over there at Marty. She's got all the tack off the horses and she's already giving them their feed."

"Oh, all right then." Grumbling, Maddie started for the trees. "I don't see what's so important about a few little pieces of wood, though."

Without Maddie there to criticize, I quickly got the sleeping bags from her trunk to air out. I don't think they'd been used since Maddie's college-student daughter was in Girl Scouts. But at least they were intact, and they'd keep my sisters and me warm.

The sun was still warm, but it was sinking. The air already carried a hint of chill. In the distance, Marty was finishing up with the horses, which meant she'd begin to feel the cold as soon as she sat down to rest. I whine like a baby when the temperature plunges, but Marty's prone to respiratory problems and strep throat. All of us worry when she gets a chill.

I called out, "Marty, why don't you put on that jacket I left under the front seat of my Jeep?"

She waved at me. "Thanks, Mace. I'm just about done."

I draped the last sleeping bag over Maddie's trunk. As I did, I noticed something dark and sinewy coiled in the back seat. I couldn't believe it! They'd brought my old cow whip, the one I loaned my niece for her film class documentary on Florida Crackers.

I pulled out the whip, running my thumb over my initials burned onto the wooden handle. *MEB*. Mason Elizabeth Bauer. I gave it a couple of practice cracks. Yep, just as loud as ever.

"Hey, Marty," I yelled over the sound.

She didn't answer.

I walked toward my Jeep, snapping the whip the whole way. It's amazing how the muscles remember; like riding a bicycle, I guess. "Hey," I shouted. "Why didn't y'all tell me you brought this?"

Still no answer.

My Jeep's door was open and Marty stood rooted, staring at my jacket unfurled on the ground. Her face was ashen and shiny with sweat. She mouthed my name over and over, like a whispered prayer.

"MaceMaceMaceMace."

And then I heard another sound. Low and menacing, it was unmistakable to a girl who grew up in the Florida wilds, clambering over piles of dead wood and turning up rocks.

Ssssttt, Ssssttt, Ssssttt . . .

TWENTY

I closed the space between Marty and me by instinct. I don't even think I was aware of the cow whip in my hand. Yet, my elbow was cocked and ready as I ran to her side.

The tail on the diamondback stood up straight, rattles vibrating. The snake's tongue darted to and fro. Its cat-eyes gleamed. Marty stood motionless, in striking distance.

I prayed that all those hours of practice I'd put in by my daddy's side wouldn't fail me. My arm tingled with the memory of knocking tin cans off fence posts and clipping oranges off their branches. I didn't want to think about the many times I'd missed my targets.

I heard Carlos shout, as if from far away: "Don't move, Marty." From the corner of my eye, I saw him edge into the campsite and stoop to get a rock. It wasn't big or heavy enough to crush the snake's head quickly. It would only aggravate him enough to make him strike.

"I've got it," I yelled, surprised when my voice sounded calm.

I snapped my arm at the elbow and let the whip fly from about eight feet out.

Crack!

Marty flinched. Her eyes squeezed shut. The whip hit a few inches behind the snake's venom glands. The force all but severed its head. For a few seconds, the body writhed across my jacket, dying. I finished it off with another whip crack. Marty probably wouldn't want to borrow that particular piece of clothing again.

"It's okay, Sister. You can look now," I said.

Carlos rushed forward to catch her before she hit the ground. I snapped the whip a third time, just to be sure no strike was left in the snake. Marty hung on Carlos' neck, her face buried in his chest. He patted her on the back.

"You're all right, Marty. Your sister killed it."

When he raised his gaze to mine, I wondered whether admiration or anger was making his eyes so dark. Carlos wasn't short on Latin machismo; I was unsure how he'd take a woman riding to the rescue.

"Go ahead and look, Marty," he urged her. "Mace was amazing."

So it was admiration. Surprise, surprise.

Just then, Mama, Maddie and Sal walked into the campsite. Maddie carried two dead sabal fronds, bushy side down, like a broom in each hand.

"Yoo-hoo!" Mama called. "Who's ready for dinner?"

At a glance, she took in Carlos supporting Marty, her tears soaking his shirt. She rushed to Marty's side. Maddie dropped the brown fronds and ran after her.

"What happened, Marty? What's wrong?" As she stroked Marty's hair, Mama looked over at me, recoiling my whip. Then she spotted the snake on the ground. Her eyes widened. A hand flew to cover her mouth.

"Jesus H. Christ on a crutch," Maddie said.

"Don't touch it," I warned them. "It's dead, but a rattlesnake has heat-sensing pits behind the eyes. Put a warm hand near it, and the head may still bite as a reflex."

Carlos swallowed uneasily and took a step back.

Sal lumbered toward us. "Rosie, you look like you met a ghost. Is everything okay?"

"It is now. Mace saved Marty's life." Carlos pointed to the snake. "She killed *that* with her bullwhip. It was like something out of the Wild West."

"Cow whip," I said. "Out west, they say bullwhip. But Florida Crackers have always called them cow whips. And we had cattle in Florida before there even *was* a Wild West."

"That's right," Maddie nodded. "Spanish explorers brought the first cattle to Florida in the 1500s. It irks Mace we never get credit for starting what the Wild West made famous."

Sal clapped me on the back so hard it nearly knocked mc down. "Cow whip, bullwhip, whaddever. You're a hero, Mace."

I didn't mind standing around basking in praise. But now that the adrenaline rush was waning, I wanted to know how the hell a rattlesnake had found its way into my Jeep.

"Marty, where exactly was that snake?"

She turned her head to stare at thc diamondback's remains, and then hid her eyes against Carlos' chest again.

"N'dyak-yak," came her shirt-muffled answer.

"Say what?" I asked.

Marty lifted her head, but still hung on his neck. Good thing she weighed no more than a flea.

"In your jacket," she repeated, more

clearly now. "It was trapped in there. The zipper was pulled all the way up. The hood was folded over the neck hole, and the two sleeves were tied together over that." She gazed at my Jeep, the passenger door still standing open. "And your jacket wasn't under the seat, like you said. It was on the dashboard."

A chill that had nothing to do with the temperature inched down my spine.

"I figured you'd wrapped it up all small like that so it'd fit on your saddle. It took me a while to unfasten everything. When I did, that's when I saw the snake." She shuddered.

"I know less about snakes than I do about horses, but they must be the acrobats of the animal world," Sal said. "How the hell did he get himself all contorted inside the jacket?"

None of us said a word; we just stared at Sal. It took him only a moment to catch on.

"Holy shit!" he said.

Standing three people back in the potty line, I shifted my weight from foot to foot. I'm calm in a crisis. But after the threat is over, the reality of what might have happened usually hits me right in the bladder. I didn't even want to think what might be taking so long with the big cowboy who'd closed the plastic door on one of the portable toilets a good five minutes before.

While I waited, I thought of how kind Carlos had been with Marty. My little sister is happily married. Carlos knows that. I knew he wasn't interested in her in that way. He'd comforted her exactly like a big brother or an uncle would. Caring. Compassionate. Platonic. As I thought about it now, it seemed awfully similar to the way he'd acted with Belle. Had I jumped to conclusions where Carlos and Lawton's daughter were concerned?

One of the toilets opened. Now I was two people back. I prayed my turn wouldn't come up on the toilet the big cowboy vacated.

Hurry, hurry, I said to myself.

"They say that guy from Miami killed the rattlesnake with his bare hands. I heard it was six feet long."

The young girl's voice was coming from the opposite side of the toilet trailer.

"Nuh-huh, Lauren. You're wrong. I heard it was seven feet. And he tossed a buck knife at it and sliced it right in half."

I didn't want to lose my spot in line. But I knew if I didn't speak to the girls, they'd turn Carlos into King of the Snake Killers before supper. Why should he get unearned credit? Craning my neck, I saw the chatty teens I'd already encountered once.

"You're both wrong, Amber," I whispered to the closest girl. "It was me who killed the snake, and I used a cow whip, like any good Florida Cracker would."

"Weren't you scared?" Lauren asked me.

"Only a fool is without fear," I said, already regretting blabbing about myself.

Amber said, "I would have been peeing my pants!"

Which reminded me of why I was there.

"We can talk later if you want, girls. But right now, nature calls."

I was up next, and a door was swinging open. The big cowboy stepped out, waving his hat and looking sheepish.

Ah, the joys of life on the trail.

I held a marshmallow on a stick over the campfire. "You're gonna love this," I promised.

"You're burning it," Carlos said.

"Not 'burning,' toasting. I can't believe you've never eaten a S'more." I rotated the stick to finish off the top side of the marshmallow.

"Mace, it's black," he complained. "It looks like charcoal."

"Trust me on this, Carlos." I pulled the stick from the fire and used one half of a graham cracker to slide the marshmallow onto the other half. Topping it with a piece of a Hershey's chocolate bar, I smashed the two crackers into a sandwich and handed it to him. "The ash only makes it taste better."

He picked up the top cracker and peered inside.

"You're not supposed to arrest it, Carlos. You're supposed to eat it."

By the time he'd "tried" four more S'mores, we were both pleasantly full and floating on a sugar buzz.

Dinner was long over. Most of the other riders had left the fire to turn in for the night. Mama and Sal were off settling Marty into a spare sleeping compartment that Mama had wrangled for her in somebody's RV. They'd moved Mama's horse and Sal's Caddy to sleep closer to Marty. The poor girl had a migraine from her near-miss. She didn't want to spend the night on the ground in a tent, and I can't say I blamed her. She'd have lain awake all night and worried about giant rattlers. And if Marty couldn't sleep, neither would I, for worrying about her.

Maddie had met up with a teacher she

knew from Seminole County. The two of them were huddled together at the woman's campsite, catching up on old times and bashing their respective school boards.

All of us were talked out over the rattle-snake incident. We argued over who might have done it and why, and whether it was linked to my shredded tent. Then, we told the trail boss what happened. He made an announcement about it before dinner.

"One of our riders had a run-in with a diamondback this afternoon," Jack Hollister had said, mentioning no names. "There's a chance someone might have put that snake there as a prank, or maybe as some kind of warning."

Several people in the crowd gasped. Lauren and Amber stepped out of the chow line to stare at me, their eyes round as saucers.

Jack's stern gaze moved over the crowd. "I can't imagine I need to say this, but I will anyway. If we find out this was intentional, the person who did it will never ride the Cracker Trail again. And we'll hand them with pleasure over to the county sheriff's office."

Now, Carlos and I were alone by the campfire. It had burned so low it needed another log. I had two final marshmallows and half a chocolate bar left in a plastic bag.

"Can I interest you in S'more, *señor?*"

"All that sugar is making you silly." Carlos grumbled, but I saw a tiny smile cracking the granite of his jaw. "I'll help you out and eat one more if you eat the other one."

"Claro que sí," I nodded, showing off some of the Spanish he'd taught me.

This time, his smile was full-fledged. "You're something, you know that?" He squeezed my shoulder. Was the touch just beyond friendly? "I still can't get over you and that cow whip."

"It was really just instinct," I said, trying to sound modest. "My daddy taught me well. Back in his great-granddaddy's day, the pioneers used their whips for everything. Scaring hogs from the garden. Snatching fruit from trees. Signaling danger on the open range or between far-flung homesteads. You know, the whip's crack will carry a mile or more through the woods."

"Is that so?" He brushed a bit of hair from my eyes.

"Yep," I answered, cursing the shiver of desire I felt at his touch.

He brought his face close to mine. "Fascinating. Tell me more," he whispered, chocolate-scented breath hot on my cheek.

I scooted backwards on the ground, pulling my knees to my chest and wrapping my arms around them. "Now, you're making fun of me."

"I'd never," he answered, rising to his knees to follow me. Suddenly, that dying campfire felt awfully hot. I stopped backing away. He cupped my chin and lifted my face. Our eyes met. Memories of his touch on my naked body washed over me.

Then, I felt someone tap me hard on the shoulder. "Really do hate to interrupt," came a nasty voice from behind me. "But I understand you want to talk to me."

I took just a second to wonder what would have happened next with Carlos. Then I turned to look up at my top suspect in the case of the planted rattlesnake.

Twenty-One

"First of all, I don't appreciate you spreading speculations around about me and some snake," Austin said, leaning into my face. "I'd sooner chew on broken glass than get anywhere near one of those horrible creatures. I'm deathly afraid of them."

"It's true, Mace." Trey tugged at his ex-girlfriend's arm, trying to back her off. "She hates snakes. Once, I took her to the reptile house at Busch Gardens. She started screaming and carrying on before we'd barely gotten through the door."

"I *told* you I didn't want to go in there, Trey."

"Well, I wanted to see the python, Austin. I didn't know you were going to freak out."

"I said I was afraid. You *never* listen!"

She tossed her curls and pouted. Trey sighed like he'd been through it before. I wondered if I'd stumbled into an episode of *Divorce Court.*

"I'm not crazy about snakes, either." Rising to his feet beside the campfire, Carlos smiled at my suspect. "I don't believe I've had the pleasure," he said. "Austin, is it?"

I raised my eyebrows. All of a sudden Mr. Rude Miami was Mr. Good Manners? "Sorry," I said, and then did some quick introductions. "Carlos Martinez, Trey Bramble. Lawton was Trey's daddy. And this is Austin Close, Trey's ex-fiancée, and, conveniently, a snake phobic."

She glared at me, and then extended a hand and a sunny smile at Carlos.

"I heard y'all were discussing me at dinner, Mace. I just wanted to come over to say I had nothing to do with that snake." I got the lower-watt version of Austin's smile. "We seem to have gotten off on the wrong foot, haven't we?"

"Well, I do tend to take it personally when someone snaps a cow whip to spook my horse into traffic."

"An accident, as I've told you," she said through clenched teeth. "And, I think I recall apologizing more than once."

"Mace is bad about accepting apologies, Austin," said Carlos, the rat. "She really hangs onto a grudge."

"I do not." I rose from the ground and crossed my arms over my chest. "And I'll prove it by calling a truce. You say you had nothing to do with my tent? Okay. And the whip was an accident? Fine. Now, you're afraid of snakes? Whatever. So if the rattler wasn't you, any idea who it might have been?"

I looked from her to Trey and back again. They both shook their heads.

"Not only do I not know who, I don't know *why,*" Trey said.

"We thought it could be a message of some sort, like someone doesn't want Mace around," Carlos said. "Maybe someone doesn't want any questions asked about your father's death, Trey."

I narrowed my eyes at Austin. "Or maybe it's someone who doesn't want me around for another reason."

She snorted. "You think I'm jealous? Of you?" Her gaze traveled from my greasy hair to my manure-caked boots, resting a moment on what were probably flecks of marshmallow stuck to my chin. "Please!"

Carlos held up his hands. "Ladies, ladies. Arguing will get us nowhere. Why don't we all sit down and start over?"

"Getting chilly," Trey said, taking a seat on the ground.

"Should be another cold one," Carlos added.

Austin sat, too. She drummed her manicured fingernails on her knee and stared up at me. I counted the stars in Orion's belt.

"Not as cold as last night, though," Trey tried again.

"The fire feels great." Carlos rubbed his hands together. *"¡Que bueno!"*

"Is that Spanish?" Austin broke her silence.

He nodded.

"That's what everybody speaks down in Miamuh," Trey said.

"What's it mean?" Austin asked, ignoring Trey's cultural commentary.

"It's like saying something is really good," Carlos said. *"¡Que bueno!"*

"I *love* hearing men speak a foreign language. It's *so* romantic." She clapped her hands excitedly, like a little girl about to kiss Santa. "Say something else."

"¿Qué quieres que te diga?"

"Ooooooh, what's that mean?"

"It means, what do you want me to say?"

Carlos' eyes crinkled into a smile. Austin laughed, too heartily I thought. My S'mores were struggling to come back up.

"So," her voice got low and sultry, "is what I've heard about Spanish men true?"

Trey rolled his eyes at me, then tugged his hat down low over his forehead.

"I'm not Spanish. That's someone from Spain. I'm Cuban, but I speak Spanish. And it depends on what you've heard." Carlos smiled devilishly.

"About how they're extra, uhm . . . sexy." She widened her blue eyes at him. "You know, in the bedroom?"

Carlos chuckled in a way I'd never heard before. Who was this guy?

"I'm going to have to plead the Fifth on that line of questioning, *niña.* I blush easily."

"Oh, you!" She gave his broad chest a playful shove. I could swear she licked her lips.

I felt around on the ground until I found a big rock. Then I tossed it into the flames with enough force to send sparks all over the two people seated closest to the fire.

"Sorry," I said. "I think I've had enough campfire chat for tonight."

Trey pushed back his hat and stood up. "Me, too." He shot Austin a disgusted look. "Let me walk you to your tent, Mace. I've got a flashlight."

I had one, too. But I decided to let Trey be gallant. I glanced over to see if Carlos noticed, but he seemed hypnotized by Austin. The hungry way he was looking at her was completely different than the protectiveness he'd shown toward Belle. Austin's eyes smoldered. The firelight reflected like a halo off her dark hair, hypnotizing him. The witch.

"Okay, then. Goodnight," I said.

Carlos mumbled, " 'night," barely looking at me.

Trey took my arm as we left. I leaned into him, purposely putting my head on his shoulder. Just before we rounded a big oak, I stole a last glance backward. Carlos was plucking a bit of spattered ash off Austin's cheek. As far as he was concerned, Trey and I could have been on the moon.

I slammed a tin cup onto the hood of my Jeep. Yanking the top off a bottle of water, I swigged, rinsed, and spit into the bushes. Then I squirted more toothpaste onto my brush and started all over. I wanted to obliterate the taste of those stupid S'mores I'd shared with Carlos.

Trey leaned against the horse trailer at my campsite, watching me.

"Take it easy, Mace. You're about to scrub the enamel right off your pearly whites."

"MmmmFFfff," I muttered, around a mouthful of brush and paste.

"You don't need to worry about Austin. Flirting comes natural to her. She hardly ever takes it to the next level."

I spit. "Why would I be worried? I couldn't care less who she flirts with."

"That's not how it seemed to me. I saw the way you and your Miamuh friend were looking at each other when we came up. And then I saw how you looked leaving just now. If looks could kill, Austin would be bleeding from the throat."

I got busy, drying my toothbrush on my shirttail.

"You're not going to deny there's something between you, are you? A blind man could see you two have a history."

"Ancient history." I put the toothpaste and brush back in the tin cup.

"He's kind of slick." Trey's lip curled. Slick isn't a compliment on the Cracker Trail. "How'd you ever hook up?"

"We met last summer when he took a detective's job with the Himmarshee police department."

"So, he's a cop. Is he looking into what happened to Daddy? Has he told you what he thinks?"

"Carlos isn't good about sharing information," I said.

"Yeah, but he must have said something."

"Well, he did tell Belle he can get some tests run on your Daddy's chili cup."

"Belle?" Trey's shoulders tensed. "What's he got to do with her?"

Good question. I'd also like to know what he's got to do with Austin. But that wasn't a topic for Trey and me.

"I think Carlos just feels sorry for your sister, Trey. He lost his wife a couple of years ago, so he knows what grief is. He offered to help. That's all."

Taking a step toward him, I put a hand on his forearm. His skin felt warm, especially as the night was growing colder. I watched him as he cast his eyes down to my hand. I was close enough to count his eyelashes, lush and black against his cheek. A tear glistened there.

When he spoke, his voice was hoarse. "Daddy and I had our problems, everybody knows that. I just never knew that losing him would hurt so bad."

I wiped at the tear, careful to avoid the jagged, bar-fight scratch on his cheek. He took my wrist, and then brought my palm to his lips. His soft kiss sent a shudder of pleasure south. The shudder evolved into a moan as Trey turned to my fingers, nipping first at one, then the next and the next. My knees became jelly. I had no idea the fingertips could be an erogenous zone.

"You know," he whispered, "I had a secret

crush on you at Himmarshee High."

Even with the electrifying effect of his hot breath in my ear, I knew that was ridiculous.

"The football star, the hottest guy in school, crushing on me? Yeah, sure."

"It's true. I think it's because you were the only girl who didn't make a big deal over me. You were strong and independent, and almost as tall as me. I always wondered what it would be like to put my arm around you and hold you tight."

Even if it wasn't true, it sure sounded good. I lifted his hand to my lips.

"I wouldn't mind if you did hold me tight," I finally said when I finished with his fingers.

I could feel him hard against me as he folded me into his arms. I closed my eyes against the image of Carlos that intruded. I knew Trey wasn't Mr. Right; but he was Mr. Right Now. He was ready for me. And I was ready for him, even if he wanted me right there, standing up against the horse trailer.

I lifted my face, and he covered my lips with his. He tasted good; salty with a hint of the banana pudding from dessert. After my marathon tooth-scouring, I was at least confident my breath was minty fresh. I'd just begun to explore his tongue with my own when I heard a loud harrumph from the far side of the campsite.

"You two might want to untangle your-selves." Maddie's disapproving scowl was clear, even in the lantern light. "Trey's sister has gone missing."

TWENTY-TWO

Maddie and I struggled to keep up with Trey. We might have lost him running through the woods if not for the bobbing light from the lantern in his hand.

"Where's he headed, Mace?" Maddie panted behind me. The beam of her flashlight skittered across the ground.

"How should I know? He didn't take the time to tell me."

When Maddie announced Belle was missing, Trey pushed away from me like he'd been slapped. He grabbed the lantern off the ground and ran off without a word.

I ducked under the low branch of a red maple sapling, and then heard Maddie hit it head-on.

"Ouch! Crap!"

I slowed a bit to let my big sister catch up. "Sorry."

"A little help would be nice, Mace. You're the woodland creature, not me. You might

201

warn me when one of your leafy friends is about to decapitate me."

I could have told Maddie she'd do better in the woods — in most places, in fact — if she'd spend more time with her eyes open and her mouth shut. But I held my tongue.

"I bet he's headed to Belle's campsite," she said. "After I checked on Marty, I was passing by and saw Belle's camp neighbors standing around like they didn't know what to do next. They called out to ask me if I'd seen her anywhere."

The bobbing light ahead came into a clearing, slowed, and then stopped.

"Watch that skunk vine, Maddie." I pointed my own light over my shoulder, illuminating a low-hanging net of green. "On your right."

She ducked, and the noxious-smelling vine just brushed her shoulder.

"Thanks." Maddie leaned over, hands on knees, to catch her breath. She gazed toward the clearing. "I think that's Belle's site. I recognize the fancy RV."

Trey stood with the lantern, talking to a man and woman next to a big RV, dark green with a white stripe. The door on the RV gaped open, spilling light from inside. A matching horse trailer butted up behind the big rig.

Maddie and I joined the three of them.

"Did she say anything to you? Anything at all?" Trey was questioning the woman, a frizzy-haired blonde with a saddle-leather face.

"She never said a word. We were watching her, wondering whether we should come over and say something about y'all's daddy. But then Bobby told me we should mind our own business, that if Belle wanted to talk, she'd come to us. Next time I looked over, her horse was still tied to the trailer, but your sister was nowhere in sight."

"How long ago was this?" Trey said.

"More than two hours now." She turned to the heavy-set man next to her, Bobby presumably. "I told you we should have come over."

Bobby studied the ground.

"What can we do, Trey?" I asked. Concern was etched on his face.

"I don't want to make too much of this. Belle has a tendency to go off on her own." He glanced toward her horse, a black-and-white gelding tethered to the trailer. "But I can't imagine her leaving Poco like that."

We all walked over to get a closer look at the horse. He stood patiently on a halter and rope, still wearing his saddle. His bridle was off, hung on a hook on the side of the trailer. Two buckets were on the ground, but neither of them held food or water.

Trey shook his head. "She'd never go off without seeing Poco was taken care of. Belle's crazy about horses. About all animals, really."

"Well, we can see to him, at least." I nodded toward the horse.

Maddie and I each took a bucket. I shone my light into the back of the trailer until I found a plastic garbage pail filled with feed. Maddie shoved the water bucket at Bobby.

"Here, you look like a big, strong thing," she said. "Why don't you take this and go make yourself useful at the water trough?"

I shot my sister a look.

"Thanks, Bobby. We'd sure appreciate it if you would," I called, as he hurried away like one of Maddie's scared seventh-graders.

"I want to help, too," the frizzy blonde said to Trey.

"You could keep an eye out to see if Belle comes back. Don't let her be alone, if she does."

I wondered why Trey feared his sister being left alone.

He continued, "Belle and I know these woods front to back. I'm going to go look for her. There is one other thing you could do, ma'am."

"Jan," the blonde said.

"I'd be grateful, Jan, if this doesn't get around camp. My sister is having an awful tough time. She might just have gone off to mourn. I don't want a lot of gossip about what Belle's done or hasn't done, or how she is or isn't."

Trey sounded more protective than the average big brother. Had there been talk about Belle before?

Jan made a zipping-the-lip motion. "You don't have to worry about me telling tales. I'm not one of them gossipy-type women. And, Trey?"

He raised his brows at her, his eyes clouded with worry.

"I do want to say how sorry I am about your daddy." She fiddled nervously with her hair. "And about us not coming over to see about your sister. I should know better than to listen to Bobby."

I quickly filled a shallow pail with sweet feed, and then started working at the cinch so I could pull off Poco's saddle and blanket. I just about had it unfastened, when I noticed a brownish-red smear halfway down the horse's neck. The stain stood out clearly against the white portion of his coat.

My mind flashed back to the merlot soaking the sleeping bag in my ruined tent. I leaned in to sniff at Poco's neck. This time the stain wasn't red wine. It was blood.

"Are you sure you don't want to get some help?" I whispered to Trey as we crouched behind Poco, hidden from Maddie and Belle's neighbors.

I'd discreetly called him over, and we'd checked for cuts or scrapes. Poco was fine. The blood wasn't his.

"No. I can handle this," he whispered back. "I don't want Belle embarrassed by a lot of fuss if it turns out to be nothing. And I know where she likes to escape to. I want to look before we call in anyone."

Maddie walked up with a dirt-streaked face and a mallet in her hand. "The ground didn't want to cooperate, but Bobby and I got up Poco's portable corral."

This was a true feat, as my sister's idea of physical exertion generally involves hefting the full slab of ribs at the Pork Pit.

"That's great, Maddie. Trey thinks he knows where Belle might be. Do you want to come with us?"

I could almost see Maddie's mind working, distaste for the woods weighed against me discovering something she wouldn't know.

Trey frowned at her. "Let's go if you're going."

She nodded, and the three of us struck out across the clearing.

The moon was high in the sky now, the air not nearly as cold as the night before. Sounds carried through the quiet woods: the bark of a dog; the lowing of cattle; faint laughter from a far campsite. We rustled through the brush without speaking, Maddie's and my flashlights trained on Trey's path in front of us. My sister breathed raggedly behind me, but she was keeping up.

Soon, we came out of the woods to the bed of a mostly dry creek. In summer, when the rains are heavy, it would be full and flowing. But now, in the dry season, it was barely a trickle in many spots. That made for easier passage. We moved quickly through desiccated marsh grasses, so brittle they crumbled to fluff as we passed. We followed the exposed bank, dark and mucky, until the water widened.

Just ahead was a stand of bald cypress, shadowy sentinels gleaming in the moonlight.

"Belle," Trey called out. "Honey, it's me. It's Trey."

No answer came from the trees.

"That's where she'll be if she left camp

under her own power." He nodded ahead as Maddie and I caught up. "We played here all the time as kids, trying to figure out which cypress knee looked like which TV star or rock singer."

"Belle," I yelled, as we started into the trees.

A night heron's squawk was the only response.

I was concentrating on the ground, trying not to trip over the root-like bumps of the cypress knees, when I heard Trey gasp in front of me. I stopped and raised my eyes to see what he had seen.

Belle lay face-up on the white, sandy soil of the creek bed. She was motionless. Her coppery hair formed a corona around her head, flowing like blood from the exposed sandbar into the water.

TWENTY-THREE

Trey splashed into the creek, moving as fast as he could in boots and jeans across a deep swath in front of Belle. In the light of the lantern, his face was drawn and pale. He looked terrified of what he'd find when he reached his sister.

Maddie and I watched from our vantage point on the high bank, flashlights trained on the water to reflect the telltale glint of gator eyes. The last thing Trey needed was a hungry alligator on his hands. As I swung the flashlight back and forth across the creek, I thought I saw Belle move. But then she was still. No noise, not even a moan, came from the sandbar.

"Belle," Trey yelled, as he thrashed into shallower water. "Belle!"

This time I was certain I saw movement. As Trey climbed onto the sand, moving on hands and knees to his sister, she turned her head away. Firmly. I looked at Maddie to see if she'd seen the same thing.

"What the hell?" Maddie muttered under her breath, her face a picture of confusion.

A gator grunted in the far distance, hidden somewhere in the reeds. I swung the flashlight about, but didn't see anything close enough to worry over.

"Belle, honey, look at me," Trey put his hand on his sister's shoulder, his voice a bit lower, a bit calmer. "It's all right. Look at me."

Belle shook her head, her fiery curls wet and glistening in the lantern light. She turned her whole body onto her side, facing away from Trey. He stood, and called to us across the creek, "She's okay. Everything's okay."

Well, not really, I thought. His sister was stretched out on a sandbar in the middle of a creek close to midnight. She'd had her head half in and half out of the water, with who knows how many alligators lurking nearby. Something definitely was not okay.

"I'm going over there, Maddie." I leaned down to unlace my boots. "I'll cross about twenty feet downstream, just where the sandbar tapers off. It's nearly dry."

"Well, you're not leaving me here alone." She grabbed me for balance as she began to take off her own boots.

Rolling up the legs on our britches, we waded into the creek.

"Ohmigod! I felt something slimy!" my sister said.

"Shush, Maddie. This is serious."

"I am serious. It felt disgusting."

When we reached the sandbar, Belle was sitting, her head resting on pulled-up knees. Trey murmured to her, too quietly for me to hear his words. As we walked up, she lifted her face. Her eyes were red and swollen. They seemed unfocused. I couldn't tell whether the wetness on her cheeks was from creek water or tears.

"I'm sorry." Her voice was barely audible. She swiped her fingers under her eyes. "I didn't mean to worry anybody. I just wanted to get away. All day on the trail, people were so nice. They said how sorry they were about Daddy; asked how I was doing. Once I got to camp, it all just hit me. He's really gone. I wanted to keep running into the woods until maybe I wouldn't think about it anymore. Then I got to this place, where Trey and I used to play, and I thought maybe the water would wash all the sadness out of my head."

"Did it work?" Maddie asked.

Belle stared into space without speaking.

"No," she finally said, letting loose fresh tears.

My sister leaned over, surprisingly tender, and stroked Belle's wet hair. I saw flecks of sand in the red curls, along with a flash of the motherly way Maddie was with her daughter, Pam.

Belle, sobbing, lifted her arms like a child. Maddie pulled her close. As Belle's hands went around my sister's neck, the lantern light revealed a dark, familiar-looking stain on the cuff of her long-sleeved, cream-colored shirt.

"What's that on your sleeve, Belle?" I asked.

Holding out her wrist, she stared at the cuff like it belonged to someone else. As she turned over her palm, we could see a red gash from the heel of her hand to her pinky finger. Trey took a sharp breath. Belle looked at the wound blankly. I began to wonder if she was on drugs.

I gently pulled her hand toward me, holding it under my flashlight. She didn't resist.

"That doesn't look too bad." I said. "You must have bled onto Poco after you did it."

Belle's eyes suddenly widened. "Poco!" she breathed.

"Don't worry. Mace and her sister and the folks next to our camp took care of everything," Trey said. "Poco's fine."

"How'd you cut yourself?" I asked.

She lifted her hand again, staring like it was the first time she'd ever laid eyes on it.

"Belle?" Trey prodded, when she failed to respond.

Maddie and I exchanged a look.

"I'm not sure," she said, slowly shaking her head. "I remember I was getting Poco's bridle off, and then I went to get something from the trailer. There's so many sharp things in there, metal edges and pointy corners. I don't even remember cutting myself. It doesn't really hurt."

That could be drugs talking, I thought. A palm cut, even when it's not deep, usually stings like the dickens.

"We should be going," Trey said. "With all the horses and riders on our property, we don't know what's been in this creek. You should get some antibiotic cream on that cut, Belle."

Belle gazed up at the moon, which had turned the cypress branches silver.

"I don't want to go yet." She leaned back unsteadily, taking two tries to balance on her elbows. "I love our family's land so much, Trey. It's the place I feel I belong. The only time I'm really happy is when I'm out here, just walking or taking photos."

Trey said, "Belle's nature pictures are in a big gallery in Stuart. Sell pretty well, too."

"Just listen to the sound the creek makes as it flows past," she said dreamily.

We were all quiet, hearing the water gurgle and sigh.

"Isn't that beautiful? That's as familiar to me as the sound of my own heartbeat," Belle said.

Trey smiled at his sister. "Belle, honey, we should go."

Ignoring him, she said, "When Trey and I were little, I'd come out here and sit for hours, wouldn't I, Trey? I used to think the cypress knees looked like all the characters from the Care Bears. I'd tell the trees all my troubles."

"My daughter used to love the Care Bears," Maddie said. "Pam's not too much younger than you, Belle. She's away at college now."

Belle didn't seem to hear my sister.

"I love the water." She trailed the fingers on her good hand into the creek. "I used to wish I could load my sorrows into a little boat, and then just watch them float away."

Trey said, "Let's go, Belle," with a stern edge to his voice. "We've put Mace and her sister out enough for one night."

"Despite everything, I miss Daddy, Trey.

Don't you?"

Trey pinched at the bridge of his nose. I couldn't be sure whether he was irritated at his sister, or holding back tears of his own.

Maddie got up and announced, "I think you two could use some time alone." Her words barely seemed to register with Trey or Belle. "Mace and I can find our way back."

What that meant was I'd find our way back. Maddie had trouble navigating from the principal's office to the parking lot. Fortunately, I'd spent a lot of time in the woods.

We'd crossed over, donned our boots, and proceeded a bit along the bank when Maddie finally whispered, "Drugs, don't you think?"

"I do," I said, "but I don't know whether that's so bad under the circumstances. She seems grief-stricken over her daddy."

We were much younger than Belle when our father died. But I remembered Mama taking a regular dose of little orange pills in those first awful days after his heart attack. Maybe Doc Abel had given Belle something similar.

"I don't disagree with you, Mace. But don't you wonder about what Belle said?"

I stopped in the clearing, trying to place

whether a fence line I saw in my flashlight beam had been on my left or my right coming in. My right, I was suddenly certain. Maddie had been to my left.

"What Belle said about what?" I asked, picking up the pace as I followed the fence.

"All that about her troubles," Maddie answered. "What kind of troubles could the pampered daughter of the richest man in three counties possibly have had?"

TWENTY-FOUR

I woke up cranky after Maddie and I fought all night over space in her moldy tent. I hated to think how tight it would be with Marty in there, too. Maddie's a bulldozer, asleep or awake. She'd probably roll our sister and her sleeping bag right out the zippered door.

"You snore, Mace."

"I do not!"

"I heard it with my own ears. Sounded like somebody using a chain saw."

"You were probably hearing yourself, Maddie. When you got going, I thought there was a wild hog snuffling for acorns in the tent."

We brushed the horses' backs and bellies, making sure there were no sweat- or dirt-matted spots to irritate them under their saddles. Despite our bickering, Maddie and I worked well as a team. We'd already fed and watered the horses, cleaned up and packed most of our stuff, and got the tent broken down. And we still had a half-hour before Johnny and his crew would start serving breakfast.

"I think I'm having the pancakes," I said. "Are you getting biscuits and gravy?"

She hefted a saddle onto her horse's back. "I'm having both." She licked her lips. "Lord knows I'm working off the calories."

Before I could come back with something sarcastic, I heard a rustle in the dry pasture behind us. My arm froze over Val's back as I wondered if a horse brush would make an effective weapon. I turned to see who was there.

"Sal! You shouldn't go sneaking up on people." I let out the breath I was holding.

He was wearing another The-Duke-Meets-Elton-John cowboy outfit, only this one was burgundy. I couldn't believe they'd made two of those rhinestone-studded monstrosities.

"Sorry, Mace. I don't know how to act around horses." He looked nervously at Val's hind end, where I was picking some burrs out of her tail.

"Don't worry about it," I said. "But it's always better to say something, give some kind of verbal warning." Both for me and the horses, I thought.

"Your mother's over at the chuck wagon. Her horse has some kind of problem," Sal said, taking a long detour around Val. "Something about a toad. She wants to know if you know anyone who might be able to loan her another horse today."

Maddie and I were saddled up and off in a flash. I asked Sal if he wanted a ride, doubling with me for the short distance on Val. He grimaced like I'd offered to pull off his fingernails.

A small crowd milled around Mama's horse, Brandy. Wynonna was there, wearing red alligator boots and tight blue jeans. Her highlighted hair was caught up in a bright red alligator-hide clip. She hunkered down next to Mama and a blacksmith. The three of them studied the soft padding on the underside of Brandy's foot. The eyes of everyone else in the crowd were on Wynonna. I wondered how it felt having people stare at you every second.

"Is everything okay?" I called to Mama.

She waved her ring hand at me. "We're fine, Mace. Brandy's bruised her frog. Mike here thinks maybe it was that patch of spilled rock we went through, where they were fixing the highway culvert. Or maybe a beer bottle tossed in the grass out the window of somebody's car. He says she'll be fine with a little rest."

Wynonna looked up, concern darkening her lovely green eyes.

"I hate to see Rosalee miss the ride," she said. "I told your Mama she can borrow one of our horses. One of Lawton's men is loading him into a trailer right now. It'll do Shotgun good to be ridden. He's getting fat and lazy."

"Shotgun?" Maddie butted in. "That doesn't sound like a horse a senior citizen should be riding."

Mama straightened, set her plum-colored cowboy hat firmly, and raised her voice to carry: "Why, Maddie, I'm still in my fifties."

That was a lie. She'd turn sixty-three on the Fourth of July.

"And I've been riding since before you girls were born."

Mama stalked off, as dignified as possible in plum-colored pants. It didn't help that she was leading a limping horse and a three-hundred-pound Bronx cowboy in rhinestones.

Wynonna laughed. "Like I told your mama, pay no mind to that name. Shotgun's the gentlest horse we have. Lawton should have renamed him, but it got to be a running joke. Not that Shotgun can't go fast when you want him to, but he's not too fond of it. And he's even-tempered. He'll walk a plank if you ask him to, just so long as he's walking."

"Well, the name is stupid, then," Maddie muttered.

"Watch it, Maddie," I whispered. "The woman is grieving."

"How's Belle this morning?" Maddie asked Wynonna.

That's my sister: From frying pan to fire.

Wynonna's mouth tightened. "I have no idea. Belle doesn't clear her schedule with me."

Maddie said, "We just hope she's all right, after last night." I jabbed her in her oblivious ribs.

"Belle's fine." The voice belonged to Trey, who had walked up behind us. "She says she's taking a break from the trail today. Wants to shoot some pictures of birds and wildlife along the Kissimmee River."

"Mornin' Trey." Wynonna's voice was as sweet as cane syrup.

He nodded curtly, but kept his eyes on me. "They're serving breakfast, Mace. Want me to get you and your sister a couple of plates?" Wynonna wasn't included in the offer.

By the time we'd eaten and cleaned up, the Bramble ranch hand was delivering

Shotgun. The pastureland was so dry, dust clouds billowed out from beneath the rig as he drove into camp.

Trey waved at the man to stop, then hurried to get the horse. The rest of us followed, watching as Trey untied Shotgun from inside, and then prodded him to back out of the trailer. Stepping calmly to the ground, the horse stood waiting — as docile as a pony in a petting zoo.

Trey patted the animal on the rump. "Shotgun, huh?"

"Is that a problem?" I asked him.

"Not at all. Sweetest horse we've got. Belle trained him, and my little sister is a real horse whisperer."

Wynonna said, "Trey's right about Belle. She and I may have our issues, but I've never seen a steadier hand with horses."

Mama and Sal were back, after making arrangements to have her temporarily lame horse trailered to the evening camp. Shotgun was saddled up and ready to ride. All Mama had to do was swing up and go. But first she needed a boost. She looked around and fluttered her eyelashes. Three cowboys, Trey included, stepped forward to help.

"Thank you kindly," she said to the Brambles' hand, who had leaped from the driver's seat of the truck to give Mama a leg up.

Only I saw the self-satisfied curve to her lips as she settled herself prettily on the horse's back. My boots would grow cobwebs while I waited for someone to help me into my saddle. Mama's power over men still held in her sixties — that decade she refused to own up to.

She performed a couple of figure-eights around the cook site, getting used to Shotgun. A chestnut-colored quarter horse, he looked responsive. Without too much urging, she got him into a lope. He seemed eager to please. She ran him at medium-speed through a barrel-racing pattern, circling around the garbage cans at either end of the site. He turned well, cutting like a charm.

Mama waved at Sal, who beamed like a proud papa at her horsemanship.

Marty, still shaky and pale from her migraine, joined us for the end of Mama's show. Wearing dark sunglasses, she nursed a cup of hot tea. She planned to drive Maddie's car to catch up with us at the lunch site. We hoped she'd feel like riding again by the afternoon.

The three of us watched our mother in silence.

"She looks good on that horse," Marty finally spoke in a whisper, wincing with each word. "What's its name?"

Maddie and I exchanged a look.

"Buttercup," I lied.

TWENTY-FIVE

The trail boss set his hat and raised the shout, "Headin' out! Headin' ooooou-uuuttt!"

The morning air was sweet with the smell of orange blossoms and expectation. Leather rubbed and creaked on the saddles of a hundred-plus horses. Riders jostled, finding their positions as the day and the trail ahead beckoned.

I glanced behind me at Mama and Shotgun. The horse plodded along steadily. Mama seemed relaxed, already chattering away to the rider beside her. I dipped my chin at Maddie, motioning for her to turn around and look.

"Mama would talk the ears off a row of corn," Maddie said, but she was smiling. "Did you get a load of that outfit on her fiancé this morning?"

"Yeah, that get-up's bad enough. Hard to believe, he has another one. Same style.

Neon blue. I'm almost afraid to see what he'll come up with tomorrow."

"You'd think Mama would have set him straight on what to wear."

"Are you kidding?" I said. "She probably helped pick them out. Did you see that plum-colored creation she had on today? Daddy would have fallen off his horse laughing."

"Nah, he wouldn't have, Mace. Mama could do no wrong as far as Daddy was concerned. Remember how they were together?"

I nodded, my mind drifting back twenty-plus years. I was just a kid when our father died of a heart attack. It was an awful shock. Daddy had hardly been sick a day in his life. But he'd gotten in over his head, trying to make a go of a cow-calf operation. Afterward, everyone said it was the stress of losing our ranch that killed him. That was one reason I was perfectly content drawing a regular paycheck from the Himmarshee Parks Department. Running my own business wasn't for me. Too many headaches and heartaches.

My sisters must have felt the same way, because the school district cut Maddie's checks, and Marty worked for the county library. None of us had set the world on fire. Then again, we all were healthy and relatively happy. Looking at the Bramble family, with all that money, I couldn't say the same for them.

A pinch on my arm brought me back to the present and the trail ride.

"Mace!" Another pinch. "I've been trying to get your attention. Look lively, girl," Maddie said. "And run a hand through that tangle of snarls you call hair. Carlos is right up there, on your left."

His thoroughbred tossed its head, raring to run in the cool morning fog. Carlos held him in with taut reins. His denim shirt strained across his muscled back and shoulders. Why did the man have to look so good?

"I don't have anything to say to Carlos," I told Maddie.

In the tent last night, before we went to sleep, I filled her in on my campfire humiliation. From Sharing S'mores to Flat-out Ignored. I don't think I'll ever be able to choke down another of those melted-marshmallow treats.

"Don't be ridiculous, Mace. If you want him, you better fight for him. He's too good of a man to let get away. You're not getting any younger, you know."

"Now you sound like Mama."

I didn't want to remind Maddie she

detested Carlos as recently as last summer. Back then, she said he was an arrogant S.O.B. with bad manners and a foul temper. Or maybe I'd said that. I'd certainly thought it plenty of times.

"Mace! Are you listening to me? This is a good time for you to talk to him. He's all alone. You can get to him before that Austin tramp comes back and starts eyeing him like he's the last biscuit in the basket." She lifted her boot in the stirrup and smacked me in the calf. "Go on. You'll hate yourself if you don't."

"I might hate myself if I do, Maddie."

I could almost hear the parts clanking in her head. She was trying to think of a way to convince me.

"Why don't you go ask Carlos what happened with Doc Abel?"

She set the hook.

"Wasn't he supposed to see Doc about getting that cup last night?"

She reeled me in.

I spurred Val forward. "You're relentless, Sister," I said over my shoulder.

"I know. It's one of the qualities I admire most in myself," she said.

I quickly caught up, slowing a few paces behind Carlos so as not to challenge the thoroughbred's racehorse instincts. I eased

228

Val alongside him.

"Hey," I said.

He turned in the saddle. "Hey, yourself. How are you this morning, Mace?"

"Fine. A little headache-y from all that sugar last night at the campfire."

He raised his eyebrows. "What sugar?" he asked cautiously.

Oh, God! Did he think I meant I saw him and Austin kissing? Were they kissing?

"From the S'mores," I blurted.

Relief flickered across his face. Bastard. He *had* kissed her. Of course, I'd been kissing Trey, and might have done more if not for Maddie interrupting us. I felt my face get hot.

"What about the cup?" I said, too abruptly.

He looked annoyed. "Do you purposely speak in riddles, Mace? You know, English wasn't my first language. You should give me a break."

"You speak English better than me, so knock it off." I made my words slow and distinct, as if I were addressing a small child: "What. Happened. Regarding. The. Chili. Cup. That. Belonged. To. Lawton. Bramble?"

"Much better," he said. "I asked Doc Abel for it, and he gave it to me. It's already at the Florida Department of Law Enforcement's crime lab."

"What . . . when?" I started to ask.

He held up his hand to interrupt me. I hated it when he did that.

"A friend of mine," he continued, "an FDLE agent, owes me a favor. He drove down to meet me last night in camp, then took the cup and its crusty chili back for testing."

"Oh," I said. "Well, thanks."

"You're welcome."

"Did Doc Abel act weird about handing it over?" I asked.

"Not at all. But if he had, I wouldn't have been surprised. Acting weird seems to be quite common around here."

I narrowed my eyes at him. "Yeah, it is. Along with acting like an asshole. Maybe you can discuss that with your new girlfriend, Austin."

He smirked at me, which really boiled my blood. I fingered the cow whip coiled on my saddle, and fantasized about snapping that smart-assed look right off his face.

"Mace, Mace," he said, with a head shake and laugh. "You are so wrong."

"Please. I have eyes," I said. "You and that girl looked like you needed to rent a room."

"It's not what you think."

"You have no idea what I think. Why'd you even come on this ride anyway?"

"I love horses. And I wanted to reacquaint myself with the pace and the people up here." He frowned. "Have you asked all the other riders so rudely why the hell they came?"

I turned Val away without answering. As I did, I saw Maddie, riding just out of earshot. She raised her eyebrows and motioned me a question: Thumbs up?

I looped Val's reins on the horn of the saddle so I could use both hands to signal my progress with Carlos: Thumbs down, definitely. Double thumbs down.

Maddie knew me well enough to know I wanted my space. And, for a change, she gave it to me. I rode the trail alone, enclosed in my cone of self pity and confusion. I wanted to make things right with Carlos again, but I didn't know how. Too proud for my own good, I didn't want to appear desperate. I couldn't stand the idea he'd see me as needy.

So where had my independence gotten me? Playing stupid games with a man I really cared about, and getting cozy with one I didn't.

As Val kept a steady walk, I leaned low

over her neck to whisper. "Like I told you before, girl, I'm an idiot."

Her head bobbed up and down, no doubt in agreement.

Before anyone could catch me discussing my love life with a horse, I closed my mouth and turned my mind to the passing scenery. We'd made our turn onto State Road 66, still moving east. Cattle grazed behind fences. A white bus from a church school putt-putted past, filled with the children of migrant workers. In an orange grove adjoining the trail, pickers climbed tall silver ladders to pluck the fruit from the highest branches.

Amid these symbols of Florida's agricultural past were troubling notes from her future: A luxury SUV roared by, its driver unmindful that a hundred-plus horses ambled close to the road. Land-For-Sale signs sprouted like maiden cane grass on a creek bank. New housing developments dotted once wild spaces. Most of them had ironic names: Eagle Trace, where no trace of an eagle remained; Oak Grove, where rows of fancy homes had replaced ancient oak hammocks.

I was contemplating a teeming Florida peninsula, paved with strip malls from coast to coast, when I heard a voice beside me.

"Penny for your thoughts, Mace," Mama said.

"You'd be overpaying."

"C'mon, honey. Cheer up. It's a beautiful day. They say it's going to get nice and warm."

"Great. That'll make that long slog we hit by the dairy smelly, dusty, *and* sweaty."

"Don't be such a sourpuss, Mace. Are you mad over Carlos and that trampy gal?"

I shot her a warning glance.

"Maddie told me all about it."

Well, of course she did, I thought.

"Honey, that Austin isn't any threat to you. Although I'll have to admit she knows how to make herself up and fix those pretty curls of hers. I wonder if she ever worked in a beauty salon?"

"Not helping, Mama."

"Sorry, honey. I was going to say she can't hold a candle to you. Carlos would never be interested in a shallow, silly girl like that. Did you consider he might just be playing her along to see what she knows?"

Mentally, I slapped myself on the forehead. I couldn't believe I *hadn't* considered that. And I didn't give him a chance to tell me, one way or the other, before Val and I stomped off. I really *am* an idiot.

"No, I didn't," was all I said to Mama.

She peered at me from under her purple hat. The rising sun threw a plum-colored shadow across her face. "Now, there's that smile I like to see," Mama said, "even if it's just a little one. We'll get all that settled with Carlos and you, honey. I can see you need a little help . . ."

"No way," I tried to interrupt.

". . . a little help with matters of the heart," Mama continued. "I do have to say that making time with Trey Bramble in the woods probably isn't the best way to get Carlos back."

Damn Maddie and her big mouth.

I steered us onto safer conversational ground. "How's Shotgun behaving?"

She leaned to pat the horse's neck. "He's a good horse, aren't you, boy? I thought I'd take him up by the wagons, see how he handles. We'll get Maddie, and ride together 'til lunch."

That sounded like a good plan. I had a bone to pick with my blabber-mouth sister.

TWENTY-SIX

"You're looking good, Mama," I called out.

"Show him who's boss," Maddie added.

I hadn't had time yet to dress Maddie down for telling my secrets. Shotgun had gotten a little skittish when the three of us drew close to the wagons. He didn't behave as badly as Carlos's thoroughbred had, but bad enough that Mama had to show him a firm hand. She spun him around a few times. Then she urged him once to the rattling wagon, and then back again.

A retired rodeo cowboy named Del, relegated by age and injuries to riding a lawn chair in the back of a mule wagon, watched as Mama worked with Shotgun. Del lifted a plastic cup to his mouth, spit a stream of tobacco juice, and then spoke.

"I've seen worse riders, I'll tell you that." His voice sounded like a truckload of rocks being dumped into a pit. "In fact, this here little ol' gal's a better rider than a buddy of mine, back in rodeo. One time, a bronc threw him up so high that a bird had time to build a nest between his hair and his hat before he hit the ground."

Del spit in the cup again.

"That's the God's honest truth."

As we all laughed, I wished Marty had been up to riding with us. I felt a rush of love for Mama and my sisters. I was even willing to forgive them for sticking their noses in my business. We were bonding on the Cracker Trail, just like Mama said we would.

I just hoped nothing happened to make us lose that warm, family feeling.

"Where are you?" Maddie shouted into her cell phone. "This signal's awful out here."

So much for Florida pioneer authenticity. I wasn't going to complain in this case, though. Maddie was talking to Marty — or trying to, anyway. And I was anxious to see how our little sister was doing.

We'd made it to the lunch site, a wide pasture ringed by hickory trees, sabal palms, and big live oaks. The smell of grilled sausage with green peppers and onions drifted our way. We sat on the ground in the shade, our horses tied nearby, as Maddie tried to decipher if Sal and Marty were going to meet us in time to eat.

"What are they saying, honey?" Mama asked.

Maddie waved her hand in irritation. "Shush, Mama. I can barely hear her as it is."

She yelled into the phone, "We're to the left of the food trailer as you come into the pasture. There's a big red pickup parked about twenty-five feet away from us."

Marty may not have heard her, but everyone else at the lunch site had. A couple seated on a fallen log frowned at Maddie before they moved to enjoy nature's glories somewhere else.

"I lost her." Maddie shook the phone and held it to her ear. "Yep. She's gone. Damn it."

"Language, Maddie," Mama said.

We always got a kick out of Mama telling us that, seeing as she could cuss a blue streak when she felt like it. But she always asked Jesus for forgiveness afterwards.

"Sal knows where he's going, right?" I asked Mama.

We were relying on him again, with Marty's help, to move vehicles and gear ahead so we'd have everything once we rode into the evening camp.

"Well, of course he knows, Mace. Sal's

made a detailed map," Mama said.

He had a map yesterday, too, and managed to get lost. I had the feeling without the Bronx Zoo or Yankee Stadium as landmarks, Sal missed his bearings.

"Well, *I* think we should go ahead and eat," Maddie said.

As soon as we agreed Maddie and Mama would line up for our food while I stayed with the horses, they were off. My sister always manages to move fast when food's at the finish line.

"Get me a lemonade," I called after them. "And extra onions on my sausage sandwich."

"I guess that means you're not planning on kissing anyone this afternoon."

Startled, I looked up to see Wynonna smiling down at me. Maybe I was distracted by my stomach grumbling and the horses moving around in the woods, but she moved with surprising stealth for a woman in red alligator boots with heels.

"Sorry, I didn't mean to scare you," she said. "Mind if I sit down?"

I motioned at the ground across from me. "Be my guest."

As she sat, she grinned and said, "So, how's your mama getting along on Shotgun?"

"He's great," I smiled back. "We sure appreciate you letting her ride him."

Wynonna waved her hand as if to say it was nothing. Then her grin faded, replaced by a serious expression.

"I wanted to ask you about Trey, Mace."

Uh-oh.

"I wondered if you've had a chance during the ride to really talk with him?"

I studied her, trying to determine her game. She returned my gaze with guileless eyes, wide with concern.

"Why?" I hedged.

"Because I'm worried about him, that's why. Your mama told me you two went to school together. I thought maybe he might have said something to you about what he's going through."

"Well, he's grieving for his father, of course." I was still being careful.

"Of course," Wynonna said. "What about his drinking, though?"

"He said he wants to quit."

"Well, I don't think he has. He disappeared about forty-five minutes into the ride this morning. Nobody's seen him since. Trey always goes off alone when he wants to get good and drunk."

I wasn't sure what to say. I hoped she was wrong, for Trey's sake. A backslide right now sure wouldn't boost his confidence. Not about his ability to quit drinking, and not about his fitness to step into his daddy's shoes. Was Wynonna driven to talk to me by compassion for her late husband's son, or by some other emotion?

An image of her caressing Trey's chest came into my mind. I wanted to question her about that night. But I had to tread cautiously, knowing she'd just lost her husband. Where was Marty with her soft touch when I needed her?

"Wynonna, please don't take this wrong, but is there something going on between you and Trey?"

Shock made a brief appearance on her face, followed by a flush of anger. "What the hell do you mean by that?"

Looks like I hadn't been cautious enough. I explained how I'd seen them on the couch.

"Are you sure about that?"

I nodded, but now I remembered the lights in the ranch house were dim that night. Had I really seen what I thought I saw?

"Mace, I was half-crazy with shock and grief. I was exhausted. I don't even remember sitting next to Trey, let alone rubbing on him. Doc Abel gave me something to help me calm down. Maybe it made me act crazy. Or maybe I fell asleep and dreamed I was with Lawton, like I've done ever since he died."

She looked wounded. I started to apologize. But Wynonna, rising and brushing bits of dead grass from her jeans, didn't give me the chance.

"Not that I feel much like eating lunch now, but I'll be on my way. I can see you're like all the others, Mace. Judging me." Her voice sounded more disappointed than angry. "But it hurts worse with you. I thought you and your mama were becoming my friends, you know?"

Tears welled in Wynonna's green eyes. And I sat there like a big, mean jerk as she walked silently away.

We'd almost finished lunch. After the sandwiches and on into the chocolate pudding, I filled in Mama and Maddie on my scene with Wynonna.

"Do you think she's lying?" Mama asked, licking her plastic spoon clean to the handle.

"I can't tell. All I know is I felt awful when she left," I said.

Maddie and I had started tidying up the lunch trash when Mama announced she'd ride out to the highway to look for Sal. That figured. She'd do anything to get out of her share of work.

After fifteen minutes or so, we started to wonder where she'd gotten to. There was no sight of Sal or Marty, and now Mama was missing, too. We decided to go find her.

"Give me a leg up on this horse, Mace," Maddie said. "I'm not as young as I used to be."

I cradled my hands, readied them under Maddie's boot, and helped her hoist herself onto the saddle.

"Oooof!" I exhaled loudly.

"I heard that!" Maddie snapped.

We'd started across the pasture when Mama suddenly called out from the edge of a woodsy hammock: "Yoo-hoo, girls! I found them. They're getting their lunch plates. Wait right where you are, and all of us will be right over."

I waved at her to signal we'd heard her. I thought for a moment she was waving back. But then I saw she wasn't waving. Her arms whirly-gigged up and down, around her head and back again. She twisted and turned in the saddle, swatting at the air.

"What in the hell?" Maddie said.

Mama's horse lowered his head and bucked. Then he reared up on his hind legs. She hung on. As Maddie and I raced our horses across the field, Mama gave a panicked yelp. She only had time for one word before Shotgun lit off at a gallop into the woods.

"Bees!" Mama screamed.

TWENTY-SEVEN

Hooves pounded. Brush crashed. Shotgun tore through the hammock — careering across the sandy path at one moment, darting through trees the next.

I kept to the path, trying to outrun Mama so I could turn and slow Shotgun as soon as I overtook them. Behind me, Maddie kept yelling "Pull back, Mama! Pull back!"

Of course, that's just what Mama was trying to do. But her hundred-pound frame tugging on the reins was no match for a runaway horse. Shotgun sped onward as if nothing but a ghost rode on his back. Mama's purple hat was gone. But still she hung on.

She leaned left, missing a low-hanging branch.

I held my breath.

She leaned right, catching a face-full of sabal palm.

I winced, as if the fronds had scraped me.

She ducked low, and the resurrection ferns growing on an oak limb grazed the top of her head.

I whispered a prayer.

Ahead, sunlight streamed through the canopy where the thicket of trees began to thin.

"Hang on, Mama. You're almost out of the woods," I yelled.

The words were barely out of my mouth when I spotted the ancient live oak, fat branches spreading low in all directions. Even if she missed the first branch or the second, the third would surely get her.

"Lean left, Mama. No, right!" Maddie's voice was frantic.

Mama had a split second to decide what to do. I saw her drop the reins and push toward the saddle's side. She was going to bail. But just as she did, her stirrup snared the heel of her boot. Hanging upside down by her foot, Mama bounced against Shotgun's belly for what seemed like an eternity. And then she dropped to the ground. I couldn't tell if the horse's churning hooves had caught her in the head. But I prayed that they hadn't.

Shotgun bolted on toward the sunlight, riderless, empty stirrups flying. Shouts of *Whoa!* and a commotion of riders rushing to stop the horse came from the clearing beyond the trees.

Maddie caught up with me, screaming Mama's name. I couldn't get my lips and tongue to cooperate on a single sound. We were off the horses and by Mama's side in an instant. The entire terrifying race had taken just moments. But that's all the time you need to have your whole life change.

"Mama?" Maddie's voice trembled, and I was suddenly ten years old again, watching with my sisters as Daddy was loaded into an ambulance after the heart attack that killed him.

As we kneeled next to Mama, I silently promised God I'd quit my every bad habit if only she was okay. Bits of leaves and twigs clung to her platinum hair. Dirt streaked her face where she'd fallen. The fabric of her plum-colored cowgirl blouse gaped open at the shoulder, showing an angry red scratch. I finally found my voice.

"Mama, wake up!" I said. "Maddie and I are here. Everything's going to be okay."

She didn't stir. She looked so small, so broken, lying there as still as death.

"Can you hear us, Mama?" Maddie's voice shook; her face was white. She looked as scared as I felt. "Please, open your eyes."

I was barely conscious of a jumble of

sounds: Someone yelled *Got 'im!* Voices filled the woods as folks spread out to search for Shotgun's missing rider. The strains of "Whistle While You Work" floated on the air.

Mama's left eyelid twitched. I grabbed Maddie's hand. As her eyes fluttered open, Mama took a shuddery breath. Then, she squeezed her lids shut again.

"Good Gussie," Mama whispered. "That hurt."

The clamor grew around us as riders, some leading horses, closed in. All I saw was a circle of blue-jeaned legs and boots, including Wynonna's of red alligator.

"Step back! Give her some air." The voice was male, ringing with authority and a slight accent. Carlos pushed his way to us and stooped beside Mama.

"What's your name?" he demanded, bringing his dark eyes close to hers.

"Rosalee Stinson Bauer Cummings Burton Deveraux," she recited.

Maddie smiled at me, and I squeezed her hand. Not a single married name missed.

"What hurts?" asked Carlos, still in charge.

"What doesn't?" Mama winced.

"What day is today?"

"February 18th. The day I wished I'd

never rode Shotgun."

She propped herself up to her elbows, legs still stretched out on the ground.

"Careful," a helpful someone said from the crowd. "She might have broken her back."

Mama straightened to a sitting position, her eyes going wide.

"You're fine, Mama," I reassured her, regaining some calm. "We just saw you use your arms. Can you feel your toes?"

She wagged her right boot back and forth. Then she yelped and grabbed at her ankle when she tried to do the same with the left.

"She probably wrenched that in the stirrup," I said to Maddie.

"Let me take a look at it," Carlos said, shouldering me aside.

"Excuse me, I'm also trained in first aid. I've handled plenty of injuries in my job at Himmarshee Park. And she's my mama. Not that we don't appreciate you taking over."

"We need to get that boot off and take a look," Carlos ordered, as he loosened her laces.

"Right." I pushed him aside and eased off her boot.

"Ouch!" Mama said.

"Careful, Mace!" Maddie scolded.

"And check the pulse at her ankle to make sure nothing's impeding the blood flow," I continued, directing my words at Carlos, "which would be a lot easier for me to do if you'd just scoot out of the way."

"Perdóneme." Carlos made a display of showing me his palms. "I forgot how much you like to be in control."

"Would you two please shut up?" Mama said. "*I'm* the injured party. How about if the both of you cooperate to help get me up and out of here?"

Before we could argue over who'd take the lead, an anguished bellow shook the leaves on the trees: "Rosie!"

"Over here, Sal," I yelled.

"I'm fine, Sally," Mama added, then lowered her voice from a shout to a whisper. "Girls, if Marty's with him, do *not* tell her how close that was."

Mama should know me better than that. I might bicker with my former boyfriend over her prostrate body, but I'd never say a word to worry Marty.

Sal came crashing through the woods like a wounded bear. Marty followed close behind, her frightened blue eyes the only color on her face.

"She's okay, Marty." Sal said, exhaling a huge sigh of relief.

"We saw your horse. People said . . . we thought . . ." Marty didn't finish before the tears started rolling down her cheeks.

"Oh, look at you two!" Mama held up her arms from the ground like she wanted a hug from each of them. "I took a spill, that's all. It's nothing but a little twisted ankle."

Sal raised his eyebrows at Carlos, who nodded in agreement.

"She'll be fine," I said pointedly, though Sal hadn't asked me.

At that, Sal leaned over and scooped Mama off the ground. He carried her out of the woods in his arms, as gentle as a bridegroom on his wedding night.

Someone had found Doc Abel. As I watched him expertly test the joint, peering at Mama's foot over his glasses, my mind went back to that long-ago day he'd ministered to a riding-related injury for me. Pronouncing nothing broken, he already had Mama's ankle elevated and packed in ice. Before he climbed aboard a wagon for the rest of the day's ride, he warned Mama, "Now, don't get back in that saddle again until I give the okay!"

We were lucky to have Doc along on the Cracker Trail.

My sisters and I skipped the after-lunch

half of the ride to help Sal ferry horses, vehicles, and our injured mama to Basinger, the next campsite along the trail. I hadn't seen Carlos since we argued over who should be in charge of helping Mama.

Now, the sun was beginning to sink in the sky. A clump of sabal palms sent long, skinny shadows across the pasture where we'd made camp. Field sparrows flitted here and there, hunting insects. Mama was ensconced on an upholstered chair Sal had scrounged up from somebody's camper. He also found a wooden chair and two pillows for her to use to rest her ankle. She was relishing her starring role in a drama.

Marty, Maddie, Sal, and I sat on the ground around her. We moved to make way as a new group of well-wishers stopped by to get the story from the horse-rider's mouth. We'd now gotten to the third or fourth re-telling, with Shotgun's speed and the perils of the woods magnified in each rendition.

"So, Shotgun and I were just standing there, pretty as you please, when all of a sudden those bees came out of nowhere," Mama said. "That horse snorted and bucked like a demon. I swear all four feet were off the ground. Then he took off, faster than a speeding bullet," she said.

Sal took his cue: "Marty and I came back with our plates, and we couldn't find her."

Marty shuddered: "We were scared to death."

"Well, not me," Sal amended. "But I was worried once we saw that horse run by without Rosie in the saddle."

I'd almost stopped listening. Until, suddenly, some fragments in my brain snapped together into one full piece.

"Did anybody hear about any other horses getting stung?" I searched the faces of the other riders gathered around Mama.

Shoulders shrugged. Heads shook.

"I wasn't too far away from that spot where your mama's horse got spooked," one cowboy finally said. "If there were bees, there couldn't have been too many. I didn't hear a hive, and I didn't see a thing."

I digested that tidbit of information.

Before Mama got wound up again to start on her story, I spoke. "I sure don't mean to be rude, y'all, but I think Mama needs to get a little rest. We'll bring her over to the campfire for dinner, and you can get all the details you want then."

Like a leading lady given the hook, Mama started to protest, "Mace, I'm not the least little bit tired . . ."

Maddie, after hearing Mama's story two

times too many, became my ally: "Mace is right. And I'm sure all these nice folks have some chores they need to get to." She leveled her sternest principal stare, and the crowd scattered like eighth-graders caught with cigarettes. "Besides, Mama, just think how many people at dinner won't have heard your story yet."

That thought seemed to cheer Mama. Her mind was probably turning to what fruit-colored outfit she'd choose for her dinner show performance.

In the meantime, I had a few questions myself for Mama. Something about Shotgun and that swarm of bees just didn't sit right with me.

Twenty-Eight

"What do you remember before you saw the bees?"

Mama and I sat in Sal's big Cadillac, alone at the spot they'd chosen for their camp. My sisters were off tending the horses. Sal had gone to find someone to help him with Maddie's tent. Carlos had remained scarce since our ridiculous spat over who'd rescue Mama.

"I don't remember anything out of the ordinary, Mace. If I'd known I was going on a death ride, I might have paid more attention."

She sat in the front seat with her ankle on her pillows. I was stretched out in the back.

"Mama, there has to be something. Sounds? Sights? Just be quiet for a minute and try to think."

She closed her eyes, leaning her head back against the driver's window.

Willie Nelson's "Mamas, Don't Let Your

Babies Grow Up to Be Cowboys," drifted over from the speakers of someone's CD player. The crack of a cow whip rang out. Cheers and whistles came from a makeshift barrel-racing course on the far edge of camp.

"I'm sorry, Mace," Mama finally said. "When I shut my eyes, all I can see is a maze of tree limbs and the ground coming at me."

I felt for her. She wasn't shying from the attention she was getting now, but she must have been awfully scared in those woods on the runaway Shotgun.

"All right, did you notice any people, then? You weren't too far from the cook site. Did you see Johnny Adams, for example?"

She shook her head.

"How about anyone in the Bramble family? Wynonna was in that crowd of people that gathered around where you fell off."

"Jumped off, Mace." She turned sideways to glare at me. "I jumped off on purpose."

"Whatever, Mama. Did you see Wynonna before you saw the bees?"

She started to say no, and then clapped a hand to her cheek. "Wait! When I was riding through the woods to holler to y'all, I saw Trey! He was half-hidden in some trees. And Mace, I think he's drinking again."

I felt my heart sink.

"He pulled a silver flask out of his pocket, and poured half of it into a plastic cup from the lunch wagon. He looked around, real sneaky-like, and then took a big swallow."

"Maybe it was vitamin water, or something like that," I said lamely.

She looked at me with pity. "Oh, honey, don't do that." We both remembered her Husband No. 2.

"And then Belle walked up to him," Mama continued, sounding more certain as her memory filled in the blanks. "I couldn't hear what they were saying, but Belle looked upset. When Trey took out the flask again, she put her hand on his arm to stop him. But he shook her off and poured in the rest of it anyway."

"What'd Belle do?"

"She turned and ran off into the trees. She had a camera case around her neck."

"What about Trey?"

"No, he didn't have a camera."

I stopped my eye-roll before it started. "I meant, what'd Trey do next?"

"Oh. Nothing. He just slid his back down the tree, swayed onto the ground, and took another big gulp from his drink. I'm sorry to have seen that, Mace."

"That's okay, Mama." I leaned over the

seat and patted her on the shoulder. "You've done real well in remembering. How long was all this before the bees?"

"I'd say five or ten minutes, maybe a little more. After I saw the two of them, I stopped to talk to that nice gal that Maddie knows from teaching school. She and her husband were sitting on a log, sharing their lunch. Sharon's her name. Or maybe it was Karen," Mama's eyes rolled toward the car's roof, like the name might be up there. "They both got cherry pie for dessert."

I knew I'd better lasso her back to the point, or I'd soon know how they liked their pie along with Sharon or Karen's life history.

"What about noises, Mama? Did you hear anything unusual?"

"You mean beside a swarm of bees?"

She closed her eyes again, trying to remember. When she opened them, they were wide.

"Right before the bees, I did hear a funny noise. It was a slapping, like someone hitting their horse with a riding crop. I remember thinking no one should have to beat on an animal like that. It was loud, like this." Just as she struck Sal's leather seat hard with her hand, a rapping on the back windshield made both of us jump.

"Sorry." Doc Abel leaned his head into the open window across from Mama. "Didn't mean to startle you. I just came to see how my patient is doing."

Mama waved her hand. "I'm fine, Doc. I sure do hate for anyone to make a fuss."

Yeah, Mama hates a fuss like Paris Hilton hates a party.

After Doc did a quick check of Mama's ankle, I said, "C'mon in and have a seat." I opened the car's door and scooted over.

"Don't mind if I do." He thudded onto the back seat, and the Caddy seesawed with his weight. "The older I get, the more it takes out of me to go traipsing around in the woods. I don't think I'll make this ride again next year."

"Nonsense, Doc," Mama said. "You're still in fine shape."

I wondered if her fall had knocked Mama's eyeballs loose.

"Well, thank you, Rosalee. But I'm fifty pounds too fat and twenty years too old. I'll be seventy-nine on my next birthday, you know."

"I hope you plan something special. Tell me, does Mrs. Abel make a big deal out of your birthdays?"

I had to admire her technique. Mama probably had Doc in mind for one of her bingo buddies, if he wasn't married.

"My wife died many years ago," Doc said. "In the year or two after I lost her, I didn't have the heart to take up with someone else. But the more time that passed, the harder it got to imagine going out and starting all over again with dating and the like. I always kept busy with my work. Now, at my age, who the hell would want me?" He chuckled, but his eyes looked sad.

"Didn't you have any kids? No grand-kids?" Mama asked.

"My wife and I only had one child. A girl. She died in a car crash up near Holopaw when she was in her twenties. It was such a senseless loss. My wife never really got over it. She got sick herself within eighteen months of our daughter's death. Cancer. She just didn't seem to have the desire or the will to fight for her life," he said.

Mama reached over the seat and put a gentle hand on his cheek. Her own cheeks were wet with tears. "Oh, you poor thing. I am so sorry."

My eyes felt hot. You never imagine when you meet somebody what kind of private heartache they've endured. I wished I could cry, or offer comfort, as naturally as Mama does.

"What was your daughter like, Doc?" I

questioned him, staying in my emotional safety zone.

A smile lit his face. "She was lovely. And smart, too. She'd just finished college, and planned to follow my footsteps into medical school. She looked a little like Belle Bramble, that same fiery hair. She was just about Belle's present age when she died. I think that's why I've always been so fond of Belle. She reminds me of my girl, Lilly."

Doc seemed happy talking about his daughter. I was just about to ask him another question, when we heard a Bronx honk across the campsite.

"I'm back, Rosie! Maddie's tent is up and I've got just the thing for a pre-dinner snack," Sal yelled, holding up a foil-wrapped paper plate like a trophy. "This coconut cream pie's got your name on it."

Doc opened the car door and eased his bulk outside. "I'll be on my way, ladies. Maybe I'll see y'all at dinner. Rosalee, stay off that ankle as much as you can, hear?"

Sal, eyes twinkling at Mama, said, "Guess that means no dancing tonight, huh Doc? Me and Rosie won't be cuttin' a rug?"

"Not unless you're doing it with a pair of scissors," Doc laughed.

As he walked away, he whistled that now-familiar tune. Off-key, of course. But as sad as Doc had seemed, it still sounded good.

I watched Sal — plumping Mama's pillows, replacing her melted ice with a fresh supply. He unwrapped the pie and loaded a bite onto a plastic fork. Then he started feeding her, as if she'd wrenched her wrist and not her foot. It was kind of nauseating, but also sweet.

We'd had our differences, Sal and I. And the sound of that New Yawk accent still grated on my Southern ears. But he took such good care of Mama, treating her as if she were a pack of precious jewels. And Mama clearly loved being cosseted. Between bites, she beamed at Sal as if he were George Clooney and Brad Pitt rolled into one. And he beamed right back.

I wondered if I'd ever find someone who cared for me like that? And if I did, would I ever let him show it?

TWENTY-NINE

Mama's accident, or her pre-dinner snack, didn't ruin her appetite.

All that was left from her fried catfish was a pile of bones. She'd plowed through grits, coleslaw, and hush puppies, too. Now, she tucked into her first slice of after-dinner pie. A second slice waited on deck. With her fork almost to her mouth, the morsel stalled in midair.

"Well, look at you! Aren't you sweet." She smiled at the big-bottomed cowgirl, who had come bearing more dessert.

"I thought this might make you feel better after that awful spill you took." The cowgirl glanced uncertainly at the brownie she was carrying.

"Well, honey, sweets are just the ticket when you've had the kind of day I had. You never can have too many, that's what I always say," Mama reassured her.

Putting down her fork, she grabbed the

brownie and plate from the cowgirl. She slid it onto an upended log beside her, next to the pie and three homemade chocolate chip cookies. If folks kept bringing treats, Mama could open a bakery right here in the woods.

Visitors had streamed by continuously. Some cared; most were just curious to see how she'd fared in her ill-fated race on Shotgun. We heard the horse was okay, except for a few bee stings.

Later, a songwriter who bills himself as a performer of Florida Cracker Soul was slated to sing and play guitar. Sal and my sisters had gone to scope out seats. I was keeping Mama company until she finished eating — which, at this rate, might be at midnight.

She invited her latest well-wisher to sit with us by the fire in Sal's vacant camp chair.

"I hate to be nosy." The cowgirl settled into the seat. "But we've been hearing all sorts of awful things about what's been happening to you or your daughters."

She glanced at me. I made my face a mask. I wasn't about to discuss our business with this stranger. Mama, of course, had no such reluctance.

"Oh, my yes!" she said, taking a quick swallow of pie. "It's been one strange thing after another ever since my middle daughter Mace and I found poor Lawton's body. This here is Mace." Mama leaned over to brush my bangs out of my eyes.

I jerked away, and then exchanged a nod with the cowgirl.

Mama began to tick off the events of the past few days on her fingers: "First, someone takes a knife and shreds poor Mace's sleeping bag and her tent."

The cowgirl looked at me and gasped. I stared into the fire.

"Oh, don't worry, honey. Mace wasn't in it at the time." Mama held up another finger.

"Second, Mace's horse got hit with a cow whip, and ran her right into the path of a semi-truck hauling grapefruit."

"Oranges, Mama," I corrected.

The woman looked at me, eyes as round as silver dollars. "I heard it was Trey Bramble's girlfriend that did that," she said.

When I didn't reply, Mama cupped her hand to her mouth and whispered, "Ex-girlfriend, honey. Her name's Austin. And that little tramp claims it was an accident."

I crossed my arms over my chest and glared at Mama. She ignored me. I knew it was useless to ask her to stop. She's the Niagara Falls of gossip.

Just then, I saw Sal, Marty, and Maddie heading our way from the other side of the fire. Happily, I'd be relieved of my nursemaid duties. I pushed myself up from the ground. "I'm going for a walk."

Mama gave me a small wave, and then raised another finger for the cowgirl. "Third, my youngest, Marty, nearly got bitten by a rattlesnake."

The cowgirl got closer, eyes gleaming. "And that good-looking guy from Miamuh killed it just in the nick of time, right?" she asked.

I tried so hard to keep my mouth shut, I bit a chunk out of the inside of my jaw.

"Oh, heavens no, honey," I heard Mama saying as I stalked away from the fire. "Carlos is afraid of snakes."

At least she didn't give him the credit. I paused to see what she'd say next.

"And then No. 4, as you know, was that terrifying ride I took today on Shotgun." Lowering her voice dramatically, she launched into her well-rehearsed monologue. "That horse and I were just standing there as pretty as you please, when all of a sudden . . ."

I kicked a rotten log as I left. It felt good to see it shatter into bits.

"Where you going, Mace?" Marty called

after me.

"Oh, let her go, honey. She's been in a sour mood all night," Mama said, raising her voice to carry my way. "I mean, really. I'm the one who should be cranky. I'm the one nursing cuts and bruises and a broken ankle."

"*Sprained* ankle!" I yelled over my shoulder.

The night was clear and getting colder. I zipped my fleece vest over my long-sleeved turtleneck. The temperature wasn't expected to plummet like it had earlier in the week, but the air still had a nip. I might be grateful for our crowded tent tonight, even if Maddie did snore like a diesel engine.

Using my flashlight, I collected some small rocks and found a log to sit on by a cow pond. Stars twinkled. A night hawk swooped low in search of prey. I started tossing the pebbles into the water. With each *plopp,* I counted another reason I had to be pissed off. The biggest reason, of course, was that my family and I had somehow become targets. That was the hardest one to understand. I didn't know who was after us. I didn't know why. And I didn't know how to stop them.

But I had plenty more reasons to be upset, and plenty more rocks.

Plopp: My inability to say or do the right thing around Carlos. *Plopp:* Mama's compulsion to tell our family business to anyone with ears. *Plopp:* My perverse desire to keep things private, but to get the credit due me as long as Mama was going to blab.

Everyone assumed Carlos had rescued Marty, which pissed me off. The man had never even seen a Florida Cracker cow whip before this trip. Then he compounded his offense by trying to push me out of the way when Mama got hurt. Of course, most normal women would be grateful for the help of a man who seemed to care about her family. Most women, that is, who aren't crazy control freaks. I hated the way he always took over, like I was some weakling.

Wrapped up in a self-righteous funk, I didn't hear someone approaching until a voice made me jump.

"Now, there's what I always loved about you, Mace: That sunny smile."

"Very funny, Carlos." I could feel the frown wrinkling my brow.

"Your mother told me you'd gone off to sulk in the woods. She told me to look for water, and I'd find you." He cupped my chin and tipped my face up to his. "C'mon, *niña,* it can't be that bad."

"Oh, it's bad all right." I knocked his hand

away. "And don't call me *niña.*"

He lowered himself to the log beside me. "Okay, I'll call you *niño,* then. But anyone who speaks Spanish is going to wonder why I'm calling you *boy* instead of *girl.*" He brought his face close to mine, breath warm on my cheek. "No one would ever mistake you for a boy," he whispered.

A shudder of desire nearly knocked me off the log. My skin burned where the side of his thigh touched mine. My mind spun with fantasies of me tearing off his clothes; of him pushing me onto the ground and having his way. For a control freak, I had an appalling lack of control over how much I wanted him. I felt like I was on fire. I lowered the zipper on my vest.

Plopp.

THIRTY

Before I could say or do something stupid, I scooted over on the log to put some space between Carlos and me. We'd tried the couple thing. It didn't work, for either of us. Now, I could read the amusement in his eyes, even in the lantern light. I decided to extinguish that arrogant smirk by doing the one thing he'd never expect.

"Listen, I wanted to say I'm sorry for the way I acted today. Thank you for trying to help Mama. I was a jerk for pushing you out of the way."

If the night had even a breath of air in it, it would have knocked him on his ass. He actually sputtered before he choked out a response to my apology. "You're welcome."

As long as I was doing the unexpected, I decided to go for broke.

"What's up between you and Austin, Carlos? I won't argue that the girl is gorgeous, but she doesn't seem like your type."

He raised his eyebrows at me. "I didn't know you cared."

"I'm not saying I care," I lied. "I just don't want to see her do you the way she's done Trey. That girl is trouble, *amigo*."

He picked up one of the pebbles from my pile and skipped it across the water.

"She's not all bad, Mace. She left the trail for a couple of days to go home and take care of her sick grandmother," he said. "But as long as we're speaking of people who are trouble, you and Trey seem like pretty good friends."

His tone gave away nothing; his face was a blank. I decided to stop playing games.

"Listen, I'm going to be honest with you," I said. "Trey was the king of my high school, way out of my league. He was gorgeous and popular, and he could have any girl he chose. I won't lie: I was flattered when he started flirting with me on this ride. But I don't feel for him the same way I felt . . ." I paused, my eyes on the ground.

Now that I was into it, I wasn't sure I wanted to confess. Honesty isn't all it's cracked up to be.

"The same way you felt about what?" he prodded, his body as still as the night.

About you, I wanted to say. I don't feel about Trey the way I did about you.

Instead, I found some words I could hide behind. "I just don't feel right about Trey," I finally said.

"Well, that's good to know," Carlos released the pebble he'd been holding, firing it into the pond. "I'm not sure I feel right about Trey either. So, would you like me to tell you a secret now?"

I nodded, not lifting my face.

"I'm not the least bit interested in Austin," he said. "You're the one who raised my suspicions about her, about how she might be responsible for vandalism and maybe more. Who knows? She may even be tied to Lawton's death. I want information from her, and I'm trying to get it." Another pebble sailed into the water. "It's called police work, Mace."

I felt like someone had just handed me a hundred-dollar birthday check with a slice of chocolate cake on the side. I even overlooked his tutoring tone.

"Well, have you found out anything?" I asked, raising my eyes to his.

"No. She's actually smarter than she seems." He dropped the rest of the rocks onto the ground and brushed his hands on his jeans. "She prattles on and acts the fool. But she never gives much away."

"Well, see if you can find out whether she

271

really is a novice when it comes to cracking the cow whip. I don't believe for a minute she *accidentally* hit my poor horse."

"Yes, ma'am." Carlos saluted me, but he was smiling as he did. "Any other tips to help me improve my interrogation technique?"

I traced the ridges of the bark on the oak log where we sat. I watched moths beat themselves against the glass dome of the lantern.

"Well, there is one thing I'd like to know about interrogations," I finally said.

"And what would that be?"

"Do you ever have to kiss a subject like Austin to get her to tell you what she knows?"

He put a hand to each side of my face and pulled me closer. "Do you mean like this?" his lips brushed over my eyelids, first one and then the other. "Or like this?" He brought the full pressure of his mouth against mine.

"Yes, like that," I murmured, tasting his tongue.

"No, I've never kissed a subject like this," he said, as he nipped gently at my bottom lip.

"Good," I said, tugging at the buttons on his shirt as I drew his body to mine. "Because I don't think that's standard police procedure."

Belle's hair gleamed like polished copper in the firelight. A camera around her neck, she sat with Trey on the ground by Mama. As I came into the clearing, Maddie pointed her chin at the beer can in Trey's hand. Beside her, Marty gave me a shake of her head and a sad expression.

"Well, there you are, honey," Mama called. "We were starting to think a gator crawled out of a pond and got you. What in the world have you been doing for all this time in the woods?"

I hoped there wasn't enough light for them to see me blush.

"Just sitting," I lied.

Maddie raised her eyebrows. "Your vest is inside out, Mace."

"It's reversible, Maddie," I lied again.

Carlos and I cut our woodsy interlude short because he'd promised to play poker with a couple of retired Miami cops now living near Sebring. I returned to the campfire alone.

"Shouldn't we be getting over to hear the Cracker songwriter?" I said, changing the subject. "We don't want to miss any of his new songs."

Sal said, "The guy who plays bass with him got a flat tire on the way here. They're going to start late. The fire's nice and warm. Why don't you have a seat with us while we wait?"

Five sets of eyes looked up at me, all except for Trey's. His hat was pulled down low, and he held onto that beer like it was an anchor in a fast current.

Belle gave me a friendly smile. "Please, Mace. Do sit down."

Her voice was strong; her eyes clear. Whatever she'd been taking last night, she wasn't taking it now. I took a seat on the ground.

"I didn't get the chance to thank you for coming to look for me last night in the cypress stand," she said

She glanced quickly at Trey, who didn't seem to notice.

"Don't mention it, Belle. I know y'all are having a rough time. Anything I can do to help, I'm glad to."

"Oh, I'm sure you are," Trey said, his words slurred by booze and what sounded like spite.

"Excuse me?" I said to him.

He pushed the hat back on his head so he could look at me. Tonight, it was Trey and not his sister who seemed to have trouble focusing. "I was just sayin' I'm sure you'd be glad to help, if only you could tear yourself away from that smart-ass cop from Miamuh."

Sal cleared his throat. Marty started fooling with the laces on her boots. Maddie, principal-style, said, "There's no excuse for foul language, Trey."

I started to defend myself when Marty caught my eye. Very subtly, she put a finger to her lips.

Belle said, "I apologize for my brother, Mace. Trey and I cut through the woods on our way here. We saw you and Detective Martinez . . ." She searched for the right word, "talking."

Sal coughed. Mama said, "Oh my!" Trey jammed his hat back down over his eyes.

"Anyway," Belle continued, before anyone could interrupt, "before Trey and I get going, I wanted to tell y'all how terribly sorry I am about what happened with Shotgun." She reached up a hand to Mama's good leg, resting it on her knee.

"Oh, honey, stop fretting." Mama gave Belle's hand a reassuring pat. "All's well that ends well, and it might have ended a lot worse."

A murmur of assent went around our little group.

"But that's just what I keep thinking about," Belle said with a shudder. "I couldn't live with myself if someone came to real harm riding a horse that I trained."

Mama was about to start her recitation about the bees, but Trey interrupted her.

"I think most people would surprise themselves with all they can live with, Little Sister. And why don't you stop making over her like that?" He pointed his beer can at Mama. "All that's happened to her is a little bitty busted ankle. Our daddy's dead, Belle!"

"I think you better quit while you're ahead, pal." Sal's voice was menacing.

Trey snorted, and then glared at Sal from under his hat.

Belle pressed on, hurrying to finish her plea on Shotgun's behalf. "He's such a good horse. Everyone says so. Don't they, Trey?"

Instead of an answer, Trey gave another snort.

"Let's go, Belle." Swaying, he pushed himself up on one knee. "These people don't want us here. You're wasting your breath."

Maddie said, "Belle is just fine, Trey. You're the one who's drunk, not to mention rude. Why don't you take Sal's advice? Go back to your trailer and sleep it off before you get into real trouble."

Trey dropped his beer can, then his hat. He cursed when he stepped on the hat while he was trying to get up.

"Just leave me alone!" he shouted, now on his knees. "Don't any of you touch me."

Sal whispered, "Why don't you let me help you get him home, Belle?"

"No," she said firmly as she stood. "Believe me, it's better if I handle him alone. I've done it before." Pain and exhaustion showed in her eyes as she gazed down at her brother.

"Let's go, Trey."

"You're the boss, Little Sister."

The way he said it, it sounded like a sneer. Then again, Trey was pretty drunk.

Belle hooked both of her arms under one of Trey's shoulders, helping him haul himself to his feet. For her size, she had surprising strength. Or maybe it was just practice.

For once, we were all silent. The fire crackled. Sparks glowed. Shadows danced. None of us said a word as the two Bramble siblings walked away, Belle staggering every so often under her brother's added weight.

THIRTY-ONE

Stomps and whistles followed the last chord of Jerry Mincey's song, "Plantin' Yankees."

"Thank you, folks," he nodded to the crowd, a smile showing above his salt-and-pepper beard. "We're gonna take a little break, but don't go away. We'll be back before you know it."

The music was almost forty-five minutes late getting started. But once Jerry launched into his Florida Cracker repertoire, the crowd was with him all the way. He sang of ancient Indian legends and modern over-development; of the days when rivers ran clear and cowmen moved herds of half-wild cattle across open lands.

"Some of Jerry's songs make me so sad." Marty took a sip from a cup of hot choco-late. "Everything about Florida has changed."

"I can think of a few more changes I'd like to see," Sal said. "Can't somebody do something about the bugs? And Florida is too hot for humans most of the year."

Maddie harrumphed. "You know, Sal, I-95 leads north just like it does south. You could always go back home, where everything is so much better," she said. "While you're at it, why don't you take about a million of your fellow transplanted New Yorkers with you?"

Mama gave Maddie's arm a pinch. "Hush! There's no call for you to be rude."

Maddie rubbed her arm. "Ow, Mama! I'm just telling him like it is. That's what Northerners like, don't they? They like people to be straightforward and direct, no beating around the bush."

"In other words, rude," I put in.

"Here we go." Sal threw up his hands. "We gonna fight the Civil War all over again?"

Maddie was winding up to defend the Motherland when a scuffle erupted behind us in the open-air theater. We all turned our heads to find the source of the shouting and stumbling.

"You're a son-of-a-bitch," Trey yelled. His face was red; his body swayed. The dented cowboy hat was crooked on his head.

"That's the alcohol talking, and I'd advise it to shut up." Johnny Adams kept his voice calm, drained of emotion. "I think you'd show more respect for your father than to get stinking drunk and go picking fights before we've even had the chance to bury him."

"We?" Trey blinked hard, shaking his head. "You don't have nuthin' to do with my daddy's funeral. You weren't his friend."

People seated nearby started standing up, moving their chairs and coolers out of the way.

"And you've got balls," Trey continued, "telling me to show *respect.*" He slurred the word. "Like you did? Oh yeah, you *respected* Daddy so much you went and sued him to try to get all our money!"

First Belle, and then Wynonna, materialized out of the crowd and sidled closer to Trey. He didn't seem to notice them. He lunged, shoving Johnny in the chest.

"You don't know what you're talking about, Trey." Johnny took a step back, his hands balled into fists at his sides. "I'm warning you: Shut your mouth and sit down."

"Or you'll do what, chicken-shit?" Trey brought his face close enough to spray Johnny with spit. "Taking me on is a little different than rolling around in the dirt with an old man with a heart condition, isn't it?" He pushed Johnny again. "Oh, I know about that knock-down drag-out y'all had the night before Daddy died."

Wynonna and Belle exchanged a confused look.

"And I know you never got over Daddy stealing the only woman you ever loved."

At this point, most of the crowd looked at Wynonna. Mama whispered to Marty and Maddie, "Not that woman; another one. Mace and I will explain later."

Slitting his eyes, Johnny stepped toward Trey. "Now, you've gone too far."

Uh-oh, I thought. I started to get out of my chair to intervene, but Sal stopped me.

"I've got this, Mace. I've had lots of practice."

Heaving himself to his feet, Sal headed toward the fight. A couple of other men saw him moving in, and did the same. Before Trey could react, they had him surrounded, arms pinned harmlessly to his sides. His right leg flew up in a kick, but the boot missed connecting with Johnny or anyone else. Sal and the other two men dragged him backwards out of the crowd, kicking and shouting all the way.

Jerry re-took the stage, starting right in with "Narcoossee Lucie." Trey yelled and cussed from outside. But his shouts quickly grew distant. By the time Jerry and his partner on upright bass got to their show-closer, "Osceola's Tears," Sal was easing himself back into his seat.

"What happened?" I whispered.

"He's fine. We got his boots off and got him into bed in his family's RV. He'll have a hell of a hangover tomorrow."

I thought of Trey's drinking; his love-hate relationship with his daddy; his squandered brains and talent. Sal may have said otherwise, but Trey was far from fine. And a morning hangover was the least of his troubles.

"There's Johnny, Mace!" Maddie jabbed me in the ribs with her elbow. "Let's go talk to him."

"Don't be so rough, Maddie! I have eyes. I can see the man."

"Stop squabbling," Marty said. "Hey, do you think Johnny has any hot chocolate left?"

The three of us had been on our way to Maddie's tent to turn in. About twenty feet from the food trailer, we stopped and watched as Johnny finished his cleanup.

The mini-concert was over. Sal and Mama had headed off to Home Sweet Cadillac. Carlos must have caught up again with his fellow lawman from the FDLE, because he hadn't come to the show. And, after Trey's drunken scene, none of the Brambles returned either.

Marty shivered in the chilly air. She's only about half mine or Maddie's size, and her body never seems to have enough energy to keep her blood circulating right. Her hands and feet, especially, are always cold.

"Can't hurt to ask Johnny for something warm," I said to her.

"Forget the hot chocolate," Maddie whispered in my ear. "I want to hear how Lawton stole his woman."

Johnny answered our hellos with a frown.

"I don't have any more pie for your mama. Tell her I said she's had enough, hurt ankle or not."

I was about to take offense on Mama's behalf, when Marty chirped, "Thanks so much for spoiling her, Johnny. Sometimes Mama's sweet tooth makes her forget her manners. I hope she didn't get too greedy?"

"Well, three pieces *is* a lot of pie," Johnny grumbled.

I didn't mention Mama had actually eaten four pieces over the day, plus the chocolate chip cookies.

"Well, we appreciate it," Marty said.

"I don't suppose you've got any hot chocolate?" Maddie asked, as direct as any

Northerner.

Johnny stopped wiping down a folding table and looked at her hard.

"Sorry," Maddie said. "I was just asking because our little sister is iced to the bone. She's prone to catching colds."

Marty gave a delicate cough. Johnny caved.

"Oh, all right. I've got about one cup left in the urn. I was just about to toss it."

He put a mug on the table and lifted a silver serving urn almost upside down. The final cup flowed. He'd stripped off his long sleeves to a white T-shirt underneath. Cords of muscle stood out on his thick arms. If Johnny had wanted to go up against Trey, he probably could have taken him, especially with all the booze Trey had obviously consumed.

"You showed a lot of restraint tonight," I said. "Trey was itching for a fight."

Johnny stared into the dark distance.

"Well," he finally said, "his father was a good friend, once. And I won't take advantage of a man who's mixed grief with liquor. That's a bad combination."

I wondered whether he spoke from personal experience.

"That sure sounded like a lot of nonsense Trey was yelling, didn't it?" I asked, watching Johnny's face to see what it might reveal.

"Hmmm," he said, showing nothing as he handed Marty the cup of chocolate.

Maddie decided to go with directness again: "Was there any truth to what Trey said?"

Johnny clattered the urn upright onto the table. I hoped its parts weren't breakable.

"Well?" I asked. "Was there?"

A vein throbbed at his temple. He looked at me like he wanted to take that swing he hadn't taken at Trey.

"I'm not in the habit of telling my personal business to strangers." His eyes were dark; his voice cold. "Now, if y'all don't mind, I've got work to do."

Marty had been quiet, sipping steadily from the mug he gave her. She drained it and put it down on the table. "Thanks for the chocolate," she said.

He turned his back, crossed the cook site, and stomped up the stairs into the food trailer.

"Well, that was rude!" Maddie said.

"Shhh!" Marty scolded. "He'll hear you."

As we left, Maddie and I each took one of Marty's elbows, pulling her close to share the warmth of our bodies.

"Did y'all notice anything funny about Johnny?" she asked, once we'd put ample distance between us and his trailer.

"He was in a T-shirt, even though it's cold," Maddie offered.

"His eyes were hard," I added.

"Think about his hands," Marty said.

I'd been concentrating on Johnny's face. When Maddie didn't speak either, Marty said, "His right hand was red and swollen."

"So?" Maddie said. "He works around hot food and fire. He probably burned it."

Marty said, "Maybe so."

"What else, Marty?" I asked.

"Well, I just thought it looked an awful lot like my hand did that time in the orange grove, when I got stung by those bees."

THIRTY-TWO

Marty crouched at the entrance to the tent, nerves showing as she shone and re-shone the flashlight into the corners. Maddie and I had already laid the sleeping bags outside, turning them inside out.

"See, Marty?" I said. "No snakes."

She peered inside a bag. "I know I'm being a scaredy cat," she said. "I'm sorry."

"Don't you apologize, Marty. The one who should be sorry is the one who stuffed that rattlesnake in Mace's jacket." Maddie gave her own bag a good shake. "And he — or she — will be sorry once we find out who it was."

"My money's on Austin," I said, tossing my bag onto the tent's canvas floor. "I know she snapped that whip at Val on purpose. She's also the best candidate for shredding my tent."

Marty followed my bag inside, the flash-light's beam strafing any possible hiding place. "Jealousy is a good motive, Mace. But what about her snake phobia?"

"Oh please, Marty! You are so gullible. Can't you just see Austin pitching a fit at that reptile house so that big, strong Trey would take her in his arms to comfort her?" Stretching my legs half out the zippered door, I pulled off my heavy boots. "Austin's exactly the type of woman who would pull that damsel-in-distress crap."

"We all know *you're* not that type, Mace." Maddie put a toothbrush and a bottle of water on top of her sleeping bag. "Would it kill you to pretend, just a little, that you could use some help from Carlos? Men like to be needed, you know. And you about bit off his head when Shotgun threw Mama."

I made a face, but I wasn't sure she could see me in the lantern light.

"I'm rolling my eyes at you, Maddie," I said. "By the way, how come you never simper around, all helpless, with men?"

"I don't need to, Mace. I already have a husband."

"It must be this relic of a tent," I said. "I think somebody just opened a time warp into 1950."

"Could you two please stop bickering?" Marty put a hand on each of our arms. "You're making my head hurt."

Maddie and I were quiet for a few moments, like two kids reprimanded by their favorite teacher. I tugged off my jeans, leaving on my socks and long undies to sleep in. Maddie went outside to brush her teeth. Marty wrapped a woolen scarf around her neck, tucking the ends into the collar of a long-sleeved thermal T-shirt.

"Hand me one of those flashlights, would you, Mace?" Maddie leaned in. "I need to use the little girl's room before bed."

I handed over a light, along with a wad of toilet paper. "Oh for God's sake, Maddie. You don't need to walk all the way to creation and back to find the portable potties. Just use that clump of brush out there by the horse trailer."

"I will not!" She summoned her most dignified tone. "Principals do not squat in the bushes, Mace. Suppose a student spotted me? They'd snap a picture on their cell phone and it'd be all over YouTube by first period tomorrow: Me, doing my business. It'd be tough after that to exert my authority."

As Maddie stalked off into the darkness, Marty and I snuggled into our sleeping bags. It made me think of when we were kids, sharing a room with twin beds. Maddie, of course, had claimed her own room.

"I've been thinking about all the things that have happened, Mace. If Austin is responsible, like you say, then how does that tie in with your notion about Lawton being murdered?"

It was too dark to see the confusion on Marty's face. But I knew it was there. I was equally as confused.

"I haven't put all the pieces together yet, Marty. Maybe Austin's not just jealous about Trey and me. Maybe she had something to do with Lawton's death, and she doesn't want me around to find out what it was."

I heard Marty's soft breathing as she pondered that possibility.

"Then how do those bees figure in, Mace? And Johnny Adams? And Wynonna and Trey?" Her voice had an uncharacteristic note of skepticism. "And what if Lawton's death was just a heart attack? What if everything is completely unrelated?"

Marty's question hung in the air. The horses noisily munched hay outside in their temporary paddock. Bullfrogs croaked from a far pond. Night creatures scrabbled in dry brush.

"I don't know, Marty," I finally answered her. "I was a lot more willing before last summer to believe in unrelated coincidences. Don't you remember all the things Jim Albert's killer did to scare us off the trail?"

"I do. I also remember the nasty notes and threats, and you haven't gotten any of those on this ride. Why do you think that is, Mace?"

Truthfully, I didn't know what to think. Maybe I was over-reacting.

"I mean . . ." Marty breathed deeply, then continued, "Shotgun running away with Mama might have been an accident, and maybe Johnny really did burn his hand. And maybe Austin didn't mean to hit Val. And Trey and Wynonna both deny there's something between them; maybe they're not lying. And suppose some teenager thought it'd be funny to rip apart your sleeping bag and soak it with red wine . . ."

"Okay, enough! Now you're giving *me* a headache."

She patted my cheek. She was wearing mittens.

"Sorry, Mace. I guess we only know a couple of things for sure: Lawton Bramble is dead . . ."

I interrupted, "And what they find in that chili cup will tell us something about how he died."

"It will," Marty agreed. "We also know

that rattlesnake was planted in your jacket. All we have to do is find out who did it and why."

Marty made it sound simple. But I remembered the case from last summer. Nothing was simple about last summer.

I awoke with a start. I was sure it was Maddie, snoring. But when I listened, all I heard in the tent was the sound of my two sisters breathing. Marty's breath was a gentle sigh. Maddie's was raspy, but not loud enough to wake me from a deep sleep.

I sat up, shook the fuzz from my brain, and grabbed my watch from the toe of my boot. The luminescent dial read one-thirty. A horse whinnied. Palmetto fronds rustled in a slight breeze. And there was that sound again: A woman, sobbing.

A man spoke over the sobs. His words were hushed, indecipherable. But the masculine timbre of his voice and the angry tone were clear. He said something, and then the woman's sobs intensified — a sad, strangled sound.

Grabbing the lantern from the corner of the tent where I'd left it, I turned it on. The light was dim, the batteries weak. Swinging the lamp inside the tent, I felt on the floor for my coat. I picked up Marty's first, which would never fit. I found Maddie's next, which would have to do.

The sobbing outside abruptly stopped. I wondered if, seeing my light, the man had clamped his hand over the woman's mouth.

I hurried into my boots, leaving the laces undone.

"Maddie!" I shook her shoulder. "I heard something. Someone's in trouble."

"Huh?" She covered her head with her pillow. "Go away, Mace."

I didn't want to waste time rousing her. I crawled out the door of the tent, and started in the direction of the sobs. But the woods were quiet now. I stopped, straining to listen. I thought I heard brush moving in the distance, but it might have been the wind.

Suddenly, I whirled around at a familiar sound. An off-key whistler was approaching our tent, coming from the opposite direction from where I'd heard the sobs.

"Doc!" I hissed. "What are you doing out here?"

"Who's there?" He shined a flashlight in my direction.

"It's Mace, Doc. I heard a woman crying, somewhere out there." I pointed my lamp into the distance. "Did you hear anything?"

"Not a peep." He shook his head. "But I

was coming the other way, from over by the campfire." He turned and aimed his light behind him.

Together, we headed into the woods to look. We made big circles with our lights, but saw nothing. Whoever had been there was gone now. No voices broke the stillness; no sobs in the night.

"I wonder who it was?"

Doc shrugged. "Probably some couple, having a lovers' quarrel. Everybody's acting peculiar on this trip. People at the campfire tonight were trading all sorts of stories. Somebody asked me about that chili cup, Mace. You should have never told people about your suspicions."

I picked a leaf from a hickory tree and started to shred it. "I didn't, Doc. But you know how people are: Somebody overhears something, and the next thing you know it's all over camp. Then you've got a crowd of people seeing clues everywhere, like they're extras on *CSI: The Cracker Trail*."

Doc huffed, "Well, I don't like it. All this speculation isn't helping Lawton's family one bit. And they need all the help they can get."

He crossed his arms and stared. I wasn't going to defend myself, since I hadn't done anything wrong. I was thinking of what to say next when Doc saved me the trouble.

"Did that policeman friend of yours get somebody to take the cup?"

I nodded, and pulled another leaf off the tree. "All of this might be moot if the state lab doesn't find anything. But a lot of strange things have been happening, and they all seem to start with Lawton's death. I think it'd be foolish of us not to wonder why."

I looked up into the black sky, just in time to spot a shooting star. My wish was for a safe ride the rest of the way to Fort Pierce. And, I wished for things to start making sense. That last part I felt I had a little bit of control over.

"Why'd you leave the campfire, Doc?" I asked.

"I got sick of hearing people run their mouths. It was awful smoky, too." He breathed deeply. "Thought I'd take a little walk and get some fresh air into my lungs before I turn in."

He shone his light on his wristwatch. "It'll be time for breakfast before we know it. I just want to enjoy the night air and these beautiful stars for a little bit longer."

He accompanied me back to the tent, where we said our goodbyes.

As he left, murdering "Whistle While You

Work," I got into the tent. It wasn't until later, as I was drifting off, that I wondered: Why would a man who claimed to detest the woods be out having a walk, enjoying all of nature's glories?

THIRTY-THREE

My sisters and I spotted Audrey sneaking a smoke behind the food trailer. It was breakfast time. But another foggy morning would delay our grub, and the ride. We decided to corner her in the meantime, to see what we could find out about her boss, Johnny.

"Mornin'," I said, as the three of us approached off Audrey's right flank.

She jumped, hiding the hand with the cigarette behind her back. "You scared the crap out of me! If Johnny sees me smoking, he'll kill me. I told him I quit two weeks ago." She smiled guiltily, took a last drag, and carefully extinguished the half-smoked butt on the trailer's metal hitch. Then she straightened the remainder and slipped it into a pocket of her server's apron.

"For later?" Marty asked.

Audrey nodded, mischief lighting her eyes.

"You really should quit, you know. Smoking is a filthy habit," Maddie said.

I ground my elbow into my sister's side. "Don't we all have habits we wish we didn't have?" I smiled at Audrey. "All of us except Maddie, that is."

Marty got to the point before Maddie could insult Audrey again. "We were wondering, how's Johnny's hand? That looked like a pretty bad burn. Were you there when he did it?"

"Occupational hazard." Audrey shrugged. "It's not the first time he burned himself on something hot. Won't be the last."

"So you saw him do it?" I asked.

"No, but I've seen it before. He cusses like a drunken cowboy and blames everyone in sight. I'm glad I wasn't around this time to catch the flak."

"What's the story with you two?" Maddie asked.

Audrey raised her eyebrows. Marty pinched Maddie's other side.

"I think what Maddie means is that you seem to have such an easy, joking way with Johnny." My smile was warm. "You two must have worked together for a long time."

Audrey beamed, her feelings for her boss shining in her eyes. "It'll be twenty years this June. I just planned to work at the restaurant the summer after high school. But Johnny needed me, so I stayed on. And on, and on."

What was the best way to phrase my next question? I wished I'd rehearsed with Marty.

"So you started working for Johnny right around the time Barbara Bramble died." I decided on the open-ended approach. "I know he was awfully close to her."

Pain flickered briefly across Audrey's face. "It about killed Johnny when Barb died."

"So tragic, too. An accident like that," Maddie said, finally climbing down off her high horse.

Audrey's face hardened. "An *accident,* yes. That's what everybody said." She took the cigarette from her apron and re-lit it.

Please don't say anything mean about smoking, I sent a silent plea to Maddie.

Marty jumped in, "You sound like you don't believe what everybody says."

Audrey took a big drag and then lifted her face to exhale, aiming the smoke to the sky. Maddie coughed and waved her arm. I gave her a warning glance.

Audrey examined the glowing tip of her cigarette. "I don't like to speak ill of the dead."

"Lawton or Barbara?" I asked.

She was silent, staring at the ground.

"Audrey?" Marty prodded, a gentle hand on her wrist.

"Honey, neither one of them is around to protest," Maddie whispered, "and you can talk to us in confidence. I'm a school principal. That's almost like being a priest."

Giving a short nod, Audrey started to speak. "I guess it depends on what you think is a worse sin: committing suicide, or pushing someone to it."

I tried to mask my shock. So did Maddie. But Marty's face was troubled.

"Johnny told me Lawton was just awful to Barb. He cheated. He cut her down. He may have even hit her a time or two. She was miserable in that marriage. She'd get drunk, call Johnny on the phone, and cry. Toward the end, Lawton had just about forgotten those two little kids."

Audrey tapped the cigarette ash, watching it fall. How hard things at home must have been for Trey and Belle.

"When Lawton went on that business trip to Tallahassee, he didn't even bother hiding the fact he was taking his girlfriend. Just about shoved it in Barb's face, Johnny said. That was when Barb had 'the accident,' as everyone calls it. But Johnny never believed it. Neither did her sister. Barb had told both of them many times how she hated her life, hated what she'd become. She told them she was going to end the misery for herself and everyone else."

She took a long drag. The smoke escaped in a cloud.

"That night, she finally did. She threw herself down those steps on purpose. And Lawton, may he burn in hell, pushed her to it."

Audrey dropped her cigarette and ground it into the dirt with her boot.

"Johnny's hated Lawton ever since. And he's hated himself, too. He's always felt like he should have won Barb back. If he had, she'd still be alive."

"And Johnny would be happily married," Maddie pointed out helpfully.

"Yes." Audrey nodded. "I guess he would."

"What I can't figure out," I said, "is if Johnny disliked Lawton so much, why'd he go into business with him?"

"I think Johnny loved his restaurant more than he hated Lawton. He was about to lose it. He needed to pay off his loan. And Lawton had more money than God. Johnny should have known better, of course. You lie down with dogs, you're gonna get fleas. Financially, Lawton took advantage of him. Just like he had when he stole Barb."

My sisters and I were quiet, mulling over what Audrey said. We could hear voices from the food line, growing impatient.

Somebody cracked a whip to pass the time. Audrey stooped to pick up her cigarette butt, and then froze at a bellow from the other side of the trailer.

"Audrey! Where you at, woman? These people are going to start eatin' the plastic plates if we don't get this food out soon."

Her smile was apologetic. "Looks like I'm being paged."

I thought of one last thing we needed to know: "Hey, thanks for lunch yesterday, Audrey. Those sausage sandwiches were great," I said. "But I never saw Johnny. Did you put on the whole spread yourself?"

"Hell, no. Johnny calls himself the Sausage Sultan. He'd never trust me to grill. He did disappear for a while, though. I remember, because that fellow with diabetes needed his artificial sugar to make sweet tea. We couldn't find the packages, and we couldn't find Johnny. Poor guy had to drink his iced tea unsweetened."

"Audrey!" Johnny yelled again. "I better not find you sucking on a cancer stick!"

She took a breath mint from her apron and popped it in her mouth.

"I'm coming, you old crab!" she shouted. "Besides, the way these folks have been shovelin' it in, it won't hurt 'em a bit to wait."

THIRTY-FOUR

The morning air smelled of coffee perking and bacon frying. Mules brayed, one answering the other, as the wagons gathered. Frank Sinatra crooned "The Best Is Yet to Come" as Sal's Caddy rolled into view.

Mama sat in the back seat like the golden car was her personal chariot. Pillows propped up her ankle. Her lemon-hued cowgirl hat outshone the fogged-over sun.

"Mornin' girls," she called from the window. "Hope I'm not too late for pancakes."

The car kept coming, rocking its way across the pasture. People and horses darted out of the way. Maybe Sal mistook the meal trailer for a fast-food drive-thru. I waved my arms at him to stop.

"Stay right there," I yelled. "We'll get your coffees."

Johnny had put out the big serving urns. He knew the campers would wait for food, but they'd storm the trailer if deprived of caffeine. After we got cups for everyone, we joined Mama and Sal.

"We're still waiting for breakfast, Mama," Marty said.

"This fog has set the whole morning schedule back," Maddie added.

Mama sipped her coffee. "Ooooh, Sal, they gave me yours!" She puckered her lips. "There's hardly any sugar in here at all."

He took a swallow from the cup in his hand. "You're right, Rosie. This one could rot false teeth."

They traded cups. Then, Sal lifted camp chairs for us from the Caddy's big trunk. We set in to wait, and he went off to find a fellow New Yorker he'd met at last night's campfire. No doubt they'd discuss how we poor, dumb Southerners couldn't do anything right.

My sisters and I filled in Mama on what we'd learned from Audrey.

"I guess Johnny really did hate Lawton," Mama said after we finished. "I found out what Trey meant, yelling about that fight they'd had. Seems Lawton threatened to call in his loan, which would have put Johnny out of business. That was two days before Lawton died. Everything between them just came to a head."

"How'd you find out?" Maddie asked.

"Well, Trey told Belle about how they'd rolled around in the dirt, fighting. She told Carlos, and he told Sal, who told me." Mama shook her head. "Imagine, girls! At their age."

Marty lowered her voice to a whisper. "Johnny must have been awful mad."

I glanced over my shoulder for eavesdroppers. "Mad enough to commit murder?"

I didn't get an answer. We all just looked at each other over the tops of our coffee cups.

Maddie finally broke the silence. "Well, if Johnny *didn't* kill Lawton, there's no shortage of other suspects."

I nodded. "Starting with Trey. He wouldn't be the first son who couldn't bear living in his father's long shadow."

"No way." Mama's voice was full of conviction. "That boy loved his daddy. You can see it in his eyes."

Maddie said, "The young widow looks most promising to me. Money's a strong motive, and she probably stands to inherit a lot."

Marty cleared her throat, like an apology. "I'm not so sure, Maddie. People with as much money as the Brambles usually have wills and trusts and limited partnerships. They have all kinds of ways to squirrel it away. It's not like Lawton would have had everything in a joint savings account with his and Wynonna's name on it."

We thought on that for a while.

"I wouldn't put anything past that Austin." Mama sipped, looking thoughtful. "She set her cap for Trey and the Bramble family fortune. Maybe she didn't want to wait for nature to take its course with Lawton."

I was more than willing to pile on about Austin. But instead I threw another name into the mix. "What do y'all think about Belle?"

Did I want their opinion because Belle's daddy died, or because Carlos seemed so taken with her?

Maddie snorted. "Belle's too fragile, Mace. She's a weakling. That stepmother of hers could knife her in the heart and then order in lunch. And, remember, Wynonna was the one who insisted Mama should ride Shotgun. She had something up her sleeve, I know it."

Mama said, "Honey, you can't blame Wynonna for those bees."

"That's assuming the bees were an accident, which I'm not sure they were," I said.

We told Mama what Marty saw on Johnny's hand.

"I'm still voting for Wynonna." Maddie pointed her cup at us like a teacher summing up a lesson. "Maybe she found out Lawton was cheating. We already know the man had a history as a hound dog."

Marty said, "And that brings us right back to Johnny Adams' hatred of Lawton."

A far-away look came into Mama's eyes. "Johnny was the sweetest thing when we were all kids. There was one real unpopular boy at our school. He never had clean clothes, or shoes that fit, because his family was so poor. I remember how nice Johnny was to him. One January, when it was real cold, Johnny brought him a coat to wear. He claimed he outgrew it; but anyone could tell it was brand new."

She stared into her coffee like the coat was reflected there.

"It made the rest of us ashamed for how we'd treated that poor child. Girls, I just hate to think a kind person like that could be capable of murder."

I was imagining Johnny's kindness to that unfortunate child a half-century ago, when a voice interrupted my thoughts.

"Sounds like you four detectives have the case nearly solved." Carlos had snuck up behind us, his hand touching just a moment on the small of my back.

"No way," I answered, hoping the others hadn't noticed the gesture.

"No kidding."

He didn't have to agree so readily, I thought.

"What you have so far sounds like idle gossip and speculation. I've warned you about that sort of thing before, Mace."

"Warning received, Investigator Know-it-All."

"Would you like to know what real police work revealed? The kind of police work that utilizes science and evidence?"

"Oh, yes! Do tell." I fluttered my eyelashes in my best Scarlett O'Hara imitation. "We're just a bunch of silly women, hanging on every word from a smart man like you."

Maddie kicked me. Marty stared at the ground. I switched back to my normal voice. "Maybe I should remind you, your 'real' police work last summer sent Mama to the slammer."

"Hush, Mace!" Mama pinched my arm. "Let the poor man talk."

"I just hate to see you wasting your time with stupid theories," Carlos said.

Last night's Carlos was attractive; this morning's version was pure arrogance. Maddie butted in before I could snap at him again. "What do you mean?"

"My friend pulled in a favor and got some quick analysis on that tasting cup Mace has been so interested in," he said. "The results are preliminary, but it's pretty clear. There was nothing in that cup but chili."

I picked at my breakfast in a sulk. My sisters and Mama tried to point out it was good news that Lawton hadn't been poisoned. And of course I knew that. But it irked me to be wrong. And it really irked me that Carlos had come to find me so he could crow about it — especially after our tender session in the woods last night. Maybe I was too sensitive, but did he have to act so superior?

"Are you going to eat that pancake, Mace?" Maddie stuck her fork over my plate and speared a piece of my breakfast before I could answer.

"Thanks for your concern, Maddie."

"Oh, stop being such a baby," she said. "You can't always be right, you know."

"That's right, Mace," Marty said. "Always being right is reserved for Maddie."

"Girls, girls. If we had rooms, I'd send you to them," Mama said. "Look over there, where Carlos is talking to the Brambles. Now, there's some people with some real problems."

Our eyes followed Mama's across the breakfast crowd. She was right, of course. Trey shook his head as Carlos spoke. Belle's face crumpled. Wynonna stood apart from the other two, head down as she listened, hands crammed into the pockets of a tight pair of jeans. Her boots were brown leather today, trimmed in fringe.

Looking around, I realized at least half the crowd was also watching the Brambles. Nothing like living your personal tragedy in public. Feeling petty, I resolved to stop acting like such a jerk. And the resolution lasted as long as it took to see Belle collapse into Carlos's arms, sobbing.

"Uh-oh," Maddie said.

Stroking her hair, he murmured something private into her ear. The bacon and biscuit in my stomach did a double back flip.

"You should go over there, Mace." A worried frown creased Marty's brow.

"Honey, she can't do that now. It would look wrong," Mama whispered.

Belle gazed up into Carlos' face. He ran a thumb across her teary cheek. I remembered the feel of his hand stroking me.

"I'm outta here," I said, pushing my breakfast plate onto Maddie's lap.

"Mace, where . . ." Marty started to say.

"Let her go, honey," Mama interrupted. "She's off to throw some rocks into water."

I picked up a handful of stones and tossed them into the high brush as I walked through the woods. *Swoosh. Swoosh. Swoosh.* It wasn't as satisfying as tossing them in a creek. But I didn't have much time to sit and stew. The fog was lifting. The ride was about to start. And I had to finish getting Val ready.

As I passed another campsite, I overheard two riders with out-of-state license tags on their trailer discussing Lawton's death: "My money's on that son. The boy probably got drunk and did him in."

One handed the other a horse brush. "Nope. There's a gal on the ride who's some kind of detective. She says the father was poisoned. Poison isn't a man's weapon. It's a woman's. Everybody knows that."

I had a momentary urge to update them. But I passed by, keeping my nose out of it.

Val raised her head as I came into our campsite. Her eyes were interested and intelligent; two bright spots in my feeling-sorry-for-myself morning.

"Hey, girl," I nuzzled her neck. "I've done it again. You know what I am, right?"

She rubbed her big head up and down on

my chest.

"That's right. An idiot."

Maddie and Marty had already broken down the tent and packed up our campsite. Before they went to the rescue group's trailer to prepare their borrowed horses, they'd saddled Val for me. She was tethered by her halter to the trailer. I felt a rush of affection for my sisters, and promised myself I'd try to be nicer, even to Maddie.

All that was left for me to do was get Val's bridle from its hook on the trailer.

As I walked around my Jeep, I spotted something white on the driver's seat. I opened the unlocked door and leaned in. On a single sheet of paper, a message was scrawled in childish block letters. I bent close and read:

Dear Mace,

Somebody wants you off this ride because you're on the right track. Lawton Bramble was murdered. Don't stop looking for his killer.

THIRTY-FIVE

I locked the Jeep's door, touching nothing else. I'd swallow my pride and ask Carlos the best way to handle the note without disturbing any possible evidence. That is, if he could tear himself away from Belle long enough to give me an answer.

By the time I finished with the horse and secured the trailer, I could hear riders shouting from the distant pasture. It was time to go. The trail boss would be gathering everyone into a tight line. He'd want us to stay close to safely cross the highway and continue on our way east to the noontime stop we'd make for lunch.

Trotting up on Val, I found my sisters easing their horses into the middle of the crowd.

"Have you seen Carlos?" I asked.

Marty gave Maddie a worried look. Maddie studied the horn on her saddle.

"Carlos went off with the family, Mace,"

Marty finally said.

"His arm was around Belle when they left. I'm sorry, honey." Maddie's kind tone sounded rusty.

I pictured Carlos the Protector taking care of Belle, and knew it was what he was meant to do. Last night had been a mistake; I couldn't compete with Belle's kind of need. I wondered if they'd send me a wedding invitation so I could see her in that size-2 dress.

"I didn't need him for anything personal." I worked to keep the hurt from my voice. "I'm just asking because I need a police officer. Somebody left something in my Jeep."

Maddie's brows shot up. Marty's blue eyes went wide. I told them about the note.

"It'll keep until we can come back for the Jeep at lunchtime," I said. "It's probably somebody playing a prank. Everyone in camp seems to know my suspicions that Lawton didn't die naturally. The news there was nothing nefarious in his cup hasn't caught up."

The Cracker Trail ride made a short detour to Dixie Springs Elementary. A student from the school was saddled up, riding with his cattle-raising father for the day. Like a living Florida history exhibit, father and son were still holding on to the old ways.

School kids lined the playground fence and sat cross-legged on the front lawn. The rancher's nine-year-old son was a jeans-and-boots-wearing copy of his dad, right down to the toothpicks stuck into the bands on each of their hats. He was the youngest in a group of whip-wielding cowpokes putting on a show.

"Do it again, Tyler," a little boy called out, as several girls put their fingers to their ears. "Make it crack again!"

Mama perched in a green wagon being pulled by a pair of little Haflingers. While whips snapped and children fed carrots to the gentlest horses, I ambled over to see how she was doing.

". . . and so that was my third husband," Mama was telling the glazed-eyed driver. "Number 3 was a nice change from No. 2. That one had a roving eye, if you know what I mean. And that wasn't his only fault." She mimed tipping a bottle to her mouth. "I was glad to get rid of him, I'll tell you that. But, anyways, back to Husband No. 3 . . ."

I doubted if the poor driver had gotten in a word since we left Okeechobee County.

"Hey," I called. "Have you heard the latest?"

Gossip, along with butterscotch anything,

is a powerful Mama motivator.

"Hi, darlin'." She introduced me to David, the wagon driver. "The two of us have been having ourselves the nicest chat."

David touched his hat brim and looked at me with desperation in his eyes.

"What's up?" Mama asked.

I told her about the note.

"I knew there was something more to that fella's death." David leaned across Mama to talk to me. "People are saying he was poisoned."

Mama waved a hand. "Oh, that's what Mace thought before. But her ex-boyfriend, who's a police detective, got a friend to test the chili in the cup Lawton was using." She shifted toward me in the seat. "I don't think Carlos would have done you that favor if he didn't still like you, Mace. I just know you two can patch things up, honey. You'll just have to try a little harder, be a little softer with him."

David pulled at his collar, looking as uncomfortable as I felt.

"Not relevant, Mama," I warned.

"Anyways," Mama turned to address David, hauling herself back on track, "Doc ruled Lawton's death a heart attack. There's no formal investigation, so there hasn't been an autopsy. And, now, with the lab tests, it looks like Lawton's chili wasn't poisoned."

I thought about that for a minute. "Well, the chili cup we *found* had no poison."

"Hmmm," Mama said.

"And the note in your Jeep definitely used the word 'murdered'?" David asked.

I nodded.

"Hmmm," he said.

"These fields are going to murder my shocks," Sal grumbled, as we jounced over pastureland torn up by wild hogs.

I rode in the front seat; Carlos was in the back. He'd agreed after lunch to return to camp with me to look at the note.

"Make a left at that clump of palmetto, Sal."

"You have to be more specific, Mace," he said. "It's all just green to me."

"The low-growing shrub with spiky fronds shaped like fans."

"Thank you," Sal said, as he maneuvered the big Caddy into a wide arc to the left.

A wallow the hogs had dug out loomed ahead: a shallow, muddy bowl. "Watch out . . ." I started to say, just before I felt the car take a dip.

"Crap!" Sal's unlit cigar fell from his mouth.

"Don't slow down, Sal!" I yelled. "Just

power on through, and you won't get stuck."

He gunned it, and came out safely on the other side.

"Does anybody know where the closest car wash is?" Sal stared out the windshield at wild land stretching for miles. "Nah, forget the car wash. How far's the nearest bar?"

Carlos leaned over the seat and patted Sal's shoulder. "Hang in there, buddy. Just one more night left on the trail. We'll be in Fort Pierce for the big parade by tomorrow."

"Hallelujah."

I said, "There's my Jeep and trailer, under that slash pine."

Sal looked at me blankly.

"Sorry. Under that tall, lonely tree that looks like a hat rack with green needles and brown hanging things."

He smiled as he eased his Caddy to a stop, parking a distance from my camp.

As we got out of the car, Carlos pulled a plastic bag for evidence from his pocket.

"Thanks for parking outside the perimeter, Sal. I don't want all of us tramping around. Mace, can you remember how you got to your Jeep before?"

I nodded.

"Try to take the same path as much as

you can. I'll follow your footsteps." Looking around the campsite, he frowned. "It's all grass here, though. Not so good for finding footprints, if it comes to that. It'd be better if it were dirt, or mud."

"I know where you can find some of that." Sal smeared at the muck on his fenders with a monogrammed handkerchief.

I moved carefully toward the Jeep, picturing where Val had been standing and what direction I walked to fetch her bridle from the trailer. Carlos followed so closely I could hear him breathing; I smelled his scent. Even without a shower, he smelled good. Musky, with a subtle overlay of the spicy, clove-scented cologne he always wore.

I'd tasted that cologne more than once as I kissed him on the neck. Which was just the kind of memory I wanted to push out of my head.

I was within a few feet of my Jeep when I noticed a slash in the old canvas top. It was cut with surgical precision above the driver-side door. As I got closer, I saw the seat was empty. Somebody had reached in and snatched the note telling me to keep looking for Lawton's killer.

"You'll never believe who stopped by with a gift for you, Mace," Mama said.

My sisters and I were gathered with Mama and Sal at Camp Cadillac. It was late afternoon, an hour or so before sunset, on the final night of the ride.

"Who?"

"Guess," Mama said, ensconced on her pillows in Sal's back seat.

"Mama, please. I'm not in the mood."

I'd had to leave my Jeep and trailer behind. Carlos didn't think it should be moved. If it turned out the stolen note wasn't a prank, there could be evidence on or in the vehicle that might be important. Better to not take any chances, he said.

I'd stowed as much of Val's supplies as I could fit into the trunk of Sal's car. He was a sport about it, even when the sticky horse feed spilled on the golden carpet inside.

"So, who left me a present?" I asked again.

Mama dug into a cooler in Sal's front seat, pulling out a bottle of white wine. "She even left a corkscrew and glasses." She presented two plastic goblets with a flourish. "Sal and I can share."

"Who, Mama?" Maddie and I screeched.

"Austin," Sal answered, fingers in his ears.

Mama gave him a playful slap. "I wanted Mace to guess!"

"Well." Marty examined the bottle. "That's strange."

"Better check the seal to see if it's been tampered with," Maddie said.

"She was really nice, Mace," Mama said. "Austin said you've had a heck of a week. And she still feels bad about that cow whip, honey."

A crack rang out just then, like punctuation. Over the course of the ride, the whips had become a background soundtrack. Novices had learned enough to make the leather snap. Old hands remembered how much fun whip-cracking could be.

Mama continued, "She was at her granny's, so she missed my terrifying ride on Shotgun. I told her how that horse and I were just standing there, as pretty as you please . . ."

"Mama, what else did Austin say?" Marty corralled her back on track.

"Well, she just said she wanted Mace and me to relax and enjoy a nice glass of wine. She even brought ice to keep it cold."

Mama hunted around until she found a cup for Marty. She handed Sal the corkscrew.

"Austin, huh?" Maddie fished out her teetotaler's bottled water from the cooler. "Will wonders never cease."

Sal uncorked the wine, and then poured a bit in each glass. Mama, Marty, and I toasted our wine to Maddie's water. We all sipped. Sal slid his cigar case from his pocket and lit up.

"Mmm-hmm," Mama said. "It's almost as good as one of those raspberry wine coolers."

Sal studied the bottle's label, and took a stab: "Sue-Vig-None Blank."

Maddie, who'd had a semester of college French, corrected him, *"Sauvignon Blanc."*

"Here you go, darlin'." Mama handed Sal her glass. "It sounds better when you say it."

Sal was about to take a swallow when a scream shattered the festive spirit of our little party. We dropped our drinks and ran to the sound, which seemed oddly familiar.

In a wide green pasture, under a sinking sun, Wynonna kneeled on the ground. She shouted over and over for help, her hands pressed to Doc Abel's stomach.

As we came closer, she looked up. Terror filled her eyes and blood stained her hands.

"Please, you've got to save him," she cried. "Somebody shot Doc."

THIRTY-SIX

Doc Abel was alive, but barely, bleeding from a bullet to the gut.

A helicopter was rushed from the hospital in Stuart. It now pounded the air above us. Riders looked to the sky, hands clamped tight over cowboy hats. The sun was almost gone now. Lanterns gleamed in the treeless pasture, marking off a makeshift landing pad. As the chopper descended, a search beam washed the scene in an eerie glow.

"Move back, people," Sal yelled as the crowd shifted, closing in again around Doc. "The medical team will need some room."

When Wynonna screamed, we weren't the only ones who heard her. People came running from all over camp. Cell phone calls to 911 must have lit up the lines at the county sheriff's central dispatch. In the crowd, I saw Austin and Johnny Adams; Trey and his sister, Belle. The big-bottomed cowgirl showed up. So did the two teenagers, their eyes bright orbs. Sal hustled over, right behind my sisters and me. He and Carlos had taken charge until deputies from the Dundee County sheriff's office could arrive at the remote camp.

"I'm a police officer," Carlos kept saying, as he elbowed his way through the jostling mass.

Carlos did what he could for an unconscious Doc. A rider who was a nurse stepped forward to help, checking Doc's vital signs and applying pressure to the gunshot wound. Then, Carlos assigned a few onlookers to help Sal with crowd control. The shooting scene was nearly impossible to secure. People had already trampled all over, beginning with Wynonna in her brown fringed boots.

As quickly as he could, with the rescue helicopter still in flight, Carlos turned his attention to her.

"Did you see who shot him, Wynonna?"

She shook her head, eyes fastened on Doc and the blood leaking from his gut onto the nurse's rolled-up towel. When Wynonna turned her face to Carlos, tears streaked her cheeks.

As she stood, he wrapped his arms around her, drawing her into a tight hug. It looked more like he was checking Wynonna for a weapon than giving her comfort.

"Did Doc say anything?" he asked, stepping away from her.

"I think he was already out of it when I found him." She rubbed a hand over her eyes, unaware Doc's blood now streaked her forehead. "He just moaned and mumbled about being shot. Then, he said something else. It sounded like 'I'm sorry.'"

I glanced at my sisters. Maddie raised an eyebrow. Marty shrugged.

Wynonna was pale, and seemed to be swaying a bit.

"Can somebody find us a chair?" Carlos yelled to the crowd.

Within moments, he had a half dozen to choose from. He took one, faced it away from Doc and the nurse, and helped Wynonna sit down. As he did, he ran his hands from her calves to her ankles, giving the top of each boot a discreet pat. He might have been moving her legs to make her more comfortable. But I'd bet he was ruling out all the places she could have stashed a handgun.

He placed another of the chairs right next to her and sat down "Why don't you tell me in your own words what happened?"

She took in a shuddering breath. Placing

her palms on her knees, she seemed to notice the blood on her hands for the first time. She scrubbed them hard across the fabric of her jeans.

"Wynonna?" Carlos prodded.

Finally, she began to speak in a robotic tone. "I left our RV, and was headed over to the trail boss's campsite. We've set all the arrangements for Lawton's funeral, and I thought maybe Jack would want to make an announcement about it at dinner."

Mama hobbled up to join us, using a hickory branch as a walking stick. Her desire to be in on the activity must have won out over her ankle pain. I leaned over and whispered, "A helicopter's on the way for Doc, who got shot. Carlos is questioning Wynonna, who found him."

"Jesus H. Christ on a crutch," Mama breathed.

"I was crossing the pasture when I saw Doc," Wynonna continued. "I ran to him. When I saw the blood, and how bad he looked, I started yelling for help."

"And no one else was around when you arrived?"

"Carlos, you've already asked me if I know who did it. I don't." Exasperation edged her voice. "When I ran up, Doc was on the ground. A cattle egret was the only other living creature I saw in this pasture."

"Did you hear anything?"

"You mean besides the sound of these stupid Crackers all over camp with their cow whips? No, I didn't."

She covered her eyes with a hand again. "I don't understand who would have wanted to shoot him, you know?"

She turned to stare at Doc, and all of our eyes followed hers. The nurse leaned over him, urging him to hang on.

"Will he be okay?" Wynonna asked Carlos, her voice small and scared.

Just about then, the *chop-chop-chop* of the helicopter sounded in the distance.

Carlos looked up with the rest of the crowd. "They'll do what they can."

Dundee County sheriff's deputies circulated through the camp, looking for a weapon, and for witnesses who might help explain the events leading up to Doc's shooting. So far, they hadn't found anyone who knew anything. Except for Wynonna, that is.

Carlos pulled me aside and asked me to take her back to her camp and keep her there while he briefed the local authorities. My sisters and Mama came with us.

The inside of the Brambles' RV was all expensive-looking dark wood. The plush carpet was hunter green. The living area featured leather furniture and a flat-screen TV. The sink in the galley was porcelain.

"Can I get y'all something to drink? How 'bout coffee?" Wynonna asked, pulling out cups from an oak cabinet in the galley.

"Hot chocolate?" Maddie asked hopefully.

Mama punched her thigh. "Whatever you have is fine, Wynonna," she said pointedly.

When the coffee was made, Wynonna started to pour the first cup. Her hand shook so much she spilled it on the countertop. Maddie grabbed a paper towel. Marty took the pot when Wynonna set it down.

"Why don't you have a seat?" Marty said. "We'll get this."

As Marty poured and Maddie mopped, I got up and opened the small 'fridge, looking for half-and-half. The only thing inside was a couple of shriveled apples and a chilled bottle of Champagne. French. I wondered about the special occasion it was intended to celebrate.

Rustling around in the galley, I found sugar, powdered creamer, and a spoon. I put out an open bag of chocolate chip cookies. Marty got up and arranged them prettily on a plate. Maddie scarfed down the first one before we even sat down again.

"Thanks," Wynonna said, looking at us gratefully. "I guess I'm in a pretty bad state."

"Not without reason," I said. "You suffered a terrible loss; and now you're the one who finds Doc. You've handled yourself better than many people could."

Marty took a bird-like nibble of a cookie. "I think I'd be in the hospital if all of that happened to me."

Mama said, "No, you wouldn't, Marty. The Lord always gives us the strength we need."

Looking at Wynonna, who seemed ten years older than she had just a few days ago, I wondered if the Man upstairs had shorted her on that ration of strength.

"Honey, I sure do hate to bother you." Mama shifted to stretch her leg. "But do you mind if I use that little throw pillow to prop up my foot? The one that says *When Things Get Tough, the Tough Go Shopping*?"

Wynonna said, "I'm so sorry, Rosalee! I plumb forgot about your ankle!"

I truly hoped that with Doc Abel underway to the hospital, Mama wouldn't launch into a dissertation about her sprain.

"Oh, it's fine, honey," she said, with a wave.

I let out a sigh of relief. Too soon.

"It's just throbbing a little with all this

walking around. Doc Abel warned me to stay off it."

At the mention of Doc's name, Mama went quiet along with the rest of us.

"I know he'll be all right," Marty finally said, patting Wynonna's hand. "Those air ambulances are something. And, they can do amazing things in emergency rooms these days."

Wynonna smiled shakily at Marty, and then turned to Mama.

"I do feel awful about what happened with Shotgun, Rosalee."

"I know you do, honey. And Belle came by to say the same."

"It's sure strange y'all ran into the one thing that poor horse can't abide," Wynonna said.

My brain sent a signal to the hairs on my neck.

"What do you mean?" I asked.

"I thought Shotgun was the greatest horse in the world," Maddie said.

"Well, he is, except for a fear of bees. When he was a colt, he knocked over a beekeeper's hive in the pasture. He got stung all over. Most horses don't like bees. But with Shotgun, it's a real terror. The creatures make him act pure crazy. Didn't Belle mention that?"

My sisters and I stared at Mama, who stared right back.

"No, ma'am," she said to Wynonna. "Belle surely did not mention that."

THIRTY-SEVEN

A hard knock rattled the RV's door.

Wynonna shook her head and whispered, "I can't see anybody right now. Tell them I'm resting, or I've gone to bed. Just tell them to go away."

All four of them looked at me, waiting. I got up and opened the door a crack. A big man in sheriff's department green and a light-colored felt Western hat filled every inch of the frame.

"I'm sorry, Ms. Bramble's had a terrible shock," I said to him. "Would you mind coming back later?"

"Yes, I would." Unsmiling, he shifted a toothpick to one corner of his mouth. "Tell her Sheriff Roberts wants to talk to her." He rose onto the doorstep, and the RV rocked with his weight.

"She's not dressed," I said quickly, closing the door a fraction of an inch.

"I'll wait." He stepped back to the ground

and crossed his arms over his chest. The toothpick seemed to migrate on its own to the opposite corner of his mouth.

I pulled the door closed, and turned to shrug at Wynonna.

She stood up, smoothed her hair, and tucked her cowgirl shirt at her tiny waist.

"Go ahead and let him in, Mace," she said. "Though the last thing I want to do right now is describe how I found Doc, you know? The sight of that blood and that poor man trying to speak is going to haunt my nightmares."

She stood up straight as I swung open the door. When the lawman came in, the spacious RV suddenly seemed tiny.

"Sheriff Roberts." She offered him her hand. "Would you like a cup of coffee?"

He shook his head and looked around. His gaze rested first on Maddie, then Marty, then Mama, then me. It made me nervous to have him looking at me so intently, even though I knew I hadn't done a single thing wrong.

"Which one of you is her lawyer?"

Wynonna's face went a shade more pale. "Do I need a lawyer?"

"No, ma'am. I only want to ask you a few questions. But I know how rich people are. You folks come prepared."

She slit her eyes at him. I saw a trace of the haughty Wynonna I'd seen that first night at Lawton's cook site. "I can assure you," she said, "I was not prepared to stumble upon a man who was my husband's doctor and a close family friend bleeding to death on the ground. Now, Sheriff, if you'd like to sit down, I'll tell you whatever I can."

His eyes showed the tiniest flicker of . . . what? Respect? Intimidation? Anger? I couldn't be sure. The glimpse of emotion was gone almost before it registered.

"I'm sorry, ladies," he said to us, sounding not at all sorry. "Y'all are uninvolved parties. I'm gonna have to ask you to leave." The toothpick bobbed as he talked. "We're investigating an attempted murder. It wouldn't be right for you to be here when I talk to Ms. Bramble."

I was relieved when he said attempted murder. Doc was still alive. At least for now.

Maddie and I each hooked an arm around Mama's waist, nearly carrying her from the RV to Camp Caddy. Marty followed, holding a paper plate with the rest of Wynonna's cookies.

When Sal saw us limp into view, the relief on his face was evident, even by lantern light.

"I was about to call in the search dogs," he said. "Where the hell have you four been?"

We told him all about Wynonna, and how shaken she'd been. We felt sorry for her, the way Sheriff Roberts seemed to attack her, so soon after she'd lost her husband. He'd hustled us out of the RV before we had a chance to ask her anything else about Shotgun's history with bees. That was definitely a line of questioning I wanted to follow up with Belle.

Sal upended my bottle of wine over one of the plastic goblets. One drop dribbled out.

"Well, there wasn't much left anyway." He looked at us guiltily. "And I sat here all alone for a long time."

"I thought you were helping with the investigation," I said, fishing a beer from Sal's cooler.

"Nah. I'll let Carlos fight it out with the locals. He and that sheriff have already butted heads. Let's just say the Dundee County boys aren't eager for outside help."

I could picture it: Carlos, with his Miami manners and know-it-all attitude, would have started off on the wrong foot with the countrified, toothpick-chawin' Sheriff Roberts. Then, the pair of them would keep rubbing each other wrong, like a wet sock over a blister. I wondered if they'd started rolling in the dirt yet, like Lawton and Johnny?

A gasp from Maddie brought me back to Camp Cadillac.

"Look lively, Mace," she whispered. "You are not going to believe who is sashaying her way into Mama's camp."

I turned to see Austin, wearing a nervous smile and carrying a second bottle of wine. If nothing else, the wine was welcome.

"You're not going to throw anything at me, are you, Mace?" She held out the wine like a shield.

"If I recall, you're the one with the killer aim, Austin."

"Be nice, Mace," Mama said, grabbing the bottle and handing it to me. "The girl has gone out of her way to make up."

I mumbled something that might have been "thank-you" or "screw-you."

"You're welcome," Austin said, choosing to believe it was the former.

Uninvited, she settled herself into one of our camp chairs. "Now." She leaned toward me, eyes burning with curiosity. "I've been hearing all about how you're some kind of amateur detective. Who do you think shot Doc Abel?"

"We haven't had a chance to discuss it

yet," Marty said, sounding snippier than I'd ever heard her. "We keep getting interrupted."

Meow!

"Well, I have a theory I've been working on." Austin plowed ahead, paying no heed to Marty's insult. "Do you want to hear it?"

"Why not?" I shrugged.

"I think Wynonna killed her husband. Doc found out; and she tried to kill him to keep him quiet." Austin beamed like a student awaiting a gold star.

"Do you have any evidence to support that?" I sounded like Carlos.

She smoothed her hair. "Woman's intuition."

Maddie snorted.

"That and a buck will get you a cup of coffee at the courthouse," Sal said.

I lifted myself from my chair. "As much as I'd like to sit around and chat, I need to check on my horse. Thanks for the wine, Austin. See you around."

She jumped up. "I'll come with you, Mace. We can talk about the case."

Maddie rolled her eyes. Marty giggled behind her hand. Mama said, "That's nice, honey. Mace could use a girlfriend."

"I've got two sisters and you, Mama. I don't need any more women in my life."

"Amen to that," Sal said.

I stalked out of the camp. Austin trailed behind me like a puppy dog.

"How'd you start solving cases, Mace?" she asked, as we picked our way through the pasture with flashlights.

"I've only solved one. And, so far, my record's not so good on this one." I shone the light ahead. "Watch that big cow paddy, Austin. It's wet."

"Thanks." She sidestepped. "But, I mean, how do you do it? How do you find the clues and everything?"

"You have to start by being quiet. You have to look and listen. You can't observe anything when you're always jumping up, getting mad and running your mouth."

She was silent behind me. I thought maybe the hint had sunk in. No such luck.

"People tell me I'm observant," Austin continued. "Maybe I could help you get some evidence against Wynonna."

"What's the deal with you and Wynonna?" I asked. "Why do you hate her so much?"

"Aside from the fact she married Trey's daddy for his money and she thinks her shit don't stink?"

I let that go unanswered. We were coming up to the scene of Doc's shooting. Sheriff Roberts must have finished with Wynonna, because there he was, arguing with Carlos. The sheriff's arms were crossed, resting on his big belly. Their faces were inches from one another. Carlos wasn't yelling. But I knew that quiet, clenched-jaw tone. I'd rather have the yelling.

I wanted to know what was going on, but I wasn't about to wander into the charged space between the two men. Even the sheriff's deputies were giving them a wide berth. Plus, if I went over with Austin, she'd surely make some kind of silly scene. So far, Little Ms. Observant hadn't even noticed the former Miami detective and the Dundee County Sheriff, knocking antlers like two bucks in mating season.

"Why don't we stop by Wynonna's, see how she's doing?" I made a quick U-turn before the crime scene. "Maybe you can ask her a few questions."

"Well, sure," Austin said, sounding surprised.

As we got closer to the Bramble campsite, I heard the murmur of voices. One man, one woman. The woman's tone was pleading, though I couldn't make out the words. I put up a hand to stop Austin behind me, and turned with my finger to my lips.

"Quiet," I whispered. "There's something going on."

I pointed to my ear, and then to my eye. Listen. Look.

She nodded, catching on quickly for once.

We turned off our flashlights and crept toward the campsite, approaching from the rear. An outside light on the RV helped us find our way. We hid in the shadows of the Brambles' stock trailer, peering at the campsite through the trailer's metal slats.

Trey was on the bottom step to the RV, with his back to Wynonna. She was just outside the door, tugging at his shirt, trying to turn him toward her. He had a beer bottle in his hand.

"I told you no, Wynonna."

"Please." She wiped at the tears on her face. "I can't help it, Trey."

"It's wrong. Daddy's not even in the ground."

Her voice deepened, turned seductive. "You know you want it as bad as me. We're both hurting, Trey."

Austin's breath quickened. She took a step toward the RV. I clamped a hand on her arm and shook my head forcefully.

"Listen," I whispered. "Clues."

She nodded, her eyes boring holes into Wynonna and Trey.

His shoulders slumped. He hung his head. Dropping the beer on the ground, he slowly turned to Wynonna. She took a step toward him. He reached out and ran his hands lightly over her breasts. The moan that escaped his lips seemed to come more from pain than desire.

Wynonna grabbed Trey's wrists and pressed his hands more tightly to her. Then she dropped her hands to his belt buckle, pulling his body close.

"C'mon, Trey." She put her lips to his, grinding against him. "Let's go inside."

When the door of the RV closed, I whispered, "Now, that's the kind of thing you see when you look and listen."

I got no response.

"Austin?"

She stared at the door, her eyes dark with fury. She pounded her flashlight against her palm, so hard I feared she'd break the lens and cut herself. Her whole being seemed focused on what was going on inside that RV. I edged away several steps. Waves of rage were rolling off Austin's body, and I didn't want to get drowned.

THIRTY-EIGHT

Whispered murmurs followed me through the crowd at the dinner site. I had the distinct feeling people were talking about me. Then again, Doc had been shot less than two hours earlier. A medevac helicopter swooped in like something out of a movie and plucked him, wounded and bleeding, from our midst. Who was I to think the conversation centered on me?

"Excuse me, Mace?" The big cowgirl put a hand on my arm to stop me. She glanced over her shoulder, seeking support from her friend with the tight curls. "People are starting to get nervous about being on this ride. We were wondering if you'd found out yet who shot Doc?"

I looked at her like she was crazy. "I have no idea. The place is crawling with cops. Why don't you ask one of them?"

"Well, the deputies are busy." She fiddled with a braid. "We heard about that note you got telling you Lawton Bramble was murdered. Everyone says you've solved a lot of murders."

I was about ready to *commit* a murder. This gossip was getting out of hand. I was certain that, somehow, Mama was behind it. I scanned the crowd, trying to spot her lemon-colored hat.

"I don't know any more than the next person about what happened," I told the cowgirl.

"So you don't know who did it?"

"Not a clue."

She turned to shake her head at her friend and who knows how many other people looking on from the crowd.

"Well, I think I know what happened," she said, turning back to me.

Of course you do, I thought.

"I think that cook, Johnny, did it. He owed Lawton a lot of money, so he killed him. But then Doc Abel saw Johnny do it, and planned to blackmail him. He had to shoot Doc."

"That sounds like a really good theory," I said. "You should share it with Detective Martinez. That's Carlos Martinez, from Miami. He's riding the big black thoroughbred."

Puffing out her chest, she strutted away.

With any luck, she'd find Carlos and the sheriff together, and regale both of them with her take on events.

Seeing Maddie and Marty in the crowd, I crossed the dinner site to join them.

"Where'd you lose your new best friend, Austin?" Maddie asked.

"You don't want to know," I said. "What's the deal with this big crowd of riders? Is Johnny getting dinner ready early?"

"No, despite the fact that a few of us are starving," Maddie grumbled. "Trail boss called a meeting."

"I'm sure Doc would feel awful if he knew that him getting shot meant you'd be forced to wait on dinner, Maddie," Marty said.

"Sisters, sisters." I took up Marty's usual refrain. "You can fight later. You'll never believe what I just saw over at the Brambles' RV."

Just then, the crowd started jostling and shushing, making a path for Jack Hollister. He climbed onto the open gate of a pickup truck and cleared his throat a couple of times.

"I'll bet he's going to announce that the Brambles scheduled Lawton's funeral services," Maddie whispered.

"He's probably going to say he's had enough," I said under my breath. "I've already seen a few folks packing up to leave. Jack's about to hand the boss's reins back to David Reed."

Marty clutched at my hand. "What if he says Doc Abel died?"

When Jack said Doc was still hanging on, applause rippled through the crowd. A chorus arose of *thank Gods.* As he announced Lawton's funeral, a week from Wednesday, people stirred. Then Jack said something that surprised some.

"We'll be riding out in the morning." He looked to his right, where Sheriff Roberts stood. The lawman nodded, toothpick bobbing. "We've got well over a hundred horses and almost two hundred people on a schedule here. All of downtown Fort Pierce is geared up for a big parade tomorrow. The food booths and craft shows and tents are already up at the city's waterfront. Everything's ready for the Cracker Trail celebration."

Jack glanced to his left. When he saw Carlos, hurling visual daggers, he quickly looked away.

"Now, many of you have said you want to finish. And this is the sheriff's decision to make." Jack paused for effect. "He says we can go ahead, so, that's what we're gonna do. In the meantime, I know him and his deputies will appreciate any information about the shooting. Anybody who plans on leaving the ride early . . ."

Jack gazed out at the crowd. A mom with two young kids nodded forcefully while a girly looking guy tugged at his hat and stared at his boots.

"That's fine. You'll just have to check in with the sheriff before you go. They'll be doing interviews all night long in my trailer. I'll apologize in advance for any of you who might lose some sleep tonight. But these questions are important to help find out who shot Doc."

Sheriff Roberts gave Jack a curt nod.

"Okay, then. Johnny will have dinner ready in an hour or so. And . . ." Jack's voice petered out. He rubbed his chin, like he was thinking of what to say next.

"How about a prayer for Doc?" someone yelled.

"Good idea," Jack said. "Let's all bow our heads and ask the good Lord to guide those doctors and nurses in doing what's best for Doc."

As we lowered our heads and closed our eyes, I wondered how many others would add my own silent plea: *Let us make it safely to the end of the trail in Fort Pierce.*

After Jack finished and climbed off the

truck, I caught up with Carlos. A bad mood had settled on him like a fog.

"You don't look happy," I said.

"That Dundee County idiot is compromising his own investigation," he hissed.

"Why don't you say it a little louder?" I said. "I don't think you've managed to piss off *all* of local law enforcement."

"Have you seen the crime scene, Mace? They didn't even have the tape up until a half-hour ago."

I thought about the note, telling me I was on the right track. I didn't suppose this was the time to remind Carlos that if anyone had listened to me about Lawton Bramble's death being suspicious, that maybe we wouldn't *have* a second crime scene.

"Well, they're doing interviews. That's a good sign, right?" I asked.

"Yeah, right," he smirked. "I'm sure those bumbling Barney Fifes are crack interrogators."

Now I was starting to get irritated. I rose to the defense of my country cousins.

"You know, Mr. Miami Big Shot, just because they're in a rural area doesn't mean they're idiots. I'm sure the Dundee County sheriff's office solves plenty of crimes."

"Hah!" he said. "Cattle rustling? Or maybe crop stealing? We handled more serious crime in Miami before lunch than they do all year."

"I'm rolling my eyes, in case you want to know," I said. "A high crime rate in your community is hardly something to brag about, Carlos. And I'd think *you* would know that better than anyone."

As soon as the words were out of my mouth, I wished I could take them back. He looked like I'd slapped him.

"I can't believe you'd bring that up, Mace." Pain laced his voice. "I told you in confidence about what happened to my wife."

"I'm so sorry, Carlos." I put a hand on his arm; he shook it off. "I didn't even know what I was saying. You made me mad by implying that all of us north of Lake Okeechobee are dumb rednecks."

"Well, if the shit-kicker's boot fits —"

I bit back an insulting retort. No sense in making things worse. I'd already taken our tiff as low as I could by bringing up the tragedy that had sent Carlos packing for Himmarshee in the first place.

"Listen, I don't want to fight with you," I said.

He looked at me, his eyes full of hurt and anger.

"Yet that's all we seem to do whenever we

see each other." He took a deep breath. "So, what that says to me is maybe we shouldn't see each other anymore."

I felt like he'd punched me. Tears gathered behind my eyes. I blinked and swallowed and willed them not to fall.

"Fine," I finally said, grateful when my voice didn't crack. "If that's what you want."

"I think it is."

Carlos reached over and gently brushed a bit of hair from my eyes. I could see him all too clearly as he turned and walked away.

THIRTY-NINE

My heart was in my stomach, and my stomach was in my throat. I felt like I'd come down with the flu, and then got hit by a train. I'd thought I was over Carlos before he showed up on the Cracker Trail; but it turned out he could still put a lot of hurtin' on me.

I wandered over to the bright lights of the dinner site, thinking maybe there would be a soda or some hot tea to help settle my stomach. The first person I saw there was Trey. He'd stuck a nearly empty beer bottle in the back pocket of his jeans. Now, he was helping himself to the coffee Johnny had put out before dinner.

Watching him, I felt a blush creeping up my face. I wished I hadn't seen what I saw between him and Wynonna at the RV. But as long as I had, I wanted to know: What the heck was up with that?

Trey swayed a little as he reached for the

sugar. I could smell the booze on him. Drowning his guilt, no doubt.

"Hey, Trey." I came up next to him. "How you doin'?"

His eyes were bloodshot. His clothes were rumpled. He needed a shave. Trey looked like thirty miles of bad road.

"Mace," he said, barely moving his lips.

"Looks like you can use that coffee."

He nodded, and winced from the motion.

"I'm sorry to see you drinking again."

"Me, too."

"You want to have a seat and talk about it?"

"Not really."

"Well, I do. And this isn't the kind of conversation you're going to want overheard."

I led him to an out-of-the-way, dimly lit spot. He carefully placed his coffee cup on the grass. Reaching around, he extracted the beer bottle from his back pocket and dropped it on the ground. We sat, propping our backs against a big rock.

When we were settled, I said, "Austin and I happened to be on our way a little earlier tonight to see Wynonna. We saw her, Trey. With you."

I had to admire his control. Even half-drunk, his only reaction was a twitch in his jaw.

"So? We're burying Daddy next week. Wynonna and I have a lot of details to discuss."

"You weren't discussing much. You were on the steps to the RV, and you had your hands all over each other. Then she tugged you inside by your belt and shut the door. Was that when y'all started talking about your daddy's funeral?"

He flinched.

"I gotta say, it doesn't look good, Trey. I have to tell the sheriff what I saw."

His mouth got hard. "What business is it of his? Or of yours? My troubles with Wynonna don't have nuthin' to do with Doc getting shot."

"That could be true. But the two of you carrying on could have an awful lot to do with Lawton's death. And if it turns out your daddy was murdered, and Doc was shot because he knew it, then that is very much the sheriff's business."

Trey looked at me blearily. "Didn't your detective friend find out there was nothing in that chili cup that could have killed Daddy?"

"Yes, but that doesn't mean he wasn't murdered." I started to tell him about the note in my Jeep, but, for some reason, I changed my mind. "There are still questions about his death," I said, "especially given everything that's happened since."

Trey dropped his head into his hands. He sat that way, rubbing at his temples, for what seemed like a long time. Finally, he looked up. Every emotion he was feeling showed in his eyes: Grief. Confusion. Guilt. I almost felt sorry for him, until I got a mental memory of his hands exploring Wynonna's breasts.

"Mace, I swear to you, I swear on my sister's life, I didn't kill Daddy. I loved that man. Which is all the more reason why I hated . . . hate . . . Wynonna. She's been coming on to me for months, and she's just relentless. Whenever we were alone, she'd be touching me, rubbing on me, throwing herself at me."

He took a swallow of his coffee. He didn't touch the beer.

"But I *never* did a thing with her while Daddy was alive," he continued. "Tonight was the first time I gave in. I'd been drinking, and I'm weak, Mace. Daddy always said it, and it's true. I'm weak. I thought it would make me feel better, just to hold someone in my arms. Just to have someone hold me. But that somebody was Wynonna, so it only made me feel worse."

He touched a thumb to the corner of his eye. It came away wet.

"When I rolled off her tonight, all I felt was shame."

Now, unfortunately, I had another mental image to add to his hands groping her.

"What do you plan to do now, Trey?"

"She's the devil, Mace. I've gotta stay away from her. I thought maybe you could help me do that. I like you. A lot. I thought there was something between us, but I can see you're hung up on that Miamuh hot-shot."

Not any more, I thought.

"It will just kill Belle when she finds out what I did with Wynonna. Can you wait to tell the sheriff until after I've told my sister? You know how word travels."

I contemplated that. I guess I owed him that much. And, knowing how fragile Belle was, I thought it would be best if she heard bad news from her brother instead of from some gossipy Cracker Trail camper.

"Yeah," I finally answered. "I'll do that. But you better make it fast, Trey."

"I will, I promise. But I sure don't look forward to it. Belle's gonna be so disappointed in me. And she'll hate Wynonna, of course, even more than she does now.

Wynonna was too smart to ever let Belle catch her chasing me. If she had, Belle surely would have told Daddy."

He sipped his coffee, probably cold by now.

"That's how close the two of them were. Much closer than Daddy and me. And I didn't mind, because I love my sister. She worshipped our daddy, and Belle was his favorite. It didn't matter that she was adopted."

My surprise must have registered on my face because Trey stopped to look at me.

"Yeah, not too many people know that," he said. "She was just an itty bitty baby when they brought her home. I was only three, a little past being a baby myself. All I remember is my parents walking in the door with this tiny, living doll. They'd wrapped her in a pink blanket, with bunnies."

"Did Belle grow up knowing?"

"Not until she was ten years old. I didn't know either, really. Daddy sat us both down on her tenth birthday. He gave us a speech, about how he and Mama loved Belle so much that they chose to have her join our family. He didn't say much about where she came from or how they got her."

"Weren't you curious?"

"Belle was, but I wasn't. As far as I was

concerned, she *was* my sister. She'd been part of the family, part of me, for as long as I could remember. She was just Belle." He stopped talking, his eyes grew distant.

"What?"

"I was just thinking about her as a little girl. After she found out she was adopted, she had a lot of questions about where she came from. But you learned with Daddy, there were certain things he didn't talk about. When Belle was younger, she tried prying out the details. As she got older, she finally accepted it and quit asking."

We were quiet for a few moments. A generator hummed at the cook site. A bobcat screeched in the distant woods. I thought of my feelings for my sisters, and of Mama's overwhelming — sometimes overbearing — love for all of us.

"Did Belle feel loved?" I asked.

"Hell, yes," Trey said. "Daddy always said he couldn't have loved her more if she was his flesh and blood. They paid all kinds of money for her to go to fancy boarding schools. Like I told you, she was his favorite. Belle could do no wrong."

I heard a trace of jealousy in Trey's voice. He'd probably deny it up and down. But it's funny how those patterns set in childhood run through the rest of your life. I wondered if Belle saw their childhood the same way he did?

I watched him in the light spilling over from the cook site. He was lost in thought. Or maybe he was still a little drunk. I guess I'm a sucker for anything wounded or hurting. I'd worried about Lawton's poor dog, Tuck. And now I felt sorry for Trey. Drunk. Hating himself for Wynonna. Failing to live up to Lawton's name.

I laid my hand between his shoulders, and gave his back a reassuring rub. I figured he could use a friend. I saw him as he was. And I wanted nothing to do with that, beyond offering simple human comfort. I swear that was the only thought in my mind.

But just before I could say, "Don't worry, Trey, everything will turn out," he turned and kissed me full on the lips. First I was surprised. Then I was turned off by the sour-beer smell of his breath. I'd just started to pull away when I heard a shriek of rage.

Austin was on us before we could react. She grabbed the bottle Trey had dropped, and smashed it against the rock where we leaned. Shards of glass spattered the ground like tiny hailstones.

"You bastard," she hissed at Trey, her mouth twisted with rage. "I hate you!"

Then she turned the jagged neck on me.

Her first pass came so close to my cheek I smelled the warm beer on the broken bottle.

And, suddenly, I knew how Trey had gotten the nasty gash we saw on his face that first night at the Bramble ranch house.

FORTY

I leapt to my feet. Austin moved with me, thrusting the broken bottle in my face.

"Back off, Austin!" Trey stumbled over the big rock as he tried to grab his ex-girlfriend's arm.

This was just what I didn't need: a jealous woman with a jagged bottle and anger issues, and a rescuer who was too soused to save me. I raised a shout of my own.

"Hey, a little help over here!" I called out to whoever might be close. "Trouble over here!"

A jumble of voices and movement arose from the dinner site. Austin looked over her shoulder, and then quickly back at me. She lowered the bottle a fraction of an inch.

"Put it down. You don't want to hurt me." I heard the tremble in my voice. I'm not vain, but I've gotten kind of used to the way my face looks without scars.

"There'll be witnesses." Trey spat the

words at his ex. "Everyone will know you're out of control."

Anger sparked again in her eyes.

"I'm not out of control," she hissed, jabbing the broken glass toward me. I reared back my head, and felt a whoosh of air as the bottle just missed slicing my nose.

"Stop it, Austin." A woman spoke behind me in a calm, steady voice. "Why don't you give me that bottle?"

"Go away, Belle. This doesn't concern you." Austin's eyes never left mine.

"Well, it concerns me," came a familiar voice, accustomed to authority. "That's *my* sister you're messing with."

Maddie.

"Oh, honey, nothing's worth getting yourself into this kind of trouble over. Give us the bottle."

Marty.

"Yeah, give it up," said a voice I didn't recognize.

I saw Austin's eyes flicker behind me, to where Belle and my sisters stood, along with an apparently growing crowd. People rustled closer, moving toward us through the grass. A new voice joined the chorus.

"I know criminals, Austin, and you're no criminal. Besides, I don't think a pretty girl like you really wants to go to jail." Carlos chuckled softly, and he switched to Spanish. "*Dámelo, niña*. Give it to me."

At that, Austin lowered the bottle to her side. She shrugged at me a little, like she was embarrassed, whispering, "I'm sorry, Mace. I don't know what gets into me. I really didn't want to hurt you. I just wanted to scare you."

Mission accomplished, I thought, my heart still pounding.

"Besides," she leaned in close, "Trey's the asshole, not you. I should have gone after him."

"Again?" I asked.

Austin didn't answer, just gave me a hard-to-read smile.

"Okay, okay," she said, raising her voice to the advancing crowd. "Show's over. Nobody's hurt." She carefully laid the jagged bottle into Carlos' outstretched palm. "I'll just be on my way."

"Not so fast," Carlos said, no chuckle in his voice now. "You know, just threatening Mace with that bottle is assault. All she has to say is she was in fear of bodily harm, and we can get one of the local deputies over here to arrest you."

Now Austin was the one who looked scared.

"Please, Mace." She put a hand on my

arm. "My grandmother's sick. I'm the one who's been taking care of her. It'll just kill her if I get into that kind of trouble."

I wanted to say she should have thought of that before she started swinging a broken beer bottle. But then I looked at Austin's face. She seemed stricken, sorry. I remembered how nutty Mama had acted when Husband No. 2 cheated on her — following his car, calling up her rival, smashing a piece of butterscotch pie into his face at Gladys' Diner. Jealous women do crazy things.

"Well, Mace?" Carlos said. "Do you want to press charges?"

The whole crowd was hushed, expectant, awaiting my answer.

"No." I heard Austin exhale. "No harm done. Let's just move on."

She put her mouth close to my ear. "Thanks, Mace. I won't forget it; I owe you one."

Belle had initially seemed so calm when I was in danger, but now she was a mess. With her arms wrapped around her knees, she was sitting on the big boulder, crying and rocking to and fro. Carlos crouched next to her, patting her shoulder and murmuring words no doubt meant to be reassuring.

My sisters and I stood a distance away,

conferring. "You're the one he should be comforting, Mace," Maddie sniffed. "Can't you act a little more upset?"

Marty chewed on her lip, nodding in agreement.

"You two know me better than that," I said. "What am I going to do? Throw up my hands and start sobbing? Besides, it's all over now. Austin's long gone. I'd look ridiculous."

"Belle doesn't look ridiculous. She looks sweet and fragile," Maddie said.

"And needy," Marty chimed in.

We were the only ones left in the clearing. The crowd had dispersed. Once Austin knew she was off the hook, she'd high-tailed it out of camp. Trey took off after her, and that was the last we'd seen of him. As far as I was concerned, those two deserved one another. Some couples feed on drama. They were probably off somewhere, having hot, make-up sex.

At the thought of sex, I focused again on Carlos and Belle. An image ran through my mind of the times he and I had made love. Soft caresses. Soulful kisses. Hot, but very sweet. And then, in my fantasy, Belle's body took the place of mine. Her hips moved under him; her mouth pressed against his. I felt a pain in my gut like a horse kick. In that instant, I knew I wasn't giving up. I wanted Carlos back, and I was ready to fight for him.

I strode toward them over the pasture, hard stobs folding like paper under my boots. My sisters rushed to keep up. When I arrived beside the big rock, I plopped myself down as if I belonged there. My sisters followed my lead.

"Well, that was close with Austin, huh?" I said. "I'm really glad all of you arrived in the nick of time."

"You probably could have taken her, Mace. You're about twice Austin's size," Carlos said.

This was going to be harder than I thought.

"No, no . . . I was really scared." I added a shudder for good measure. "Belle, you seemed very brave when you ordered her to hand over that bottle."

"Very brave," Marty echoed.

Maddie slapped her on the back. "We were proud of you, Belle."

I thought we might be pouring it on too thick, until Belle raised hopeful eyes.

"Were you?" she asked. "I was trying to help Mace."

"And I appreciate it," I said. "So, why are

you so upset now? I'm fine. Everybody's fine."

Belle wiped at her teary cheeks. "After it was over, I just started thinking about all the terrible things that have happened, and I got so sad. Daddy dying, Doc getting shot, my brother caught up with that awful woman."

For a moment I wondered if she meant Wynonna.

"Austin is so bad for Trey; and he really needs somebody good right now." Belle looked at Carlos. "We both do."

I wasn't about to let her go there.

"I can think of a few other bad things that have happened," I said. "Marty almost got bitten by a rattlesnake. I nearly got flattened by a truck hauling oranges. And the horse you trained went nuts and almost killed Mama."

Belle waited a beat. "I feel so awful about Shotgun, Mace. How's your mama's ankle? Any better? I know Doc told her to stay off it."

When she mentioned Doc's name, Belle started sniffling again.

"See?" She gulped back a sob. "I can't stop thinking about poor Doc. Do you think he's going to make it?"

Carlos said, "They're doing everything

they can."

To me, it sounded reflexive, like it was something he'd said to friends and families of a hundred crime victims in Miami. But the words seemed to cheer Belle. Marty placed a gentle hand on her arm, and then went in for the kill.

"You know, Belle, we heard something strange from Wynonna. She told us you knew Shotgun was terrified of bees. Why didn't you say anything about that after he ran away with Mama?"

Belle furrowed her brow in confusion. "Of course I knew he hated bees. All of us did. What's that got to do with anything?"

"That's what set him off," Maddie said. "Bees."

A look of surprise raced across Belle's face. Then, realization.

"No one said a word to me about bees." Her voice rose in anger. "I had no idea that's why Shotgun took off with your mama."

"Oh, sure," I interrupted. "Mama's told her bee story to everyone in camp, most of them twice, and you hadn't heard word one about it?" My tone was sharp, just as I intended it to be.

Carlos put up his hands like a referee. "Wait a minute, Mace. Let Belle finish."

"Yes, Mace, why don't you shut your mouth and listen?" Belle displayed a trace of that Bramble family haughtiness. "That way, I could tell you this is the first I've heard of your mama and bees. Rosalee didn't mention it when I stopped by to apologize. And people haven't really been coming up to me to share the latest gossip. I guess that happens when someone has suffered the loss of a loved one."

My sisters glanced at me.

"No one knows what to say," Belle continued, "so they say nothing. Except for some sympathetic words and a lot of staring, everyone on the trail has been staying away from Trey and me. People act like we're carrying the plague."

Marty bit her lip, looking guilty.

Maddie said, "We're sorry, Belle. We know you've had a tough time."

Carlos glared at me until I chimed in.

"Maddie's right," I said. "We're sorry."

Belle clamped her lips shut and smoothed her curls. Our encounter wasn't proceeding like I wanted it to.

"Everybody's been under a lot of stress," Carlos said. "Fortunately, Rosalee's doing fine, Belle. She's bruised, and her ankle's hurt. But why don't we talk about something else?"

"Good idea," Maddie said. "What do y'all think of Sheriff Roberts?"

I saw that little vein in Carlos' temple start to pulse. Maddie couldn't have raised a worse topic if she'd studied on it. His lips looked glued shut.

"Carlos and the sheriff don't see eye-to-eye on investigations," I answered for him.

"I'm out of my jurisdiction," Carlos raised his palms in a shrug. "It's different up here, that's for sure."

Belle said, "But it's different in good ways, too, isn't it?"

"Amen, Belle," Marty said.

"Like our family land," Belle continued, her eyes all dreamy and distant-looking. "There's such beauty and peace there. It's like nowhere else in the world, at least not for me."

She reached out a hand to Carlos, laying it just above his knee.

"I just know you'll love it as much as I do. I want to take you there sometime, show you the creeks and the birds and the trees. The trees will knock you out. You'll see a million shades of green." She looked into his eyes. "I want you to see what I see there; feel what I feel."

Carlos placed his hand over hers. "I'd like

that, Belle," he said softly. "I'd like it very much."

The two of them seemed lost in each other's eyes.

Marty shook her head at me, and worked on chewing a hole through her lower lip. Maddie mimicked holding a tiny fishing rod in her hands, casting out the line and reeling in the fish.

FORTY-ONE

Frank Sinatra's voice floated toward us on the evening air. "I've Got You Under My Skin." A moment later, Sal tapped the horn on his Caddy a couple of times, spooking whatever horses weren't already nervous about all the whip-cracking in camp.

"Yoo-hoo, girls!" Mama waved from her backseat throne. "Please tell me dinner is on."

"Just about, Mama," Marty answered. "Johnny's crew is setting out the steaks now."

"Thank goodness! I could eat a cow, hooves and all."

I guess the bag of Wynonna's cookies Mama had polished off earlier had worn off.

Once we all had our dinner plates and Mama was settled comfortably by the fire, Sal went off to find his New York buddy. My sisters filled her in on my near-mauling by Austin.

Mama speared a piece of steak and a stray green bean on her fork and pointed it at me: "I knew that girl was trouble!"

She'd conveniently forgotten she invited Austin into my life by chatting her up on the trail and welcoming her — and her bottle of wine — into Camp Cadillac.

"Mace says that Austin and Trey deserve one another." Marty delicately bit a green bean in half. "I think she's right."

"As far as I'm concerned, that whole Bramble family is a nightmare," Maddie said. "If I had them as students, I'd put the whole lot in permanent detention."

I figured it was a good time to tell them about the scene Austin and I had witnessed at Wynonna's RV. I looked for eavesdroppers. Most people were hunkered over their plates. Dinner was just an hour late, but you'd think we were lost for weeks in the woods without food.

"Speaking of the Brambles," I began in a whisper, and Mama and my sisters crowded closer to listen.

"Did you stay long enough to see if the RV started rockin'?" Maddie asked when I'd finished.

Mama slapped her wrist. "That's just crude!"

Marty said, "It may be crude, but Maddie raises a good point. There's clearly something between Trey and his daddy's widow. They could have conspired together to get rid of Lawton."

"I don't buy it," Mama said firmly. "That boy is purely grieving over his daddy. As for Wynonna, I've gone back and forth on the way I see her. But I'll tell you one thing: Her mourning strikes me as more for show than for real."

All of us were quiet for a bit, thinking. I played back in my mind the way Wynonna had been after she found Lawton's body. I saw her climbing that log again, and crying as a sympathetic crowd surged forward. I heard her screams after Doc was shot, and saw the shock on her face again and her hands smeared with his blood.

I remembered how hurt and disappointed she'd seemed when I confronted her about rubbing Trey's chest at the ranch house. Talk about acting!

"I don't know, y'all," I finally said. "Maybe she's a sex addict."

I must have said those last two words louder than I meant to, because the conversations around us suddenly stopped. I looked out the corner of my eyes, and actually saw people holding their forks in midair, quiet as barn mice, to see what I'd say next.

"Who's a sex addict, Mace?" Sal boomed, as he returned to the campfire.

I cringed. It got so quiet around us I could hear Maddie chewing her steak.

I raised my voice, "We were just talking about something I saw on TV, Sal."

"Cable, huh?" He stole a buttered roll off Mama's plate.

"Sal, honey, would you mind an awful lot finding me a jacket?" Mama asked. "I'm getting a bit chilled out here."

Mama watched him go then whispered, "Big pitcher *and* big ears."

I took up where we left off before she banished Sal. "I wish we knew who left me that note about Lawton being murdered. That might tell us something."

"And I wish we knew who came along afterwards and stole it from your Jeep," Maddie added. "That'd tell us something, too."

My thoughts went back to Carlos, and our search for the note. When I thought of how closely he'd trailed my footsteps through the pasture, I could almost smell his familiar scent. Had that only happened this afternoon? So much had changed in the hours since then.

As if my head were attached to strings, pulled by a force beyond my control, I turned to the spot where I'd glimpsed Belle earlier. Sure enough, she wasn't alone. Carlos the Protector was by her side. Even in the firelight, I could see she looked pale and shaken. Fragile. Carlos, his muscled arms and broad chest stretching the fabric of his denim shirt, would have to be strong enough for the two of them. He'd love that.

"Mace, we're talking to you!" Maddie's sharp voice interrupted my mental pity party.

When she noticed where I was staring, she said, "Uh-oh." Mama's and Marty's eyes followed hers.

Carlos leaned close to Belle, his head cocked to catch her soft voice. Her hair glowed like autumn leaves in the firelight, a tumble of golden red curls. I ran a hand through my own greasy snarls, and clamped the cowboy hat in my lap back onto my head.

"I'll tell you what you have to do, Mace . . ."

As Maddie started in, I snapped at her.

"I don't remember asking you what I *have* to do, Dr. Laura. If I wanted your advice, I'd call into your radio show to get it. Oh, wait a minute. You don't have a radio show.

You're not Dr. Laura. You just think you are."

Maddie looked wounded. I didn't feel as good as I thought I'd feel for biting her head off. Before I could say I was sorry, Mama started lecturing.

"Mace, your big sister only wants what's best for you. You ought to listen to Maddie. *She* has a husband. And he loves her like the cat loves the cream jar, even after all these years."

"Which is a mystery to me to rival the pyramids," I said sourly.

"Mace!"

"Oh, let her pick, Mama." Maddie waved the roll in her hand at me. "Mace has to take it out on someone. I'm a school principal. I think I'm tough enough to take my sister's sniping."

Marty had been quiet throughout our exchange. She was watching Carlos and Belle.

"I don't think he's as taken with her as he's making out to be, Mace," she said.

I cursed my heart's hopeful little flutter. "Why do you say that?"

"Because he's looked over here at you at least three times since he sat down next to her."

I fought the urge to swing my head toward

Carlos. "He has not."

"Hush, Mace," Mama said. "You know Marty's good at reading people. She's quiet and shy and before you know it, she knows everything she needs to know about anybody. She's like me that way."

Mama? Quiet and shy? Maybe in a parallel universe. But I didn't correct her. I needed hanging-on-to-a-man advice, and I needed it quick.

"What should I do?"

"Where should we start?" Mama said.

"Not helping, Mama," Marty said. "Now, listen, Mace. I know you don't like to play games, but you need to do just a little of that right now. If you can make Carlos just a little bit jealous, make him realize he doesn't want anyone else to have you, it might knock some sense back into his head."

"I tried to see if he'd get jealous over Trey. That didn't go so well."

"Let's find somebody else," Maddie said. "Somebody without a drinking problem and a crazy ex-girlfriend and a questionable relationship with his dead father's widow."

"I've got it," Mama slapped her hand against her thigh, jostling a pile of fried potatoes on the plate in her lap. "It's perfect girls: He's strong, silent, and unattached."

All of our eyes followed her gaze across

the fire. The trail boss was sitting off by himself, staring at the stars. He looked happy. He was probably dreaming of a day coming soon when he'd be out on the range with the cattle again, with just his horse and a cur dog for company.

"I don't know, Mama . . ."

"Nonsense, Mace. You don't have to fall in love with the man," she said. "You just have to flirt with him a little bit. It's a piece of cake, honey."

Easy for her to say.

The Committee to Fix Mace's Love Life voted to send Maddie along with me on my mission. Given the choice between looking at me or Marty, any man would choose Marty. And Mama, with her gimpy ankle, would have slowed me down or distracted Jack. We only had so much time.

"You can do this, Mace," Maddie pep-talked into my ear as we rounded the fire. "It's easier than wrestling gators, and you're good at that. At least Jack Hollister doesn't have seventy-five razor sharp teeth and a tail that could break a man's leg."

"Hey, Jack," I said as we got closer.

So far so good.

He lowered his eyes from the night sky and frowned at me.

Uh-oh.

"I was just wondering if you'd heard anything about Doc," I asked.

He shook his head. "Nothing yet." He returned his gaze skyward.

Maddie gave me a little push and an opening. "We saw you looking at the stars, Jack. My sister Mace loves astronomy. When she was a kid, she had a poster with all the constellations on the ceiling over her bed."

"Really?"

"No." I glared at Maddie. "But I do love looking at the sky."

I sat down next to him. "Look, there's *Canis Major*." I pointed overhead.

"The bigger of Orion's hunting dogs," he said, smiling at me. He looked up again and outlined *Canis Minor*. "And there's the little dog."

Maddie stood out of Jack's view, tapping her finger to her eye and pulling out the lid. I couldn't believe she wanted me to try that old chestnut. I mouthed *No way* at her. She fisted her left hand and pointed to her wedding ring. She'd been with Kenny since high school.

"Ouch," I said, feeling like a simple fool. "I think I've got something in my eye."

"Let me take a look," Jack said, putting a calloused finger to my cheek. "Probably some dust and grit from near the dairy. That was a mess out there, wasn't it? I thought it would never stop blowing."

Those were the most words I'd heard him speak when he wasn't standing on a log, addressing the assembled riders.

"Sure was a mess," I agreed.

He lifted my hat off my head and turned my face toward the light of the campfire. Then he peered deep, searching for the nonexistent speck in my eye.

"Listen, Jack, I wanted to tell you how well you've handled everything that's happened on this ride. I don't think many trail bosses would be up to dealing with all that."

"Well, thanks, Mace." He pulled his face back a bit from mine and smiled. "That means a lot to hear you say that. I'm sorry about that scare with your sister and the rattlesnake, and then your poor mama and Shotgun. Is everybody okay?"

I nodded.

"Hold still, now. I think I see something." He barely brushed my bottom eyelid with the tip of his finger, a surprisingly gentle touch. "Got it." He held up a black, buggy speck. "Looks like a gnat."

Who knew?

Reaching down for my hat, I took a furtive glance at Carlos and Belle. She was talking, but he was frowning at Jack and me. As I straightened my hat on my head, I sneaked a look at Maddie from under the brim. Her face was creased in a big smile and her hands were nearly hidden in the folds of her riding culottes. But she sent a signal for my eyes only.

Two thumbs up.

FORTY-TWO

I heard *whir, snap!* A flash of light nearly blinded my gnat-invaded eye.

"Got it," Belle said, lowering an old-school camera from her face. "That was a good one. You and Jack were really lost up there in the stars, Mace."

The trail boss looked irritated. "I don't like having my picture taken, Belle. I wish you'd have given me some warning."

"Candid shots are much better, Jack. People look unnatural when you give them time to think about being shot." He raised his eyebrows. Belle realized her turn of phrase. "I mean 'shot' like shooting a picture, not shot like what happened to Doc." She sat down next to us. "How is he? I've been thinking an awful lot about him tonight."

I guess she meant she was thinking of Doc when she wasn't pouring out her heart to Carlos or walking around "shooting" with her camera at anything that moved. I glanced across the fire to where he'd been sitting with Belle a half-hour before Jack and I got caught up in star-gazing. Carlos had disappeared.

"Still no word about Doc," the trail boss answered Belle. "The hospital said he'd probably be in surgery for several hours."

Belle lifted the camera to her eye again and shot something arty through the flames of the campfire. Jack used that moment to plead he had business elsewhere. He escaped, leaving Belle and I alone.

"How long have you been taking pictures?" I asked, making conversation.

She turned and shot another frame of me, then lowered the camera. It dangled from a strap around her neck.

"As long as I can remember," she said. "Photography has always been my escape valve. Whenever anything was going wrong in my life, I'd get my gear and head for the woods. I've always been able to lose myself behind the viewfinder."

I could relate. Shooting photos must be Belle's version of tossing rocks into the water.

"I'd love to get a picture of you with your family, Mace. Would you mind?"

I hesitated. I'm not a big fan on my best

day of having my picture taken. But she was making an effort. What was I going to say? No?

When I didn't answer immediately, Belle said, "Listen, Mace. I know you don't like me very much."

I started to protest, but she held up a hand. "I can tell, and it's all right. You can't be friends with everyone. I just want to make sure you don't dislike me for the wrong reason." She paused. "You know, there's nothing going on between Carlos and me."

Now she had my attention.

"It's just that he's a good listener," she continued, "and I've been so sad. It helps to talk to somebody else who's been through an awful loss. You know about his wife, right?"

I nodded.

"He's a good man, Mace. And he's still hurting. You ought to cut him a break."

I was too surprised to speak.

She lifted the camera back to her eye and smiled slightly as she snapped off three or four quick pictures. I looked where she aimed, and saw a teen-aged cowboy flirting with a pretty girl. He was teasing her with a blackened marshmallow on a stick. Their young faces were laughing, and rosy in the firelight.

"Nice photo," I said, thinking of Carlos and me eating S'mores.

"Yep," she said. "That'll be a good one. Happy times."

We sat in silence for a few moments. Her eyes never stopped roaming, looking for scenes she could capture. I wondered how it would feel to have that kind of talent, to know instinctively what would make a good picture. Whenever somebody asked me to take a snapshot, I always aimed wrong and cut off significant body parts.

I reconsidered posing for her with Mama and my sisters. Belle was a professional, with her photos on exhibit in fancy galleries in Stuart and Palm Beach. It might be nice to have a memory of us together on the Cracker Trail. No telling when we'd ever make the ride again.

"Belle," I finally said, "I'd be honored if you'd take my family's picture."

I was rewarded with a smile that transformed her somber face into something approaching happy. "Glad to do it. And I've got another idea, too."

I raised my eyebrows.

"I'll get some shots of you and Carlos."

"I don't really think . . ."

"I won't take no for an answer. From you,

or from him. Trust me. It's a great way to get the two of you back together. I'm good at this. I can make anybody comfortable in front of a camera. You two will forget I'm even there. You'll be laughing and fooling around before you know it."

"I'm not sure . . ."

"We'll do it in the morning," she cut me off, "before the ride starts. The light will be perfect. You two will be perfect. You'll see."

Belle was so determined, I ended up agreeing to meet her by the mule wagons before breakfast. She said she'd handle getting Carlos to show up. I was blown away by this side of Belle. She made Maddie the Bulldozer look reticent.

Within fifteen minutes, Belle was moving Mama and the rest of us around, instructing us to relax. Which, of course, was the cue for us to do anything but. Mama primped. Marty fastened her eyes on the ground. Maddie looked annoyed at being told what to do. I clenched my jaw into a smile that felt more like a grimace.

"This isn't working, y'all." Belle sighed. "Mace, you look like the governor just signed your execution order. Marty, honey, you're a beautiful girl. Don't you ever look anybody in the eyes? And Rosalee, I'm shooting old school, with black-and-white film. No digital, no color. Nobody will know whether you have one coat on or six of that orange lipstick."

Mama snapped shut her compact and returned her tube of Apricot Ice to her pocket. Maddie gave an exasperated sigh. Belle told us to go ahead and sit down while she thought of another way to get us to pose without looking like somebody's prisoners. Just then, Sal returned, with desserts for all of us.

"Oooooh." Mama lifted her hands and squealed. "Butterscotch pie. My favorite."

Whir, snap!

Maddie took a plate and handed Marty and me one. We all dug in.

Whir, snap!

"That's perfect," Belle fired off frame after frame, her face shining with glee. "Now, y'all look like a family!"

Figures food would be the secret ingredient to get us all to relax.

The air was growing colder; the evening winding down. After she took what seemed like an album's worth of pictures, Belle went off, alone, with her camera. We'd finished dessert.

Carlos hadn't returned to the campfire. I pictured him lurking outside the interview trailer. He was probably making himself crazy over how badly Sheriff Roberts' deputies were bungling the investigation into Doc Abel's shooting. I hoped that, in at least one tiny corner of his brain, he was chewing over that image of me looking skyward with Jack Hollister. I wondered how Belle's plan would go to get Carlos and me back together, at least inside a picture frame.

"That was some camera Belle had around her neck." Sal tossed his toothpick into the fire, and extracted a fresh one from his neon-blue breast pocket. "Must have cost a fortune."

Maddie edged her boots closer to the campfire. "It's not like the Bramble family can't afford it."

"Still," Mama said, "you'd think she'd want to take better care of it. When I saw her before, she had it protected inside a leather case that hung around her neck. Suppose she hit the camera against something, or dropped it? There goes a couple hundred dollars."

"More like a thousand, with that special lens," Sal said. "My son's into photography. It's an expensive hobby."

"I don't think it's a hobby with Belle," I said, remembering how shooting pictures had transformed her. "I think it's more than that."

Later, on our way to Maddie's tent, we decided to swing by the dinner site. My sisters and I were still curious about Johnny Adams and that "burn" on his hand. If we saw him, I planned to flat-out ask him if he'd been stung by some bees.

Our secondary goal: Seeing if we could scare up another slice or two of butterscotch pie before bed.

As we drew closer to the food trailer, I heard murmured voices. They were almost drowned out by the loud hum of the generator. But it sounded like a man and a woman.

I held up my hand to my sisters to stop, and put a finger to my lips. They cocked their heads to listen, and we crept closer.

The site was spic and span, not a stray utensil or slice of pie in sight. Everything looked cleaned and closed up for the night. The voices were coming from the dark side of the food trailer, shadowed from the generator-powered lights. We stuck close to the trees, staying out of sight, as we worked our way to the rear of the food camp.

I recognized Johnny first, facing us and tossing a long-handled serving spoon from palm to palm. The woman's back was to us. Her slight shoulders shook with what looked like sobs. I couldn't see her face, but I definitely knew those boots: Brown, with a leather fringe up the sides.

As we watched, Johnny stuck the spoon in his back pocket. He cupped Wynonna's chin in one hand, and with the other, tenderly wiped what must have been her tears. Her arms went around his waist. She pulled him close. They kissed.

Even in the dim light, I saw Marty's blue eyes widen. She breathed, "No way!"

Judging by the enthusiasm of their kiss, I don't think Johnny was offering Wynonna simple human comfort. Plus, she'd lowered her hands and was now busy massaging his rear end.

"Yes, Marty," Maddie whispered. "Way."

FORTY-THREE

"I still think we should have said something to them." Maddie spoke between brush strokes, through a mouthful of toothpaste.

I handed her the bottled water we were sharing as we prepared to turn in.

"What were we supposed to say, Maddie? 'Excuse us, we're over here peeping at y'all, and we just wondered if you'd clue us in. What in the Sam Hill is up with you two?' That's not the best way to go about getting information," I said.

The three of us had stood there in shock, watching Wynonna and Johnny. Then, suddenly, Audrey's voice rang out, calling his name. He jumped away from Wynonna like she was hot grease. She slipped away into the night.

Now, at our tent, Maddie swished and spit into her camping cup.

"But, Mace," Marty said, "we could have acted like we just stumbled upon them at the food trailer and were really shocked."

"That wouldn't have been acting," Maddie said, patting her mouth dry.

"I just don't think it was the best time to confront either one of them with questions," I said. "I wanted to ponder on it a bit, try and figure out what was going on. You know how our cousin Henry always says he never asks a question in court he doesn't already know the answer to? Well, I think it's the same when you're investigating. I want to do some snooping first before we show them our hand."

"So now you're a big investigator. Detective Mace Bauer." Maddie tossed her toothpaste water out the tent's flap.

I shook my head. "No. But I try to find ways to get information without making folks so mad they'd never tell me anything. Unlike some people I could mention."

"Is that a shot?" Maddie slapped the water bottle back into my outstretched palm.

I shrugged. "If the mule-wagon sized shoe fits . . ."

"Cut it out, you two." Marty wound her wool scarf around her neck and up her chin. "We need to stick together. Tomorrow's the parade in Fort Pierce and the big barbecue afterwards. We'll have plenty of time to nose around and find out what's what."

We were all quiet for a bit. Pulling off jeans and boots. Unzipping sleeping bags. Getting ear plugs ready to deaden the rumble of Maddie's snoring.

"I just feel sorry for Audrey," Marty finally said, her voice wool-muffled. "She really seemed to care for Johnny, and not just as her boss."

"Well, what did we really see between Wynonna and him?" I asked. "Maybe he was just trying to comfort his old friend's widow, and she caught him off guard."

"Donftinkzo." Marty's voice came from beneath the sleeping bag she'd pulled over her face.

"What?" Maddie and I both said.

Marty peeked out to enunciate. "I don't think so. Johnny looked like a willing participant." She shivered. "Aren't you two cold? It feels like the walk-in freezer at the Speckled Perch in here. My nose is a frozen fish filet."

I leaned down and breathed some warm air on Marty's nose. "Better?"

"Yes, thanks." She sniffed. "And now I'll go to sleep dreaming of butterscotch pie."

I took the hint, brushed my teeth, and zipped myself into the cocoon of my loaner sleeping bag. Marty was right. It had gotten chilly. Now, Maddie's crowded tent didn't seem so bad. Even so, it wasn't nearly as cold as the socks-on-my-hands night my tent was shredded.

My mind raced. Sleep seemed impossible. Disjointed thoughts and images galloped through my brain. Lawton's body, the chili cup, and Wynonna. Wynonna with Trey. Now, Johnny and Wynonna. I'd been half-kidding when I proposed that she was addicted to sex. But maybe she was. Had she also had a thing going with old Doc Abel?

I thought of Doc, whistling in the woods. Then an image of him collapsed in the clearing, a bullet in his gut, pushed into my head. I saw Mama, lying still and broken in the dirt. Austin's whip snapped at Val, and I stared head-on at a semi-truck. Marty stood, paralyzed with fear, as a rattlesnake prepared to strike. Trey and me. Carlos and Belle. Belle at peace with her camera.

I heard Marty sleeping beside me, her breath soft and even. No snores from Maddie yet.

"Pssst," I whispered. "You awake, Sister?"

She twisted in her sleeping bag toward me. "I feel like a sausage stuffed in a nylon casing, and this ground is like granite. Of course I'm awake," Maddie grumbled.

"What do you think will happen tomorrow?"

"I imagine we'll get through the day. Then we'll return our horses and the three of us will squeeze into my car and we'll head home."

Maddie's tone was practical; matter-of-fact. I didn't buy it.

"So you don't think anything bad will happen?"

She was quiet for a long time.

"I pray it won't, Mace," she finally said. "Now, try to get some sleep, Sister. We've got an early morning to make Fort Pierce."

I lay there, awake, until Maddie dozed off and began to snore. She started quiet, and then got going loud enough to shake the stakes in the ground. She was definitely Mama's daughter.

I fumbled in the corner for my boots. That's where I'd stashed my ear plugs so I could find them easily in the dark. I plucked out my watch: seven minutes past one.

The night was still, aside from Maddie's snores. The air in the tent felt close, stinking of mildew and horse hair. I peered at Marty's face. She looked peaceful, untroubled. I hoped she *was* dreaming of butterscotch pie. Maddie's mouth was creased in a frown. I wondered if she was worried about the parade, or just scolding some eighth-grader in her dream.

Every so often, voices crackled in the distance over police radios. Sheriff Roberts' deputies still combed the camp, looking for the weapon used to shoot Doc. I planned to speak to the sheriff before we left, tell him what I knew about Lawton's widow and her various liaisons. Trey should have had enough time by then to confess to Belle about his wicked ways with their stepmother.

Surely, given everything that had happened since Lawton died, there'd now be an autopsy to prove what killed him. It may not have been the chili in the cup we'd found, but I was certain it wasn't a heart attack. And I was at least halfway certain Wynonna was involved.

I shifted, trying to get comfortable. Maddie was right about the ground. Had it been that hard when we were kids? Hoots of laughter drifted over from somebody's camp. I wondered who was still up, and what was so damn funny. A dog howled. A whip cracked.

I looked at my watch again. One twenty-three. Jeez. Give the cow whip a rest.

As if in answer, the loud pop came again. Funny how much it sounded like a gunshot.

FORTY-FOUR

I waited at the mule wagons in a fragrant cloud of roses, vanilla, and a hint of butterscotch toffee. Mama insisted on dousing me for my sunrise photo session with her favorite perfume. I smelled like a florist sharing space with a candy factory inside a horse stable.

"Trust me, Mace," Mama had said. "Carlos won't be able to resist you when you smell so sweet."

I wasn't sure about Carlos. But the closest mule sneezed as I drew near.

For the photos, I'd chosen my last clean shirt. Denim, of course, which Marty claimed brought out the blue of my eyes. Even Maddie contributed, tying a bandana at a jaunty angle inside my collar.

"It'll hide the dirt creases on your neck," she said.

I glanced at my watch. Again. Six-forty a.m. Belle had said she'd bring Carlos. We were supposed to meet at six-thirty. Just as I was wondering if I'd been duped, she called my name.

I turned, and my heart sank. Belle's face was full of pity. She was alone; and she didn't have her camera. I cursed Mama's stupid cologne and the jaunty neckerchief. I smeared the back of my hand over my mouth to wipe off the lipstick Marty applied. I felt like a perfect fool.

"Listen, Mace, I'm so sorry."

Belle looked at me like I was six years old and she had to break the news that my puppy just died. She put a hand on my wrist. I shook it off.

"It's fine. I didn't want my picture taken anyway. Plus, I left my sisters with all the work of getting the horses ready. I better get on back to help them break down camp."

I hoped she wouldn't hear the tears trying to force themselves into my throat.

"I tried really hard to talk Carlos into coming, Mace." Belle, too, seemed on the verge of crying. "He just flat-out refused. He's very stubborn."

Was that supposed to make me feel better? I wondered if Carlos asked about me, or even bothered to make up an excuse. But I was too proud to find out.

As if she read my mind, Belle said, "For

what it's worth, I think he still cares about you. Otherwise, why wouldn't he just walk over here, smile, let me shoot a few photos, and then walk away? I think it hurts him too much to be around you."

When I still hadn't spoken, she said, "Do you want me to tell him anything?"

I shook my head, not trusting my voice.

"All right, then. I'm really sorry, Mace." She rested her hand on my arm again. This time I left it there. "Maybe you two will iron things out once you get back to Himmarshee. I hope so, anyway."

Me, too, I thought as I nodded. Still I said nothing.

"Goodbye then." Belle patted my arm and then dropped her hand, looking at me with kind eyes. "Maybe we'll see each other again after the ride."

The next time I'd see Belle would likely be at her daddy's funeral. The thought sobered me up quick. Here was a woman mourning that kind of loss, and she was comforting me over boyfriend trouble. I suddenly felt pretty stupid. I found my voice.

"Thanks, Belle. I know you tried. And you're right: Carlos is as stubborn as a . . ."

The animal closest to us picked just that moment to stamp his foot and shake his harness. Belle looked at him and laughed. Bad as I felt, I had to laugh, too.

"Sheriff Roberts?" I knocked on the side of the interview camper. "Mind if I come in?"

He got up to open the door, rocking the trailer with his weight.

"I was wondering when I'd hear from you. Weren't you one of the gals with Ms. Bramble yesterday when I stopped by to talk with her?"

"Yessir," I said, feeling that sudden flush of nerves again.

"I hear you're some kind of Jessica Fletcher."

"Pardon?"

"*Murder, She Wrote.* On TV?"

"Oh, yeah." I nodded, politely, I hoped. "I've caught a couple of old reruns. It's not really my kind of show. Doesn't it seem unrealistic that everywhere that woman goes, someone up and gets killed?"

"It's just TV." He gestured for me to sit across from him at Jack Hollister's fold-down dining table. "Now, who do you think shot Doc Abel?"

Over the next fifteen minutes or so, I told the sheriff everything that had happened before Doc got hurt, beginning with Wynonna finding her husband's body. I told him how she was involved with Trey, and maybe Johnny, too. I mentioned somebody trying to scare me and my family off after we started asking questions about Lawton's death.

"I think Doc knew too much," I wrapped up. "Whoever shot him must have wanted him out of the way."

The toothpick between the sheriff's lips had barely moved as I spoke. He listened closely, hardly uttering so much as an "uh-huh," or a "Go on." Finally, he shifted the toothpick.

"What time do they start serving breakfast at the food trailer?"

"Come again?" I said.

"Breakfast," he repeated. "It's been a long night and I've had enough coffee to float a battleship. I need some food in my stomach."

Maybe Carlos was right about Sheriff Roberts.

"Don't you want to follow up on any of the leads I've given you? Don't you have any questions?"

"Naw," he said. "The hospital called about an hour ago. Doc Abel came through surgery like a champ. The doctors say him making it through the night is a real good sign. As soon as Doc can see us, my chief deputy's going over to the hospital in Stuart. Doc can tell us himself who put him there."

He leaned in close. His breath smelled like twice-used coffee grounds and toothpick wood.

"I'd watch my back if I was you, though," he said. "I heard you stole Trey Bramble away from some gal who's meaner than a pit bull. I've seen more deadly violence over jealousy than just about any other reason."

I rose to let myself out. "I'll keep that in mind, Sheriff."

Just as I opened the door, he said, "Hang on a minute, Mace."

His voice carried an urgency I hadn't heard before. I turned.

"What time did you say breakfast was again?"

"Mace, honey, that's just awful. So Carlos never even got to smell my perfume?"

"No, Mama. Not unless he could smell it over at his camp, which he might could have, considering you about emptied the bottle on me. But he never showed for the pictures."

Picking half-heartedly at my breakfast, I related the details of my humiliating morning. It wasn't even eight a.m., and already

I'd been dissed by Carlos and dismissed by Sheriff Roberts.

"We're gonna fix things between you two," Marty said.

"Please don't," I said. "He already told me our relationship is too complicated. Having the family circus ride to the rescue is the last thing I need."

Maddie said, "I'll go talk some sense into him."

God, no! I wanted to scream. But all I said was, "I don't think it would help, Maddie."

She harrumphed. "What about Belle? I bet she was gloating."

"That was the shocking thing," I said. "Belle was really sweet. She felt just about as bad as I did about Carlos standing me up."

Mama's fork hovered over my plate. "Well, honey, at least you got everything off your chest with the sheriff." She speared a sausage I hadn't touched. "All you can do is give him the information. It's his job now to try to make sense of it."

We all glanced toward Sheriff Roberts. He devoured a sausage biscuit in two bites, then gulped down a forklift-load of eggs and pan-fried potatoes with ketchup.

"Well," Mama said, "maybe not him. I hear his chief deputy is a real hotshot, though. He's got a criminal justice degree and everything. Poor old Sheriff Roberts should have hung up his holster ten years ago. Let the young blood take over."

"That's not always easy for the old blood to do," Sal said.

He'd been quiet, fooling with his beloved cigar case. He lined up his cigars on a log, and then loaded them into the leather case. Then he removed them again. He likes to play with the stogies as much as smoke them.

He peered inside the empty carrier. Up-ending it, he shook it hard.

"My stars and garters, Sally! What are you doing?" Mama asked.

"There's some tobacco caught underneath one of the seams on the bottom," he said. "I'm trying to get it out."

"It's a cigar case, Sal. It's bound to collect tobacco," Maddie said.

He knocked the carrier against his camp chair, looked inside, then knocked it some more.

"I know that, Maddie. I want it to be clean!"

He hit it firmly against the chair again. I'm sure the final few taps were solely to annoy my big sister.

I glanced at Mama to see if she thought

so, too. Her head was cocked to listen, and she wore a puzzled expression.

"What?" I asked her.

The expression was gone as quickly as it came. Her blank eyes now focused on me.

"Nothing," she said. "I was about to think of something important, but then I lost my train of thought. I guess I'm having one of those senior moments a few years early."

"Fuhgeddaboutit, Rosie. You'll be the world's sexiest senior citizen." Sal planted a loud, sloppy kiss on Mama's lips.

"Ewww," my sisters and I groaned.

FORTY-FIVE

A stiff wind blew off the Indian River, snapping parade flags and banners, and carrying the smell of the sea. Some of the horses pranced about, nervous over new sounds and scents. Their riders worked to steady them. Nobody wanted to make headlines as the Cracker Trail participant who plowed into a group of parade-goers in Fort Pierce.

We were mounted and waiting for the signal to go, assembled in a large field serving as the parade staging area on the outskirts of downtown. I watched a petite rider wrestle with a big, skittish Appaloosa. The poor girl had probably spent the last week getting her horse accustomed to the crack of cow whips. Now, the Appaloosa looked ready to bolt for the bridge over the Intracoastal Waterway, not stopping until it got to the wide beach and the Atlantic Ocean beyond.

I heard a syrupy voice beside me.

"That's a lot of animal for such a little girl." It was Austin, sounding like we were the very best of friends.

"Hmmmm," I answered.

I edged Val away from Austin's Arabian. She'd braided golden thread in the horse's mane, a match to her own sequined hat-band. She also wore a glittery gold vest, showing off her tiny waist and ample bust-line. So much for authentic Florida Cracker garb.

"Are you still mad at me, Mace?"

"Not mad. Just wary."

"I'm sorry about the bottle." She looked down and picked at the leather of her reins. "I don't know what gets into me. When I get angry like that, it's like a spell takes over. I'm not myself."

"You ought to try to find the antidote for those spells, Austin. They're pretty scary."

She ignored my advice-giving. "I really did appreciate it that you didn't make a big deal about our little scuffle the other night."

"By 'little scuffle,' you mean when you threatened to fillet me with a broken bottle?"

She nodded, casting her eyes down at the reins again.

"Forget it," I said. "It's over."

She raised her pretty face at me. "That's

what I wanted to talk to you about, Mace. I feel like I blew it. I was hoping you and I could still be friends."

I stared at her. Sincerity oozed from every pore. And, finally, I was fed up. I was fed up with all the crazy and dangerous things that had happened on the ride. I was tired of people who lied and left out and twisted the truth. And, especially, I was sick to death of the nutcase now smiling at me hopefully from under her stupid, sparkly hat.

"We're not gonna be friends, Austin," I said flatly. "I'd sooner jump naked into a swimming pool filled with snapping turtles than spend another second with you. In fact, I think you need to get yourself some psychological help before you wind up killing somebody. If you haven't already killed anybody, that is."

The smile left her face like a shift in the wind. Anger sparked in her eyes. Uh-oh, I thought.

"Looks like the parade's getting started." I began to maneuver Val into the line of horses and wagons that was forming.

Austin screwed up her mouth like she was going to spit at me, and then turned her horse into my path. Val was blocked in by riders on either side. Austin kept pushing her Arabian closer, forcing us to the gutter of the street. Val stumbled over a high concrete curb. I bobbled in the saddle, but held on as she regained her footing.

"You crazy witch," I said to Austin. "I should have sent you to jail."

"Oh, don't be so dramatic, Mace. What's a little horseplay between friends?" Her smile was chilling.

Spurring her horse, she yelled over her shoulder, "And you better watch who you call crazy."

Maddie rode up. "Who's crazy?" She watched Austin dart away through the crowd.

"She is." I was shaking, more from anger than from fear. "Austin's a total head case."

"I'm so glad we made it, girls!"

My sisters and I flanked Mama in her mule wagon, as we made our turn onto Orange Avenue. We were on horseback. Mama was in the passenger seat with her ankle on a pillow, doling out waves like Queen Elizabeth in a peony-pink cowgirl hat.

Spectators lined both sides of the parade route, whooping and cheering as the Cracker Trail riders streamed past. Historic murals and sturdy brick buildings hinted at olden times. Waterfront condos and sleek yachts in the city marina spoke to the new Florida.

Ahead, the crowd erupted into shouts and loud applause. Maddie's eyebrows went up.

"You got me," I shrugged.

We angled our horses for a better view. Wynonna had reached the downtown roundabout on Indian River Drive. She reared up on a perfect palomino, the animal's forelegs pawing at air. The breeze ruffled the horse's golden mane and tail. Wynonna, dressed all in white except for her red alligator boots, demonstrated complete control. She waved her white hat over her head.

The crowd roared its approval.

"So much for the ban on theatrics in the parade," Maddie said dryly.

"She's a heck of a rider," Marty said. "You've got to give her that."

"That horse is gorgeous and well-trained." I sniffed. "He'd make anybody look good."

Mama said, "Speaking of Wynonna, what did y'all find out about that business with Johnny?"

I hadn't had time to snoop. I looked at my sisters. They shook their heads.

"Well," Mama said, "I saw Johnny's food trailer pulling into the park where we'll have our picnic. I'm betting we'll get the full scoop before dessert."

I wasn't so sure. Johnny hadn't been inclined so far toward revelations. I didn't think our quadruple-teaming him was going to change his mind.

"Ooooh, look girls! There's Sally!" Mama doffed her pink hat, shaking it frantically in his direction. "Yoo-hoo! I'm over here, honey!"

He aimed a video camera at us. He needed an extra light to compensate for the glare off his neon Western wear. "You're looking good, girls," he yelled. "Now, everybody wave hello! Smile, Mace!"

Like kids in a school play, we followed his instructions. I felt a pang of envy for the original Florida cow men. They'd faced hurricanes, heat and humidity, and mosquitoes so fierce they could down a cow in a blood-sucking cloud. But at least as they rode into P. P. Cobb's old trading post at Fort Pierce, they hadn't had to grin and wave for the cameras.

"*Niña,* you should listen to Sal. Where's that lovely smile that I know so well?"

I felt a flush spreading fire north from my neck. Maddie's eyebrows shot up. Marty's hand darted over and gave my knee a surreptitious squeeze. Mama was otherwise occupied, still striking pretty poses for Sal's camera.

Fearing my voice would come out in some kind of awful squeak, I cemented my lips.

"What? No smile at all this morning?" Carlos flashed his white teeth at me, looking so handsome on that big, black horse that it about took my breath away.

Maddie leaned forward in her saddle, shooting him a murderous glare. "Mace was all ready to smile at sunrise. But then somebody plucked out her heart and stomped on it."

He struck a fighter's pose, jokingly raising a fist. "Who broke Mace's heart? I'll teach them some manners!"

Even Marty was mad enough to be mean: "You're not in any position to teach anybody manners, Carlos."

He leaned back in the saddle, taking all three of us in. "Did all the Bauer girls get up on the wrong side of their sleeping bags?" He yelled over the squeaks and rattles of the mule wagon toward Mama, "Rosalee! What's up with your daughters? They're acting like I'm the one who shot Doc Abel."

The flirtatious smile Mama had been wearing for Sal's camera died on her lips. She turned eyes like stones on Carlos. "You don't want to come around here all sunny and smiling after what you did to Mace this morning. Any real gentleman would have posed for Belle for a couple of pictures."

He frowned at each of us in turn, puzzled. I studied the horn on Val's saddle, stealing glimpses of him from under my hat brim.

"I have no idea what you're talking about," Carlos finally said. "What pictures?"

FORTY-SIX

The parade was the best ever for the Florida Cracker Trail ride. That's what everybody in Fort Pierce said. When we made it all the way back to Harbour Pointe Park without death or injuries, I sent a little prayer of gratitude heavenward.

At the waterfront park, the bands and the barbecue were in full swing for our after-party. The sun shone. The breeze blew. Puffy clouds raced across a brilliant blue sky.

The air was a bit chilly, so I'd run back to the vacant field to get Mama a sweater from Sal's Caddy. The staging area was chock-a-block with pickups and trailers. Riders fed, watered, and groomed their horses. Country songs blared from truck stereos. Pop-tops on beer cans went *Ssstt.* Cow whips ripped.

I stopped first to check on Val, who was contentedly munching hay by the horse rescue group's trailer.

"Hey, girl," I called, and added a whistle.

She raised her head, her bright eyes tracking my approach.

"You are the best horse in Florida, maybe the world," I whispered, running my hand under her dark mane. "Thanks for getting me here safely."

She bobbed her head before returning to her hay. I think she was acknowledging the compliment.

I leaned over to inspect her legs and feet, making sure she'd be sound when I returned her to her owner. Aside from some major wear on her shoes, Val looked great. There was barely a mark where Austin "accidentally" smacked her with the whip. I could let myself think about Austin, and get mad all over again. Or I could breathe deeply and let it go.

"What do you think, Val?"

She chomped her hay.

"You're right. She's so not worth it."

I was busy dusting my jeans of the dirt I'd gotten checking Val's hooves, when I heard a rustle in the grass behind me. Discounting the prickle at the back of my neck as nerves, I slowly turned toward the sound.

"Jesus, Trey!" I exhaled. "You scared the vinegar out of me."

"Sorry," he said, coming close enough to rest a hand on Val's back. "I wanted to catch you before you left for home."

He was unshaven. Black circles underlined his eyes. His shirt looked slept in. But he didn't smell of liquor, so I guess that was an improvement.

"Is your sister around?" I asked. "I'd like to speak to her about something."

"What about?"

"I'd rather talk to Belle about it," I said.

Carlos had told us that she never even asked him to meet me for the photo session at the mule wagons. It seemed that, like her stepmother, Belle was one hell of an actress.

"You can tell me," Trey said. "Belle and I don't have any secrets."

"Everybody has secrets, Trey."

He took a step closer. "Do you?" His voice was husky; his breath hot on my face.

I flashed back to the Golden Boy I remembered from high school. What I wouldn't have given then to have Trey Bramble pressed up next to me, breathing heavily. Now, I turned away. Too much had happened for me to see Trey the way I used to.

"So that's how you're gonna be, Mace?"

His voice had turned rough, menacing. I stepped away, but not before he snatched at my wrist. I tried to yank back my arm, but he held tighter.

"Stop it, Trey. You're hurting me."

"You don't know pain." He intensified his grip. "I want to know what you need to see Belle about."

I'd had just about enough of Trey's crap. I grabbed his wrist with my other hand and hissed at him through my teeth, "You'd better back off unless you want my kneecap rammed clear through your groin."

He looked at me in surprise.

"I'm as strong as many men, and you've let yourself go — physically, along with every other way. You do not want to test me, Trey."

Just as the pressure eased on my wrist, I heard someone call my name.

"Over here, Sal," I yelled.

Mama's sweater looked like a doll's wrap in Sal's big hand. His eyes darted quickly from me to Trey. I rubbed at my wrist. Trey stuck his hands in his pockets and stared at his boots.

"Everything okay, Mace?" Sal missed nothing.

"Fine," I said. "Trey was just leaving."

Trey made no move to go. Sal waited a beat.

"Then I'd say he better get to it." He clapped a hand onto Trey's elbow, nearly dragging him off his feet. "Why don't you and me take a little walk, okay pal?"

I watched the two of them move across the field, Sal three or four inches taller and nearly twice as wide as Trey. With his size, and the popularity of books and movies about New York mobsters, Sal rarely had to ask anyone twice to do his bidding. He never actually claimed to be connected, but he never denied it, either.

"What do you think, girl? Sal's turned out to be a pretty good guy, hasn't he?"

Val swished her tail from side to side, chasing flies.

"Yeah, I think so, too. Mama's lucky to have him."

The wind was gusting off the water again. The smell of barbecue drifted over from the park. I looked around the field. The crowd had thinned out, lured by the promise of dinner. I could nearly taste the swamp cabbage and smoky beef brisket.

I was almost finished sprucing up Val. Starting from the left, I began a once-over with a brush I pulled from the trailer. To make sure the saddle's cinch hadn't left sores, I stooped to check under her belly. That's when I saw a pair of blue-jeaned legs standing on the other side of Val. They ended in tiny, mud-caked boots.

I straightened to see Belle Bramble staring at me across the horse's back.

"Boy! You sure sneaked up on me."

"I photograph a lot of wildlife in the woods, Mace. It's taught me to move quietly."

"I spend a lot of time in the woods myself. And I've never heard anyone that quiet."

Belle's camera dangled from a neck strap. The afternoon sun glinted off the lens. A tiny alarm pinged in my head, though I wasn't quite sure why.

"I saw your Mama's boyfriend dragging Trey off," Belle said. "Is everything okay? Where was he taking Trey?"

What was it with these two?

"I don't know, Belle. Trey went kind of loco on me when I told him I wanted to talk to you. Sal came along and figured he'd take him away for a little cooling-off."

"Will he hurt him?"

"No." I grinned. "Sal's not as sinister as he looks."

She seemed relieved, but awfully jumpy. She looked around the field like she was waiting for someone.

"What did you want to talk to me about?" Belle asked.

I was done treading carefully. "Why'd you lie to me about Carlos and the photos?"

She tucked her hair behind her ears, and then rubbed her hands up and down the front of her jeans. Her eyes darted in every direction except to mine.

"Well?"

No answer; just more fidgeting. She ran a finger under the strap of her camera, easing its weight from her neck.

It was that camera that was bothering me. "I've been meaning to ask you, Belle. What happened to the nice leather case you had before?"

She looked down like she'd never seen the camera before. She seemed spacey again, like she had that night we'd found her in the cypress stand. I almost felt sorry for her. Belle had issues.

"What?" she asked.

"Your camera case." I pointed at her chest.

She took her time before answering, "I must have lost it."

"What's wrong with you, Belle?" I could hear the exasperation in my voice. "Did Doc Abel give you some kind of drugs?"

Her eyes jerked toward mine. "Don't say that!" she nearly shouted. "Doc didn't give me anything!"

"Okaaaay," I said slowly, wondering why she sounded so defensive.

"What about this morning then?" I asked. "Why'd you have me show up like a fool?"

She bit her lip and studied the parade

staging area. A CD of Kenny Chesney's "Don't Blink" ended, mid-song. A truck door slammed. Aside from some whooping trick-riders at the far end of the field, nearly everyone had left for the barbecue.

I felt a prickle of nerves at the back of my neck.

"Can we go somewhere to talk, Mace? I feel awful about misleading you this morning."

"We can talk right here, Belle."

"Fine." She sank, cross-legged, to the ground. "I guess this'll have to do."

I looked down for a moment to check the grass for horse paddies before I sat, too. When I glanced again at Belle, her green eyes burned into mine. She wasn't fidgeting anymore.

She held a firm grip on a .22-caliber pistol. When she fired, it sounded like the crack of a whip.

FORTY-SEVEN

"That was to get your attention," Belle said.
"You got it."

After shooting once in the air, she'd lowered the gun. It was now aimed directly at my gut. I swallowed a couple of times, forcing my fear back down my dry throat.

"It was you," I said. "You shot Doc."

She nodded. Her eyes, hard as jade, showed no remorse.

"You've known him since you were a baby, and you left him in a pasture to bleed to death. How could you do that, Belle?"

She shrugged one shoulder, like I'd asked why she chose scrambled eggs over fried.

The black lens of her camera was like a magnet, drawing my eyes in. Suddenly, some of the disjointed images in my head clicked into place.

"The bees were you, too, weren't they? Mama heard leather slapping before they swarmed. You had them in your case. You must have smacked it against something to rile them up."

She nodded, with a crazy smile. "I used a broken bottle to scrape at Brandy's frog. I thought the bruise would sideline your mama, and maybe the rest of you, too. But then I got lucky when Wynonna suggested she ride Shotgun instead."

"Because he's terrified of bees."

"Right." Another smile. "Beekeepers have boxes all over our orange groves. All I had to do was scoop some out and trap them in my case until the time came to make them swarm."

An image of Mama lying still in the dirt flashed into my head.

"You could have killed her." My voice sounded small.

"I didn't want that to happen, Mace. I like Rosalee. I just did what was necessary to get you to leave. I thought the rattlesnake would be enough, but y'all don't scare easily."

All the questions I wanted to ask felt trapped in the parched gully behind my tongue.

"So now you plan to shoot me?" I managed to choke out.

She didn't answer, just rested her wrist on her crossed leg, keeping the gun low and trained on me. It wasn't big, but at this range it was deadly. "I'll scream and yell." I swallowed. "You'll get caught."

She tilted her head toward the far end of the mostly empty staging area. Whistles and hollers came from the riders showing off fancy moves.

"Between that noisy bunch and this gusty wind, no one will hear you, Mace."

I weighed that, knowing she was probably right. I decided not to press my luck. If I made no sudden moves, maybe I could talk Belle out of whatever she had planned. Or, I might overtake her, if I got the chance.

"Was all of this to cover for killing your daddy, Belle?"

"You'd never understand."

"Try me." I looked deep into her eyes, trying to appeal to whatever feeling might be there. They looked empty, cold as green ice. I pushed away the thought that if Belle shot me, those might be the last eyes I'd ever see.

She gave a little sigh. "Doc betrayed me, Mace. He helped me get rid of Daddy, and then he wanted me to confess. I couldn't do it. If I went to prison, who'd take care of our land?"

I didn't answer. My mind stalled on what Belle said about Doc and her daddy.

"We argued and argued about it. You heard me with Doc that night in camp, near your tent. I ran off before you could find us fighting."

"But what . . ." I started to say.

She interrupted, words rushing out like a dam had burst. "Doc kept pushing me, Mace. I had to shoot him, before he told and ruined everything. I learned something, though. It wasn't smart to leave Doc out in the open like that."

"Wynonna found him."

She nodded. "So, this time, you and I are going to take a walk. You stick real close. Pull anything, and I'll shoot you where you stand. You know I'll do it, too."

I had no doubt she would.

"Get up." She lifted the gun's barrel, gesturing at me to rise.

"You should do like Doc said. Turn yourself in. He survived, and he'll talk. What will Trey think of his little sister then?"

Something flickered in her eyes.

"Trey doesn't know, does he?"

She shook her head. "No. But I did it for both of us. Trey couldn't have done it. I love my brother, but he's weak. Daddy always said so. And Trey'll be the first to agree. Now stand up."

I did as she said. With her gun in my

spine, Belle marched me toward the water. I took a last look at Val. I smelled sea air and the smoke from the brisket I wouldn't get to eat. Spotting a channel marker in the waterway, I wondered if my body would float past it to the ocean on an outgoing tide.

My mind raced furiously, thinking up and discarding hopeless plans. I'd find a rock, I thought, and then realized Belle would shoot me in the back as I stooped to get it. I'd whirl, and kick the gun from her hand. And wind up shot in the face, with Mama mourning over my unsightly corpse.

When we got to the bank of the river, every detail imprinted itself on my brain. The purple flowers of a railroad vine, tangled in green leaves against the sand. White sails catching wind on a catamaran, heading for open water. The screech of a seagull, crying a warning.

In reflex, my bird-watcher's eyes shifted for a moment toward the gull's call. And that's when I noticed the sun glinting off something golden. In the near distance, Austin crept toward us in her sparkly vest and sequined hat. She laid a finger to her lips, just as I'd done to her that night outside the Brambles' RV. She lifted her other hand to show me a cow whip, tip snaking off onto the shell-flecked ground.

I raised my voice to Belle over the wind, hoping my face hadn't betrayed what I'd seen.

"Please, Belle! Don't do it!" I prayed that between the gusts and my yelling, she wouldn't hear Austin sneaking up.

Belle cocked the hammer and put her finger on the trigger.

Austin streaked forward like a golden arrow, cow whip unfurling in a graceful arc.

I heard a loud pop, and my eyes involuntarily squeezed shut. Was I saved or was I shot?

FORTY-EIGHT

Belle screamed in pain as the whip lashed her hand. Her shot went wild and she dropped the gun. I dove to the sand, rolled, and hit her legs with the full force of my body. Knees buckling, she went down hard. The breath left her lungs with a *whoosh.*

"I've got her gun," Austin called out. "You all right, Mace?"

"Yes, and I've got her." I straddled Belle's body wrestler-style, my thighs pinning her thin arms to the sandspur-studded ground.

Sticking Belle's .22 into her waistband, Austin worked the whip again, and then again and again. In olden times, three cracks of a cow whip signaled danger or an emergency. In this case, I think she was showing off. But I didn't mind. Austin most likely saved my life.

"I see you got your whip back. You're awfully good for someone who was just 'practicing' the day you 'accidentally' hit my horse."

"Yeah." She studied the whip, looking ashamed. "I'm sorry about that. Your tent, too."

"I think this makes us even," I said.

Austin shifted her gaze to Belle, who turned her head away. She pressed her cheek into the coarse sand and sobbed, narrow shoulders jerking.

"A little late for crying, isn't it, Belle?" Austin sneered. "Mace had Carlos first. He's not worth getting yourself thrown into jail over. I've been mad at Mace, too. But I'd never pull a gun on her. What in the hell is wrong with you?"

Austin thought my near-murder was over a man! I was grateful for her timing and expert aim. But if brains were blue ink, she didn't have enough to dot an *i*.

"Oh, honey. I can't believe I almost lost you!"

Mama sat with me on a bench by the river, stroking my hair. She fluffed, and then re-fluffed my greasy bangs, and I didn't even pull away. Maddie pressed herself against my other side, clutching my hand. Marty had flitted around nervously, finally lighting on the ground at my feet. She gripped my knee with both hands, like a bird hanging onto its perch in a hurricane.

"I'm fine, y'all," I told them for what seemed like the hundredth time.

Austin had left me pinning down Belle while she ran for help, spreading word through the picnic grounds as she went. Mama and my sisters rushed over as soon as they heard. Sal wasn't around, as he'd disappeared with Trey on a mission to find a cigar store. Neither was Carlos, who hadn't even finished the parade before rushing to the hospital to try to talk to Doc.

The Fort Pierce police came and took Belle into custody. She sat now in the back of a squad car, ducking her head from the stares of a growing crowd of riders and parade spectators.

"I knew all along it was one of the Brambles," the big-bottomed cowgirl said to her friend with the permanent curls.

"Is it true Belle shot Doc Abel?" I overheard a latecomer ask her.

"That's right." The cowgirl spoke with the authority of someone who'd learned the news a few moments earlier. "And killed her daddy, too."

I still didn't know exactly how, or more importantly why, Belle had done the things she did. She'd clammed up after Austin hit her with the whip.

"Are you sure she said she 'got rid' of Lawton, Mace?" Maddie looked at me doubtfully.

"Yes, Maddie. With Doc's help. Like I told y'all, I didn't find out more because it's hard to think of follow-up questions when you're counting down your final seconds on Earth."

Marty squeezed so hard I knew her nails would leave marks on my knee. "Maddie, stop badgering Mace. We're lucky she's even here."

"You're absolutely right, Marty."

Both Mama and I stiffened in surprise. Maddie giving in so easily? My formerly imminent death must have scared her pretty bad.

"There'll be time to figure everything out after we've gotten something to eat." Maddie was signaling that, at least for her, things were returning to normal.

"Speaking of food . . ." Mama nodded toward the crowd, where Johnny Adams approached with Audrey. Each of them carried two foil-wrapped plates.

"Audrey thought you might be hungry." Johnny's gruff voice had gone soft.

"Don't listen to this old crab." She poked him with an elbow. "Johnny's the one who insisted we come over to check on you."

Mama and Maddie reached up for the plates. The hand-holding and bangs-adjusting was over, which was fine with me. Still, I couldn't eat. The top and bottom halves of my stomach were holding a tug-of-war. I toed a pebble loose from the ground, and then leaned to pick it up. I stood, and found another and then another buried in the sand.

"I'll get something later." I slipped the rocks in my pocket. "I'm going to the river."

Marty's eyes went wide. "No, Mace! You should stay here with us!"

Mama stroked her fine blond hair. "Honey, don't worry. Mace'll be okay. She's just going off to toss some rocks into the water."

"Maybe I could go with her." The voice was masculine. Slightly accented. I looked up from searching the ground to see Carlos, his eyes dark with emotion; his face full of relief.

"We could toss rocks together," he said softly, holding out his hand.

I took two steps toward him. He took one to me. And suddenly I was in his arms. I buried my face in his clean denim shirt, inhaling the smell of laundry soap and safety. Wrapped in his tight embrace, I didn't feel weak. I felt cared for, and doubly strong.

He lifted my chin. We kissed, and he nipped at my bottom lip with his teeth.

"I almost went out of my mind driving back here," he whispered. "Belle poisoned her father. Doc said she tricked him to get an extra prescription for digoxin, the medicine Lawton took to regulate his heart."

"And she used the drug to give him a fatal overdose. In his chili. Was I right?"

He nodded, and his smile was sad. I didn't feel triumphant.

"Belle had a second, identical cup," Carlos said. "She mixed in more and more of the drug over the day, and then took Lawton's tainted cup. She left the clean one to be found."

I thought of all the devious planning Belle must have done. Somehow, her mind had become as poisoned as that cup.

Carlos touched my cheek, looking deep into my eyes. "I flew back from the hospital, praying all the while I wasn't too late. Then, when I arrived, someone said you'd been shot . . ."

"Shhh." I put a finger to his lips. "I was right here, waiting for you."

As we turned to the water, Carlos' arm close around my shoulder, I glanced back at the bench. I had to smile at Mama and my sisters. They each sent a silent signal: Six thumbs up.

FORTY-NINE

"Can I warm that up for you, hon?"

The waitress hovered over my table at Gladys' Diner. I covered my cup with my hand and shook my head.

"No thanks, Charlene. I'm fuller than a drainage ditch in the rainy season. But you can bring me a tiny slice of that peanut butter pie."

I was too nervous to eat much. Trey Bramble had called and asked me to meet him. He had something for me, he said. Just as I began to wonder if he was standing me up, the door opened and in he walked. He'd probably dropped ten pounds in the month since the Cracker Trail ride — weight he couldn't afford to lose from his lean frame. His jeans hung low on his hips; his slim-cut Western shirt bagged across his chest. The dark smudges under his eyes attested that sleep was hard to come by.

Every head in the place turned as Trey

walked to my table.

"Hey," he said as he leaned in and kissed my cheek.

"Hey yourself," I answered.

Lowering himself onto a chair, he put the stares and whispers behind his back. He slid an envelope toward me across the table.

"Thanks for meeting me, Mace." He dropped his eyes, touching a finger to the envelope. "I thought you might want these."

Opening it, I swallowed a gasp. Inside were the campfire pictures Belle took of Mama, my sisters, and me. They were really good. She'd captured us completely. I traced Mama's mischievous smile in one photo as she snatched a bite of pie from Marty's plate.

"Wow," I said.

"I know.' Trey looked at me sadly. "Belle had real talent. What a waste."

Then both of us started to speak at the same time: "Trey, I'm so sorry . . ."

"I feel just awful . . ." he said.

I motioned for him to go first.

"I can't even say how terrible I feel about what Belle did, Mace. I'm glad Austin was there with that cow whip. By the way, you might be interested to know she's signed up for anger management sessions."

I had to smile at the image of Austin,

deep-breathing and chanting her calming word.

"And I'm sorry, too, Trey. For everything. You lost your daddy, and now your sister, too. It's a lot to bear. How you holding up?"

He drew a circle in the condensation my water glass left on the table. "You mean am I drinking?"

"Not only that."

Charlene bustled by, raising her coffee pot to Trey. He nodded, and she poured before dashing off again.

"I went on a week-long drunk after Belle was arrested. I barely got myself together for Daddy's funeral."

I remembered. Trey stumbled into the church service, twenty minutes late and stinking of booze. Head-shaking and tongue-clucking followed him down the aisle like wake from a boat.

"When I woke up the day after we buried him, I decided enough was enough. The family business needs me. Belle still needs a brother. I haven't had a drop since. Now, I know I've quit on my own before and always slid back. So, this time I'm getting help. I start on Monday at some fancy rehab place in Orlando."

He pointed at the sugar shaker on the table. I passed it over, and he dumped what looked like a quarter of it into his black coffee.

"I'm proud of you, Trey. I know you'll kick it this time."

"I don't have a choice, Mace. It's all on me now."

Was responsibility what he needed all along? Or would the extra weight prove too much for Trey to carry? I guess we'd just have to wait and see.

His eyes went again to the pictures spread out in front of us. "Belle made some beautiful photographs on that ride," he said. "She took some awful ones, too. I wish I'd thrown away the film she left in her camera; never had it developed. The police have most of those pictures now, anyway."

The hair rose at the back of my neck.

Stirring the coffee he'd already stirred, Trey whispered, "She shot a picture of Daddy dying." When he looked up, his blue eyes, his father's eyes, were wet. "How could she do that, Mace?"

I had no answer to that.

"This psychologist says it was wrong for Daddy to keep so much from Belle about being adopted. It made her feel like she had a secret she had to be ashamed of. The doctor says it made her become disconnected, family-wise. And that got all tangled up with

Belle's feelings about Bramble land. When she found out Daddy planned to sell a good portion of what we own, something just went wrong in Belle's head." He rubbed his eyes. "She wasn't herself, Mace."

I couldn't tell which of us he was trying to convince. I put my hand over his on the table.

"I'm sorry, Trey."

What else could I say?

"There were other pictures, too. The rattlesnake. The bees crammed into her camera case. Doc with his hands up and fear in his eyes. The last one she took was of you, brushing your horse after the parade in Fort Pierce."

I felt a sudden chill, and it wasn't from the diner's rattling air conditioner. Given enough time, Belle might have snapped a picture of my gun-shot body sinking into the Indian River. I knew Trey still loved his sister, despite everything. But if I had my way, they'd lock her up and lose the key.

"Didn't you ever suspect anything, Trey?"

He blew on his coffee and sipped, a stall before answering.

"I think I did." He nodded. "But I didn't want to face my suspicions. I left that note for you to keep looking for Daddy's killer. I hoped and prayed it'd be anybody but Belle.

But the more I thought about it, the more afraid I got that you'd keep asking questions and they'd lead you right to her."

Trey traced the map of Florida on his placemat. When his finger got to the star north of Lake Okeechobee that marked Himmarshee, he spoke again.

"I'm the one who broke into your Jeep and took back the note."

I looked at him. Youth and joy were gone from his eyes. They looked pained. Empty.

"I'll pay for the damage, Mace."

"I'm not worried about the top, Trey. It already leaked like a sieve. We're in the dry season anyway."

"No," he said firmly. "I'll get you a check. I'm just beginning to iron out Daddy's business dealings. I'm getting Johnny Adams back his money. Daddy shouldn't have done him like he did. And I'm going to buy out Wynonna's half of our cattle business."

"Where is your step-mama anyway?"

"Off to Paris, alone," Trey said. "We had us a long talk before she left. Wynonna's got issues with men."

No kidding.

"She said she's having herself one last fling before she moves back home to North Carolina and settles down. She claims she saw a therapist back there who deals with

439

people with her problem. So I guess she'll go back and hope the treatment takes."

So Trey was going to dry out. Austin was combating her rage. And Wynonna was working on her sex addiction. Maybe Jerry Springer should do a show next year from the Cracker Trail.

I glanced at my watch. It was just past noon. The diner was filling up. Ranchers and citrus growers in boots and jeans strode in. The courthouse's suit-and-tie crowd filed to tables. My eyes flickered to the entrance every time the bells on the door jangled.

"You waiting on somebody, Mace?"

I felt a flush. "Kind of," I answered.

Just then, Carlos passed by the plate glass window on his way to the door. I figured I had a fifty-fifty chance of seeing him since downtown Himmarshee's dining choices were either Gladys' or the Dairy Queen on US Highway 441. I waved him over. The two men shook hands warily.

"How are things down in Miamuh?" Trey asked.

"I'm living up here now, becoming an authentic Himmarshean."

"Don't let him fool you, Trey. He still hates sweet tea and craves Cuban coffee," I said. "But we'll make him into a good ol' boy yet."

Carlos flashed me a smile. My stomach did a high dive.

"I keep telling you, *niña,* I'll be as country as you want, just as long as you don't make me eat grits."

Trey's gaze went from one of us to the other, understanding dawning. He pushed back his chair and stood. "I was just about to git," he said to Carlos. "Why don't you take my seat?"

He held out his hand again; the two men shook. "You take good care of Mace, hear?"

Carlos raised an eyebrow. "She doesn't need anybody to take care of her, do you Mace?"

I took a moment to think about that.

"You're right. I don't *need* it," I said. "But I've learned it's not a sin to *want* it every now and then."

ACKNOWLEDGMENTS

I owe a debt to the great folks on the Florida Cracker Trail, who welcomed me on the Twentieth Anniversary of the cross-state horseback ride. Everyone was uniformly nice: not a greedy, murderous, or crazy character among them. Just as my books' fictional town of Himmarshee is inspired by Okeechobee, the Cracker Trial served as muse. I shifted Florida geography to suit the story. The characters, good and bad, came from my imagination.

Some real people, however, deserve a tip of this cowgirl's hat.

Judge Nelson Bailey educated me on Florida's cattle history, which the ride honors, and loaned me his horse, Domino. Carol Bailey helped me resurrect long-dormant riding skills.

Mitzi Webber and the Miami crew rescued me one wet, frozen night, providing horse trailer and portable heater. Apologies to

Mitzi's horse, Poco, who had to sleep outside.

Florida's fine cattlemen and women hosted the ride, keeping agricultural traditions alive. Special thanks to Duck and Susan Smith for a ranch house tour and family tales.

Pat's Bar-B-Que, the chuck wagon crew, fed us so well I forgot my aches and pains.

The mule- and horse-wagon drivers offered a few rides, giving my bottom a break.

Deputies and police across Florida helped keep us safe; all were competent pros, unlike the sheriff from fictional Dundee, Florida.

Dr. Robert King briefed me during the ride on medicine and matters of the heart (Dr. David Perloff did the same, back in Fort Lauderdale).

Bit of Hope Ranch loaned a rescued horse for the final day's parade. Thanks to Karl, a peach of a plow horse!

As always, I want to thank my husband, Kerry Sanders, and the original Mama, Marion Sharp, for their love and support; Joyce Sweeney and the Thursday group for writing help (super title, Audrey!); and my agent, Whitney Lee, for being in my corner.

I'm grateful for the talented staff at Midnight Ink, especially Connie Hill, whose editing skill saves me from looking stupid; Courtney Kish, who gets the word out; and Lisa Novak, whose designs make my covers pop. Illustrator Mark Gerber is an added gift.

To those I've named, to anyone I missed, and especially to you, for reading *Mama Rides Shotgun* . . . THANKS.

ABOUT THE AUTHOR

Like Mace Bauer's, **Deborah Sharp**'s family roots were set in Florida long before Disney and *Miami Vice* came to define the state. She does some writing at a getaway overlooking the Kissimmee River in the wilds north of Okeechobee, and some at a Starbucks in Fort Lauderdale. As a Florida native and a former longtime reporter for *USA Today,* she knows every burg and back road, including some not found on maps. Here's what she has to say about Himmarshee:

Home to cowboys and church suppers, Himmarshee is hot and swarming with mosquitoes. A throwback to the ways of long-ago southern Florida, it bears some resemblance to the present-day ranching town of Okeechobee. The best thing about Mace and Mama's hometown: it will always be threatened, but never spoiled, by suburban sprawl.

We hope you have enjoyed this Large Print book. Other Thorndike, Wheeler, Kennebec, and Chivers Press Large Print books are available at your library or directly from the publishers.

For information about current and upcoming titles, please call or write, without obligation, to:

Publisher
Thorndike Press
295 Kennedy Memorial Drive
Waterville, ME 04901
Tel. (800) 223-1244

or visit our Web site at:

http://gale.cengage.com/thorndike

OR

Chivers Large Print
published by BBC Audiobooks Ltd
St James House, The Square
Lower Bristol Road
Bath BA2 3SB
England
Tel. +44(0) 800 136919
email: bbcaudiobooks@bbc.co.uk
www.bbcaudiobooks.co.uk

All our Large Print titles are designed for easy reading, and all our books are made to last.

65

68

185

309

131

968

145